Time, Distance, and Shielding
Radiographic Thriller – Book 1

PAT SETTEGAST

TIME
DISTANCE
AND
SHIELDING

A RADIOGRAPHIC THRILLER

Published by Pathologic Publications.
This work is protected by copyright. No part of it may be reproduced in any manner without written permission. All rights reserved. © 2019 by Benjamin Roberts.

For Jessica

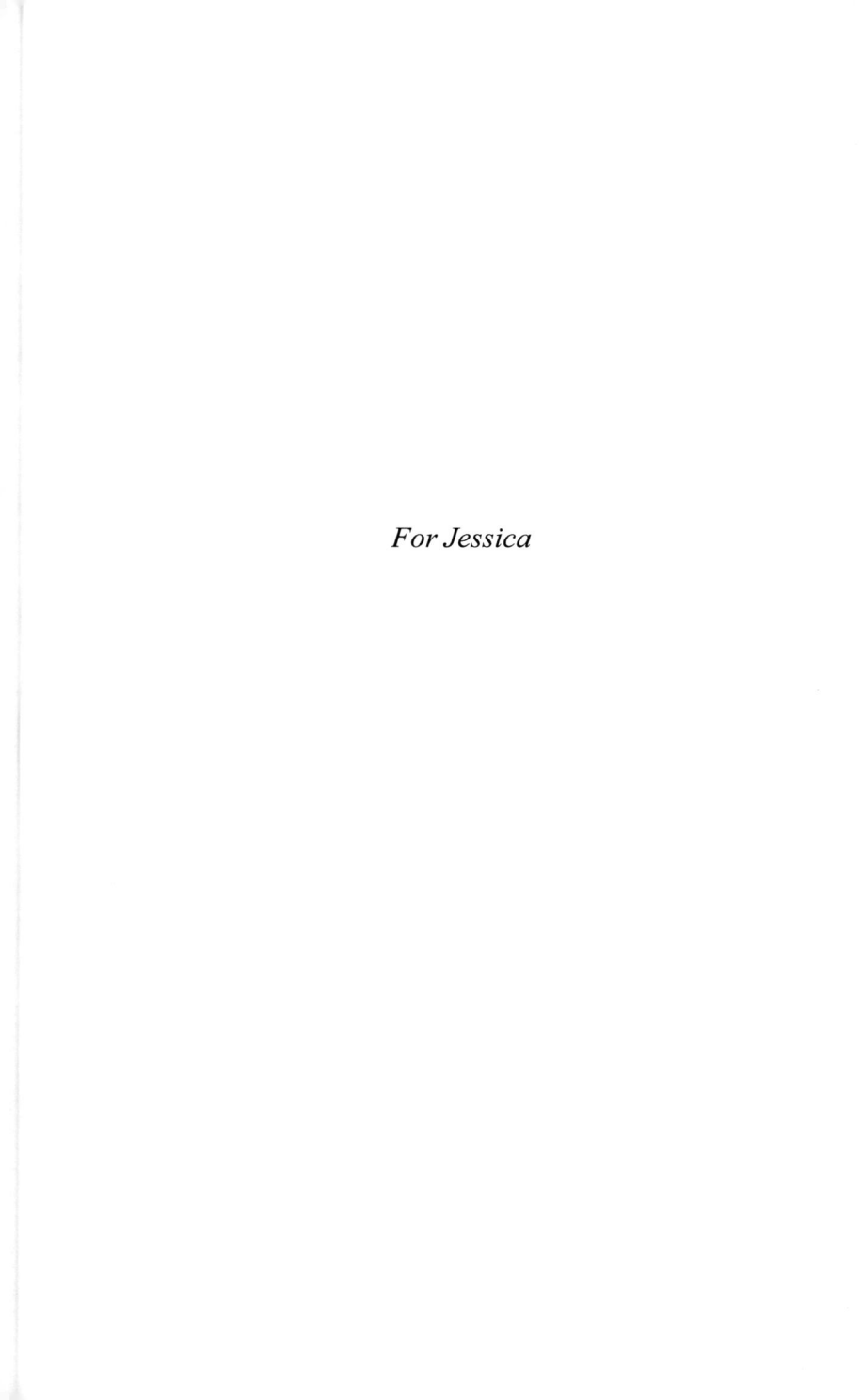

1

Dr. Richard Dortman wrote the order for the STAT portable L-spine x-ray. Dr. Dortman performed the patient's laminectomy, but M was the first to see what Dortman did to the patient's lumbar spine. Then she crashed the portable x-ray machine into a wall in the ICU hallway.

M is a pale, somewhat vampiric, kind of androgynous person. Black hair, cavernous eyes. I can imagine the look on her face as she backed the portable x-ray machine out of the massive hole in the sheetrock. She tends to chew her lower lip.

The portable was fine. It's a boxy piece of work, built to survive the apocalypse. For all its actuated motors and wheels, it handles like a bad shopping cart. A cart full of steel, lead, and tungsten because that's what a portable x-ray machine is – that and a giant, high-voltage DC battery. I could drop the portable off the hospital roof, and it would still pump out x-rays.

The damage to the wall was cosmetic. Nothing some new sheetrock and paint couldn't cover. The wreck was the patient's spine on the x-ray image.

That's the problem with patient care. It's clumsy, slows your role as a rad tech. Care too much and you won't finish a single exam. X-rays don't lie.

2

In x-ray school, I learned, if you really care, care to keep your distance. Something like that was in our textbook, Selman Brookes' *Radiography for Technologists*.

Good patient care begins with professional boundaries, but professional boundaries get tricky when a person's a spinal cord is half-severed right in front of your eyes.

Wheeling the portable down the hall, M sent the L-spine exam to PACS. PACS stands for Picture Archiving Computer System (aka Pain And Constant Suffering). She texted the radiologist for a STAT read. Two more STAT exams dropped.

STAT derives from the Latin for "needed it like yesterday" (aka Stop Thinking About Sanity).

M had a little cry, which is on the security feed for anyone to see and draw whatever conclusions they'd like. Then she moved on to the next STAT exam because everything is STAT at 400 hours.

I've known M going on five years. She put herself through x-ray school working as a mortuary make-up artist and stripping at the Rhino Club. The point is a little cry does M's morbid little heart good. Toughens her up.

According to the powers that be, that was the problem. Rather than crying about the wrecked lumbar spine she'd committed to radiographic imaging, M should have completed an incident report on the hole in the ICU wall. M figured she'd report it to Shelly, the lead tech, once the day crew arrived. M was busy.

That was a mistake. Because Vanessa, Dr. Dortman's nurse, saw M wreck the portable, and

Vanessa completed an incident report of her own. Then, according to M, Vanessa called Dortman.

2

This is where it turns he-said-she-said. M says Dortman pounced on her while she was alone in the portable storage room. There's nothing on the security feed, and according to the proximity cards, Dr. Dortman left the hospital shortly after ordering the STAT L-spine exam. That's what Timmy the Fearless, our department manager, told M.

Dortman doesn't have to prove anything. He's St. Rafael's chief surgeon. He has the backing of the entire hospital. He is god. He can do whatever he wants. That's what Dortman told M as he leaned against the storage room door, trapping her in the small room with him.

M and her partner, Janet, are the kind of grrls who leave Halloween decorations up year-round. The first time I saw M scared was when she told me about Dortman in the portable storage room. That's why I believed her. I didn't press for the dets.

In the world of infectious diseases, there are numerous pathways of spread. Direct contact is when the infected person passes the disease through blood, hair, mucus, and assorted bodily fluids. It's the reason you shouldn't go around kissing and hugging everybody. Work in a hospital long enough, even handshakes are suspicious.

What I'm saying is, M appeared compromised. Dortman directly transmitted something infectious to her. I mean metaphorically. No, spiritually. That's the kind of thing you think but don't say.

3

Caring is kind of masochistic. Real caring requires sacrifice. Instead of care, most people cope. When you care about someone who is hurting, a part of you dies, but that self-death feeds the soul.

I was conked out in Exam Room 1 when the Dortman stuff went down. M woke me up and immediately started talking. She followed me into the bathroom, jabbering as I splashed water on my face and picked the sleep from my eyes.

I have a boyish face. It's something with my cheekbones and nose. I have freckles. My yellowish hair is pixie cut so I don't have to mess with it. I've never liked the color, but I don't dislike it enough to pay to change it. I shave my legs and pits once a month. Granted, I might look odd in an evening dress but wake me up in the middle of the night and I'm ready for the world in under a minute. No make-up required.

The first thing I thought was M must have a fever. Her hands were shaking. I had the hardest time following her story. I checked her radial pulse. Counted ninety-two beats per minute resting. A little high. Sixty to a hundred is normal. Her tympanic body temperature was ninety-nine. Also normal. Her blood pressure was elevated – 124/77.

She said, "Claire, you're weird. You know that, right?"

"I need coffee."

"You're the only person in the world who checks vitals on someone because they're pissed."

"You look feverish."

M rolled her cavernous eyes.

5

I figured the story was straightforward: M was in a hurry to send the L-spine to PACS, she hit the wall, Nurse Vanessa electronically wrote her up, and Dr. Dortman personally busted her down – but there was still that sense she'd been compromised, contaminated.

She said, "I should have told her not to do it."

"Who?"

"Duh," M said. "The patient, Jess Walden. When I did her pre-op pictures, they were normal. I said, 'Jess, get a second opinion.' But that's what everybody says."

I said, "Since when is it our job to dispense medical advice?"

"She's up there in agony, Claire, gorked out of her head on pain meds."

"Do you know her?"

M shrugged, "She works with Janet. Her back started hurting. Jan told her I was an x-ray tech here, and she signed up to see Dr. Dortman. He tells her – before he's ordered any tests — that a spinal fusion could end all her problems."

I see what's she saying. Spinal fusion isn't a black-and-white decision. Most folks want to see health as a binary – like this woman's back problems – pain bad, surgery good.

That's the thing about being an x-ray tech. You become religiously committed to seeing all the grays in the gray. That's what a diagnostic x-ray is.

M said, "I did her pix. She was starry eyed about the surgery. Claire, there was nothing wrong with her back losing twenty pounds couldn't fix. Now, she's in a living hell because of Dortman."

4

My smartwatch alarm rang 530 hours. This was the Thursday before Halloween. I was due at the gym in thirty minutes. I told M I had to go. That's the difference between caring and taking care. Maybe that seems heartless, but the first step in caring for someone else is to take care of yourself.

I couldn't do anything about Dortman. I'm a nobody – sleeping on an x-ray table because the department's short on graveyard techs. Until Timmy the Fearless hires someone, I'm the only tech stupid enough to work doubles for coverage.

At Rafa, my preferred M.O. is like an x-ray photon. You don't see, hear, or feel anything but you're ionized. Walk silently and carry big data.

For the last two months, I've been at the hospital close to ninety hours a week. Last night was slow. M offered to run portables while I napped with the ER pager. I felt partly to blame. If I had been driving the portable, we would have maintained invisibility. We would have avoided this mess.

5

I made it to the gym with five minutes to spare. After the workout with my roommate, Alex (in which she gave me all the glorious details of her evening with Tucker from yoga), I ran five miles along Shoal Creek and biked home. I was in bed by 900 hours and up at 1300: shower, protein, scrubs, and bike back to St. Rafa.

The swing shift was quiet. Dani and I took a late lunch so M could join us before she clocked in for the grave. It's our time. We walked a block down 32nd to

7

El Burrito Volador. It's not Austin's finest dining, but it beats the hospital cafeteria, and it's open 24/7.

I ordered black coffee and vegan breakfast tacos. Dani ordered a beer and folded his arms over his chest, studying his biceps like – "I dare you to say something." Every time I think I could maybe be attracted to Dani, he does something stupid like order a beer while he's more-or-less on the clock.

Dani's parents are from Jordan. He was born in Memphis, Tennessee. He's medium height, really into his muscles and Gucci Mane. I think he lives in a strip club the months outside of Ramadan. Very Mid-South meets Mid-East, but shot-for-shot Dani is the most accurate, detail-obsessed x-ray tech I've ever met. M, for her part, is the fastest.

She launched into a story about Timmy the Fearless writing her up for crashing the portable.

She said, "He did it over the phone."

Dani said, "A shining example of rising to the level of your own incompetence."

M looked like she hadn't slept much, but with her that might be the look she was going for – difficult to say.

I said, "Now what?"

M said, "Exactly. You tell me."

Dani said, "Suck it up. I'm sure the portable is fine. Maintenance will handle the wall."

"Dr. Dortman is out to get me."

"Don't go down that road, boo," Dani said. "Listen. We can't take care of you if we're too busy caring about you."

M said, "Do you think about what you're saying? Or does your mouth just string words together?"

"The way I see it," Dani said. "To really care I have to kind of not care."

He motioned to me for confirmation.

I made my best don't-look-at-me face and pulled absentmindedly at the broken heart pendant I've worn since Dad left, sliding it back and forth on my necklace.

M said, "Dani, eat your damn tacos."

He said, "It's complicated."

Turning to me, she said, "You are now officially the only person at St. Rafa who gives a shit."

Like I said, she's quick.

6

I studied M for a moment, trying to gauge the level of the infectious process I sensed that morning in Exam Room 1, the disease spread by Dr. Dortman. It was like I could feel the contagion sweeping toward me, but I was clueless how to stop it.

M held a coffee mug in her small, pale hands, studying the dregs.

I said, "The only way out of this is deeper in."

Raising her cavernous eyes, M bit her lip. She glanced at Dani.

I said, "You can trust us."

Dani said, "Maybe me and the Clairista –"

"– Please don't call me that."

"Maybe we ain't your first choice for compadres, but you need to find folks you can trust up in this bitch. If it ain't us then who?"

M shook her head, laughed, and pushed a tear out of her eye.

"You're such a bonehead."

Dani nodded, "That's right, but you know this bonehead got that pale, vampire ass of yours."

"Gross. OK, shut up. Here's what happened. Dortman blocked the door. It was just me and him in the portable storage."

Dani popped his knuckles, "What'd you do?"

"I freaked. I wanted out of there. I wasn't thinking straight, and he kept going on and on about who was going to pay for the wall and where did I learn to drive and anyways I lost it. I said, 'At least I didn't botch a surgery.' I blurted it out. I said a few curse words too, sorry Claire."

She smirked at me. I rolled my eyes.

Dani said, "What'd Dortman do when you hit him with the botched surgery line?"

"He stared at me. Just kept staring. That's when I realized he was on something. Cocaine or meth. He wasn't drunk. He was wired. I wanted out of that room. I wanted him gone, out of my way. I knew I wasn't helping anything, but I started shouting at him, accusing him of malpractice. I couldn't get the patient out of my head. That's when I saw his scrubs. There was blood on them, y'all. Her blood. He was spun out of his head and still wearing those nasty scrubs. I tried to push passed him. He grabbed me and slammed me against the wall."

As she confessed this, M held it together. She's stronger than the post-goth façade suggests, but she couldn't meet our eyes. She stared into her coffee mug.

Dani tilted his head from side-to-side, popping the joints in his neck.

He said, "We got you."

10

She said, "The look in his eyes. He had his forearm across my throat. I don't know what happened. I froze. I couldn't move a muscle. I wanted to kill him. I wanted to die. He leaned in close. I could feel his stinking breath on my face, and he said, 'I can make it to where you never walk again.'"

I glanced at Dani. The wheels were turning in his head, but he was afraid. His face gave him away – the flesh bloodless and slack. This was the contagion without sign or symptom. I asked myself, what is it about Dortman that low-key makes me reach for the PPE just talking about him? That's PPE, as in personal protective equipment, as in plastic gown, nitriles gloves, N95 mask, and splash shield, just for your standard bitch session.

M said, "When he let go, I fell on the floor."

She spat the words out, clutching her coffee mug like she wanted to tear it in two, staring into that small empty space. Her silence was abrupt.

I don't remember what platitudes we offered. There's nothing to say to make that sort of thing go away.

Dani rubbed his face with both hands. "That douchebag really said he'd make it to where you'd never walk again?"

The words were shocking. We all struggled to believe. Even M.

She nodded, "I don't remember him leaving. I don't know how long I sat there on the floor. Listen, this stays here. I haven't told anyone except y'all. I can't tell Janet. She'd go ballistic, hire a lawyer. I don't want any of that. I just want Dortman to go away. Either that or I'll find somewhere else to work. I'm sick of this stupid town anyways."

I stared out the dirty window. Behind El Burrito Volador, there's a little white cottage hidden in a dense garden. It's the kind of place I imagine I might live someday. Tiny, close to town, surrounded by scrub oak, agave, and palms. I could walk to work.

From where I sat, I saw the patio behind the cottage. Hanging on the wall was an old light box. It was old school. The sort of thing techs hung x-rays on when we shot film. It was at least ten years ago. Maybe twenty or thirty. Before my time.

The light box glowed, displaying two rows of hand x-rays. The bones were visible through the twisting branches of the garden.

By the light of the glowing x-ray images, I saw a little old woman sitting at a wrought iron patio table talking to herself. It was Dorothy Hicks. She was a receptionist in the imaging department. What was she doing sitting at a patio table lit by the light of hand x-ray films? It almost looked like she was praying. The whole thing was odd.

Not far from where she sat, there was a statue of an angel. I often biked by on my way to St. Raphael's. I liked to glimpse the angel through the foliage. Maybe crazy, old Dorothy Hick was praying to the angel statue.

It's an old statue. The base is covered in moss. The angel isn't a man or a woman. It's something of both. Its wings are folded behind. It holds a fish – carrying the fish like a baby – in that detached, disembodied way of a saint.

Looking out the grimy window at Dorothy sitting there alone in the dark, lit by glowing bones, I said a prayer for all us poor sinners. That we will be able to help each other. Or, at least avoid causing more hurt. I also prayed to not become an old woman who prays by the light of glowing bone pictures to an angel statue in the middle of the night.

7

Maybe the angel in the garden heard my prayers because that graveyard shift was one of the best nights of my life. M and I stuck together. The patients were mostly easygoing, appreciative types. The exam orders were steady without being overwhelming. M was excited about the new *Halloween* movie.

Between exams we talked Jamie Lee Curtis. How Jamie Lee was the first crush M ever had and how she was trying to convince Janet to do her hair like Jamie Lee's aerobics mullet in *Perfect*, which M believed could have literally been *the* perfect movie if Michael Meyers had killed John Travolta in the first act instead of not appearing in the film at all.

I was happy to listen. We were moving – each in our own way – to overcome a real obstacle. We were closer for it. I didn't know how to change anything with Dortman or his nurse, but I knew we were a team. We'd figure it out.

My alarm rang at 530 hours. I hugged M. She kissed my cheek, and I jumped on my bike to meet Alex at the gym. Neither of us suspected that was the last time we'd work together.

8

In high school, I was completely self-absorbed. I liked three things: soccer, reading, and staying up late. I "hated" my parents. I was a walking, talking defense mechanism against their crumbling marriage.

Dad left the day after high school graduation. I've seen him a handful of times since. We connect online some. He moves around. He's not a drug addict or a deadbeat or whatever. He's a burned-out nerd who temps IT jobs and plays too many video games. When he left, I hardly noticed he was gone.

Mother lives in Pflugerville with a real estate agent named Collier who I guess is my step-dad but who seems more like an advertisement. Sometimes I think Mother wishes she was a drug addict, but she's your basic pseudo-hippy narcissist. Super into Fleetwood Mac. Walks like she's floating on a cloud, like Stevie Nicks. Drives an old Mercedes-Benz with an "Honor Mother Earth" bumper sticker. Insert whatever weird affectation here.

Two months after Dad left, it dawned on me that he was gone for good and that he'd split mostly because Mother and I were selfish, mean, hurtful people who spent his money and treated him like a non-entity. How he stayed around as long as he did is a testament to willpower and the amount of video games the man plays. Anyways, his departure was my first lesson in caring.

Because it hurt that he left. At first, I tried burying the pain beneath layers of annoyance and Vietnamese sandwiches. (We lived a couple of blocks from Chinatown Center.) I read the *Hunger Games* ten times.

14

Then I stopped reading, stopped eating, became this anorexic fixture at Barton Springs, but Dad's absence still hurt.

Nothing I did helped; so I stopped trying. I let myself hurt. I worried whether he was OK. I hoped he wasn't lonely. I wondered if he found what he was looking for. I still wonder that.

What I'm saying is I allowed myself to hurt. I didn't try to hide it. I emailed him over and over and called and called until he finally answered. I told him I missed him, and that I was sorry I hurt him.

Allowing myself to feel hurt was like stepping into uncharted territory. Feeling hurt wasn't something I was raised to do. I tried talking to Mother about it. She would dodge.

Her line was "Someday, in heaven, we'll know who was right and who was wrong."

This was around the time she found religion. Then, she found Collier, and it was back to her old ways, piling one quirky affectation on top of another.

Neither of us understands how I'm her daughter. For my eighteenth birthday, Mother bought me an all access pass to the Austin City Limits Festival. I sold the pass to Zoey, my high school bestie, and bought my broken heart pendant and chain.

I left home around the time Mother and Collier became a thing. My BMI was pushing 30 (the threshold between overweight and obese) because Mother insisted I take antidepressants if I stayed under her roof.

Zoey and I found a house for rent on the upper east side, and Alex – who I met in English class at community college – followed a month or so later. Thanksgiving will be five years we've lived together.

Alex was the one who pulled me out of my funk and into the gym. I dropped sixty pounds and the antidepressants. I don't work out to lose weight. I work out because it keeps me sane, clears the cortisol out of my brain.

Mother and I have a standing date for brunch first Sunday of the month. I love her, and she loves me, but we don't get each other.

It goes back to the hurt. She chose to cope. I chose to care. It's a choice we all have to make every day of our lives. To be fair, Mother cares as much as she can. I believe that's true for everyone.

I love my parents. There's nothing I can do to change them, and I'm OK with that. Alex and Zoey are my family now. They've got problems, sure. Alex is one hook-up shy of needing to attend sexaholic meetings. Zoey is "you do you" to the point of nihilism, like an evil Emma Stone, but with my roommates I feel like there's hope.

It's the same with M and Dani. We're young. We can learn. That's why I thought the situation with Dr. Dortman – as unhealthy as it might seem – would be another step toward becoming better.

My cell rang through the do not disturb setting, waking me up at 1100 hours. It was Timmy the Fearless. He was calling to tell me I'd be working the grave solo.

I said, "What?"

Timmy smiled and sighed. It's an audible thing. I could hear his khaki smile and the sigh over the phone. I swear it's even attached to his emails.

Timmy said, "We had to put Melissa on investigatory probation."

It took me a moment to realize he meant M.

I said, "Why? She's one of the best techs we have."

He said, "I can't say more than that. You understand."

I said, "I don't understand."

Timmy said, "We hope to have this resolved in a week or two. Until then I'm going to work nonstop to find coverage."

All the moves were planned out ahead of this call. That was Timmy. A master of self-preservation.

"Who put you up to this, Tim?"

He sighed. Dani claims the man's sighs inspired the smiling poop emoji. I was starting to agree.

Timmy said, "I know it's rough. Stick with us through this, and we can discuss cross-training in CT."

Meaning, if I didn't stick with him on, we wouldn't discuss computed tomography. Timmy knew I wanted to be a CT tech. He was using it against me. It was both bribe and threat. Timmy calls it leverage. It's not a bad strategy. I only wish he had the guts to use it on the people over him – not just the people under him.

Timmy said, "Make sure to get plenty of sleep."

I hung up. Sleep was the furthest thing from my mind.

9

Alex and Zoey were both in the kitchen when I stumbled down the hall in my PJs and in desperate need of coffee.

My roommates, like most people, could not understand why a healthy individual would want to go

17

anywhere near a hospital let alone stay there overnight. Zoey would joke about having her empathy glad surgically removed, scrunching up her cute little face. Alex liked boys – a lot – which was not the same as caring. Her hair is blonde and long right now. That will last until her next big crush.

Zoey said, "Aren't you up early?"

I nodded and said, "Couldn't sleep."

She said, "Are you on meth? You were out for, like, two hours tops."

That's the thing about working healthcare. A jacked-up circadian rhythm is the least of your worries.

Alex said, "That can't be healthy."

We lived in a small house inside the loop. It was pre-fab. Stamped out from the same mold of every other place on the block. A sad corner of town. The police were at the apartments across the street twice a week.

From the little window above the sink, I surveyed the small bamboo forest in the backyard. Bamboo is super invasive in Austin. The bamboo forest was the kind of thing I would never want if I owned the place, but since we were renting, I loved the bamboo. The shady paths, the small sunny opening around the patio were alive with unending shades of green.

The bamboo forest was what I loved best about our little prefab home. It was a sanctuary, transplanted and incongruous with the chaos and noise outside our front door.

Someone punched my arm. Alex.

She said, "Are you listening?"

I shook my head and said, "Sorry, y'all I'm asleep on my feet."

18

Alex said, "Go back to bed."

I took a sip of coffee.

Zoey said, "This is about work, isn't it? First they put you on graves—"

"I volunteered."

"Whatevs. Now they've got so far inside your sweet little unsuspecting head that you can't sleep. What next, Claire? Are you going to check yourself into the hospital and spend half your time a patient and the other half working?"

"I don't work as much as you do."

It was true. Even as she was talking, Zoey had one earbud in, watching a fashion video on her tablet.

"My work is my passion," Zoey said. "You're not doing anything anyone is truly passionate about."

"Please, tell me how you really feel."

She said, "You're a slave."

"Ouch."

Zoey paused the video, pulled the earbud out, and turned to me with her best, most convincing look of caring.

"I'm trying to help."

Alex said, "She's right. The protestant work ethic is overrated."

Turning to her with exaggerated surprise, I said, "What?"

Zoey said, "She met a poet last night at Spider House."

Alex said, "The skinny jeans on this guy left nothing to the imagination. Plus, his name's Tucker."

I said, "Aren't you already seeing a Tucker?

She nodded, "Don't judge. It's less to remember. I like to keep things basic with guys because guys are basic – even the smart ones. I'll save the complicated stuff for us girls, OK? Anyways, according to Tucker, you can forget work. It's way too 20th century."

Zoey said, "What we're trying to say is we're worried about you. I know that's hard for you to understand because you're used to being our mom, and you can't believe you might need to be mommed, but that's what's happening."

Alex said, "Before you protest, I want to make it perfectly clear that neither of us is getting paid to worry about you. We don't want to worry about you. We love you, but worry doesn't cut it for this girl."

I said, "What do you want me to do?"

"Duh," Zoey said. "Work less. Party more."

Alex said, "When was the last time we all went out together? When was the last time you got stoned?"

I said, "I don't smoke."

Zoey said, "That's why there's brownies, darling."

Alex said, "When was the last you were with a guy?"

"That isn't up for discussion?"

I meant it as a statement, but it sounded like a question. The tag team wore down my defenses.

Zoey said, "Do you want to die a virgin?"

I said, "I don't want to die at all."

Alex said, "Keep working too much at the hospital and that's what's going to happen."

Zoey said, "Can you stop thinking about yourself long enough to wonder how we feel?"

Maybe they were right. They weren't going to hear it from me.

10

St. Rafa has a trauma level-two emergency department. We handle anything short of a mass bombing, and we don't do burns. That'd be trauma level-one ED. Give us your car crashes, stabbings, shootings, overdoses, and heart attacks.

The ED has a stroke protocol, which means we admit, diagnose, and treat a cerebrovascular accident in under two hours. Anything we can't treat we stabilize for transfer to the university hospital.

Sometimes – especially weekends in the fall when all of Texas drops everything to watch football – you go a whole string of shifts without seeing anything worse than a kidney stone. Then, I don't know what happens, the gates of hell open and spew carnage down these fluorescent lit halls.

You see things you'd never think possible, for example a circular saw blade somehow lodged in the frontal bone without injuring the brain, and then you'll see two more of them. Like there was a sale on saw blades on Idiot Avenue.

Some folks say it's the full moon. Most everyone in the hospital believes in some form of luck: knock on wood, fortune cookies, spirit animals, horoscopes. Antonio, the graveyard respiratory therapist, is convinced his nights go according the scratch-off ticket he buys at the corner store five minutes before his shift. He doesn't have many good nights.

That night Antonio must have pulled a particularly bad ticket. I didn't have time to ask. It was me versus the entire underworld minus M. I was slammed. Each injury weirder and bloodier than the last.

21

More than once, as I wiped down my examination room and washed my hands, I wondered whether Zoey was right to call me a slave. I pulled some hefty paychecks, but I didn't feel like a big girl in the big city. Not anymore. I felt like a grunt down in the trenches, slogging through gore under dubious orders.

Lesson learned working trauma: know your baseline. When you walk into that room where everyone is yelling and the patient is dying, it's no time to practice your etiquette. It's go time.

In the trauma room, the first thing I check is my own heartrate. Anything over 99 beats per minute, I know I'm amped. I gauge my moves accordingly.

The virtues of an x-ray tech are speed, accuracy, and care. We get in, get good pictures, and get those pictures to the doc fast. And, we do it all without harming the patient or delaying the work of others.

To accomplish this, I had to train my eyes. I need the big picture. How the team is working. How the patient is situated. What's my entry point? My exit? But I also have to see through it all.

The best superpower an x-ray tech could wish for is x-ray vision. I'm not going to go full mystic on this, but my superstition, the thing that gets me through a spell of bad luck, is the belief that I can see through it all.

Maybe it's imagination, fantasy coupled with a little anatomy and physiology. I don't think my power is literal like that girl in Russia with the x-ray eyes, but there is a perspective I can adopt where I can see all your insides laid out in front of me. Any picture the doctor wants, even something that's not in the textbook, I'll get it in a single shot.

Granted, I'm not at fast as M or as accurate as Dani, but we've each adopted the x-radiation perspective as our own. The fancy word for it is "radiolucent." It's what separates technologists from button pushers.

We can see through you.

11

I survived the night. There was a point – when the floor kept calling about a standing portable order, while I was pinned down in the ED – I may have slammed down the department phone hard enough to crack the earpiece, but I was simultaneously trying to keep a very sweet, very confused granny from falling off the table between x-rays.

I've never been happier to see Shelly, the day lead, in my life. She wasn't happy to see me, but that's Shelly. She isn't what I would call a fulfilled individual.

When I was a student, I rotated on clinicals through St. Rafa. Shelly was the first tech I met. She wasn't happy to see me then, either. Shelly seldom is happy about anything. Fifty-something, she still lives with her parents.

M thinks Shelly is closeted and super repressed.

"How else do you explain the crimp curled hair and Dallas Cowboys Starter Jacket?" M once asked me.

I said, "That's mean."

"You didn't disagree."

The thing is I don't agree, either. M is right about one thing. Somehow Shelly missed out on being the person she truly is. The thing that makes her most unhappy is when someone else is being who they truly are. Whether it's the way they walk or the place they go on vacation, Shelly snipes.

The sad thing is Shelly is a natural leader and exceptionally organized. She runs a tight ship, expects a lot from the techs – while at the same time giving everyone the freedom to do things their own style. It's like Shelly knows she's a downer; so she stays out of the way. She takes her breaks only when the breakroom is empty. She says it's because she wants everyone to eat before her, but I've seen the way she flinches and apologizes for the smell of the tuna fish salad she eats day-after-day. I like Shelly, but I don't think Shelly likes Shelly.

She helped me catch up with the outstanding ED orders, and sent the early morning tech up on the portables. Once the dust settled, we reviewed the completed examination report.

She said, "Busy night."

I nodded.

"Why'd you do it?"

I asked, "What do you mean?"

"Take the slack for Tim? We all heard about Melissa. It's total garbage. You know he's going to fire her, right?"

It felt like she'd shocked me with a defibrillator. My heart heaved against my ribs.

She said, "It's garbage, like I said, but she got on the wrong side of Dortman. You of all people know what a bad idea that is."

I shook my head and said, "What do you mean?" Shelly said, "You went to his high school, didn't you? Fellowship Christian Academy?"

"Dortman went to FCA?"

Shelly leaned in conspiratorially and said, "I heard he raped a girl. Then worked it to where the school expelled her. He graduated with honors."

"What?"

"Don't tell me you never heard?"

I kept my face as neutral as possible and said, "Must have been before my time."

She shrugged, "He can't be that much older than you."

12

I said a hurried good-bye and walked up the stairs to the third floor where the spine doctors have offices. Shelly's words made the hospital walls feel thin. The concrete stairs vanished beneath my feet.

There was a guy who graduated four or five years ahead of me at FCA. The stories about him didn't stop at rape. Everyone called him Suicide Steve because the girl, Peggy Nash, wasn't simply expelled, she died from complications during the pregnancy. Her family was never the same.

I know because I was friends with Peggy's younger sister, Beth. She became suicidal after Peggy and the baby died. Beth spent half the fall of her freshman year in a psychiatric hospital. They kept it quiet.

The only reason I know is Beth was kind of, maybe my first girlfriend. We made out exactly twice. This wasn't the type of thing you allowed yourself to be consciously aware of at a small, private Evangelical Christian school.

Whatever may have been between us died in the rumors that went around FCA about Suicide Steve. There were these jokes that bordered on urban legends. It all centered on how massive his dick was. Awful stuff you'd hear leak from the boys locker room. Suicide Steve wasn't a person. I couldn't remember a face or anything, just a giant penis in prep school polo shirt and khakis.

And, I couldn't remember the guy's last name. It was a blind spot in my memory. I knew it once, but I had repressed it.

I repressed a lot in high school. Repression was part of survival at FCA because FCA was uber repressive. A lot of the girls wore wedding rings to indicate they were married to Jesus, which is just weird. Shouldn't the boys be married to Jesus, too? Sex ed was more like abstinence class.

I will never forget the first day of sex ed. We were all in the gym, the girls and boys, sitting on the bleachers. Coach Pitts passed around a paper plate with white cheese cubes. He told us to chew up the cheese and spit it into a clear glass pitcher he passed around. It was disgusting. The boys competed to see who could produce the most cheese spit.

Coach Pitts had another pitcher filled with water.

He said, "Man, I'm thirsty. Are any of y'all thirsty?"

He poured a glass from the cheese spit pitcher. The girls screamed. The boys howled and laughed. Cindy Jamison nearly passed out.

Coach Pitts held up the cheese spit and said, "Anyone want a drink?"

He said, "Imagine these pitchers are the person you're gonna marry. The person you're gonna kiss in front of God and everyone assembled on your wedding day."

That was sex ed.

Anyways, Suicide Steve was partly why I decided on x-ray. I always wanted to do something medical; so I figured nursing. I saw some x-rays on a TV show, and I thought, 'That's it. That's the best way to stop the Suicide Steves in the world. Build a better way to see through people.' I checked radiographic technology on the community college application and never looked back.

I hadn't thought about Suicide Steve in years, but everything snapped into focus when Shelly started dishing the dirt about M. If Dortman was the same guy, I was going to be sick, but it still didn't answer the bigger question – why would a guy like that want to be a doctor? Bigger still, who would let him be a doctor?

13

I found Dortman's name on the office list of physicians. Richard. My unease persisted. Where was his middle initial? The other doctors had all sorts of names and titles and initials. Doesn't everyone have a middle name?

I pushed my way through the door and into the waiting room. It was full of patients and family members. A line stretched to the receptionist. I took a place and waited.

I felt like an idiot. I didn't know what to say. 'Is Dr. Dortman sure his first name is Richard'?

I removed my badge from the collar of my scrubs and stuffed it in my pocket. I'm sure that made me look even more suspicious.

As I stepped up to the counter, I put on my emptiest, most basic smile. I should have paid more attention that time Alex spent an entire night at the club teaching me how to be more basic.

The receptionist greeted me with a professional smirk and said, "May I help you?"

"Hey, this is like crazy, I know, but I think I went to school with Dr. Dortman? And, he was like friends with my friend's sister."

I couldn't bring myself to lie.

I said, "Anyways, the sign out front says his name is like Richard Dortman, and I'm thinking how many Dortmans can there be? Wouldn't it be cool to see this guy I knew in high school who's a doctor now?"

The receptionist was about my age. She could clearly comprehend what I was asking. That might have been the problem. I was angling along her line.

She said, "Oh darling. Isn't that cute?"

I might not speak basic fluently, but I know "isn't that cute" translates to "step the fuck off."

I said, "Is his name Richard Dortman. Like just Richard Dortman?"

She said, "Yep and if you don't have any other questions, Ms…"

She was trying to get my name. I was glad I'd hid my badge.

I said, "Yeah, but it's weird, right? There's no middle initial. And everybody else on the sign has all sorts of names and initials because they're important doctors. You know. Everybody except Richard Dortman. See, the guy I knew. His name was Steve."

I watched her face carefully when I said this. I saw the briefest flicker of what might have been recognition. Then perhaps fear, but it was difficult to say. The receptionist drew her face down into a mask of acute boredom. She was good.

She said, "Dr. Richard Dortman's name is clearly indicated on the sign. Are we done here? Thank you."

I walked away with my head bent low. I almost didn't see Dortman coming down the hall. He was in the middle of a heated conversation with a 30-something woman in a business suit and a techie guy about my age dressed in black jeans and a black tee shirt that read "Big Doctor." The conversation grew more heated, and the guy in black wandered off. He just pivoted and was gone, lost in thought.

Dortman and the woman exchanged looks of exasperation. Seeing them standing there. It made me pause. His wavy brown hair was perfectly disheveled. He was dressed for the office in a tie and a lab coat. The woman's suit cost more than I made in a month. She had black hair, expensively styled. There was a line of gray – perhaps an old scar – that ran through the hair from above her left eye to her ear. If I had to guess, I'd say she liked him. Maybe even loved him.

They looked like they were in a movie, and it wasn't a movie with people like me or the guy in black jeans. At best, we were extras, added color for the scene. Dortman didn't even notice me as I strode their direction. I wanted to keep it that way.

14

As I powered past Dortman, I caught the scent of cologne. Something pine-scented and expensive. I immediately felt dizzy. I don't know if it was the cologne or the two hours of sleep I'd had in the last three days, but black stars swung across my vision. I stumbled into the nearest bathroom and braced myself against the sink. Gradually, the nausea subsided. I needed to eat, but the thought of food made me sad. I splashed water on my face.

As I dried my face, the sleeve of my scrubs rose over my right bicep, and I saw the edge of my tattoo. I pulled the sleeve higher to examine the art in the mirror. I forget it's there.

It's my only tattoo, a portrait done in the Victorian style with floral designs around an oval frame. At its center is Anna Bertha Roentgen, wife of Wilhelm Conrad Roentgen, the man credited with discovering x-rays on November 8, 1895.

Below her picture the tattoo reads in German: "Ich habe meinen Tod gesehen." Translation: "I have seen my death."

Reportedly, Anna Bertha said that after beholding the bones of her hand on the world's first recorded x-ray image.

I know my tat is weird, but I like it. I got it when I graduated x-ray school. I like Anna Bertha because she was smart and tough. She had a hard life, chronic kidney disease. And, while the whole world was bowled over by her husband's discovery, she was the first person to understand it must have some drawbacks. In fact, she might have been the only person alive at that time who suspected that invisible rays, capable of revealing so much, might have a hidden cost.

Someday I want to go to Germany and see where the Rontgen's lived. I listen to German lessons while I run.

As I was collecting myself in front of the mirror, Alex was blowing up my phone, asking whether I was coming to the gym.

I texted, "No," with an exhausted emoji and took a last look at my reflection, wondering whether I had the strength to bike home. In moments like this, Anna Bertha's dire words feel too on the nose to be inspirational.

15

I made it home blasting *Dream Wife* on my bike's Bluetooth speakers. I drank a protein smoothie, jumped in the shower, and turned off my phone before falling into the bed. I almost overslept.

As soon as I punched the clock, I went to Timmy's office. It's nothing fancy, but he has a window. That makes his office better than any other room in radiology. Every inpatient radiology department I've ever been in has a subterranean feel – like working in a fallout shelter, which is pretty much right.

Timmy's administrative assistant, Gail, was at lunch, and Dorothy the outpatient receptionist was sitting behind the admin's desk, reading a continuing education article from *Radiologic Imaging*.

She looked up at me. Her eyes were baby blue, and her face was as wrinkled as fried chicken. I remembered her sitting in the backyard praying to the angel statue in the middle of the night and shivered.

Nodding at the radiography magazine, I said, "I thought only techs read those."

Dorothy said, "I am a tech."

"Really? Why are you at the reception desk? We need warm bodies in the department."

Dorothy shook her head and said, "I'm retired."

I'm sure she could read the confusion on my face, but she didn't explain.

She said, "He's in there."

Tim was looking at reports when I knocked on the door.

He said, "Dorothy? I thought I said no interruptions."

I glanced back at her.

She rolled her eyes and said, "Ignore him."

I nudged the door open and said, "Hey, I'm sorry."

Tim looked up from the reports on his desk and said, "Oh, it's you. Come in. I tried calling you a couple times earlier, but it went to voicemail."

I was glad I'd turned off my phone. I'd have to remember that going forward.

Through the door, Dorothy said, "You do know that some people have to sleep during the day, right Tim?"

Timmy the Fearless motioned for me to close the door, but he did not indicate I could sit. Whether he was being dumb or deliberate was impossible to say. Perhaps both. Tim tilted back in his chair and put his hands behind his head.

He said, "I wanted to let you know, HR has given priority status to the review of Melissa's file. This stays between you and me. The only reason I'm sharing this is because I know you're picking up the slack."

"Thanks," I said.

I didn't feel grateful. Timmy the Fearless earned his nickname doing his best impersonation of a tough guy within the department and caving anytime he had to face-down hospital administration.

He said, "I'm looking at these reports right now to find a way to justify another full-time employee so we can have more coverage in situations like this."

"About that. I've been thinking. I have a solution. Take the cost for damages out of my paycheck and call it good."

Timmy pulled his hands from behind his head and rocked forward in his chair. He's the kind of guy who never completely lost his baby fat. His hair was starting to thin, and the image of a giant baby in a Joseph A. Bank suit was difficult to shake.

He said, "I'm confused. Can you elaborate?"

I shifted on my feet, trying to hide my frustration. This was a pet peeve of mine: people intentionally acting confused. I knew Tim wasn't actually dumfounded. It was just a stupid communication technique he learned at a management conference.

I said, "M is on probation because she crashed the portable into a wall in ICU, right? So, take the costs for repair out of my paycheck, and we're good."

Timmy shook his head and said, "I wish it were that easy, Claire. While the situation you mentioned does color the review slightly, the accident with the portable is not the reason for Melissa's probation."

I started to speak, but Timmy the Fearless held up his hand.

"More than that I can't say. Anyways, the hole in the wall is small potatoes. Look, I appreciate your concern, but the department has a budget for incidental expenses. Can you imagine how it would look if we docked tech pay every time someone made a mistake?"

I wanted to say, can you imagine how it would look if you stood behind techs and supported us rather than caving to administration's every whim? I held my tongue.

Respondeat superior is an oft misunderstood and misapplied legal term. It's Latin for "let the master answer," and the concept guides civil legal cases in which an employee causes harm due to instructions given them by their employer.

Too often *respondeat superior* is a cop out for the spineless. It provides a rationale for caving in. I'm sure the Romans or whoever came up with *respondeat superior* didn't think about it that way. They probably imagined anyone with sense enough *wants* to be the master. Unlike Timmy the Fearless, they want to answer.

That's what I want at least. I want to master the art of taking x-rays. I want to answer for myself, but that's a totally different read on *respondeat superior*. A way of thinking I doubt Tim is capable of understanding.

These were the kinds of things I told myself while ignoring whatever Timmy the Fearless was rambling about. His fall back was always policy. Lots of policy. Anytime Tim starts talking policy, it's like an anesthetic gas. My brain goes off line.

At some point he must have dismissed me because I found myself wandering out his office door in a sort of painless haze, uncertain about anything. I had entered with a great deal of clarity. I exited in a fog.

16

Dorothy was waiting for me outside Tim's office. She kicked the door closed hard enough to knock a picture off the wall. I didn't hear anything shatter, but it snapped me out of my stupor.

34

Before I could say a word, Dorothy threw a wrinkly arm over my shoulder and guided me out into the hall. At this distance, I could smell the patchouli oil. It seemed out of place with her tendency to violence.

"Why'd you do that?" I said. "He'll think I slammed the door."

Dorothy said, "Figured that's what you wanted."
She smiled blithely.

"That was stupid, you know. Telling him to dock your pay. Dumb move."

I said, "You were listening?"
Dorothy ignored the question.

"Now, he knows your weak spot."

I said, "Everyone knows I'm friends with M."

She pinched my shoulder hard and said, "No, your weak spot is you don't know dick about policy. Plus, you just showed him you're willing to think outside the box and stand-up for people. Two strengths that are diametrically opposed to that gutless wonder."

I was increasingly uncomfortable with the tenor of this conversation. I couldn't help but agree with what Dorothy was saying, but she had to be crazy, slamming doors and throwing her weight around.

She said, "I know what you're thinking. What the hell does a secretary know about the price of beans? Old witch ought to mind her own business."

She pinched me again. It hurt. I wanted to knock her hand away, but I was afraid she'd fall. I'd wind up doing a hip x-ray on her. She was that old. It was kind of a miracle she had the dexterity to pinch so hard.

Dorothy said, "I used to run this department. Back when administrators gave a shit. I had a department full of headstrong dumbasses like you. The best goddamned bunch of misfits who ever screwed an anode with an electron. I keep telling myself if I had just one of those jackasses with me we'd turned this place upside down."

She was crazy. That was the only explanation, and the only reason I didn't tear myself out of her grasp and run screaming down the fluorescent lit hall was I felt a begrudging responsibility to determine if she posed a threat to herself or anyone else.

In my best, most placid voice, I said, "I understand. How does that make you feel?"

She stopped, spun me on my feet, dropped her free hand on my other shoulder, and stared me in the eye for a long hard moment.

Dorothy laughed and said, "Get out of here, you dipshit."

She shoved me down the hall in the direction of the bunker.

As she walked away, I could hear her muttering, "She thinks we're crazy. They fucking all do. Jesus, is it even worth the effort?"

Her rant almost sounded like a prayer.

17

Most every radiology department is set up in a hub and spoke design with exam rooms surrounding a long central hallway. This layout was essential in the days of film. On one end of the hall was the darkroom, on the other the radiologist reading room. Between the two was a line of exam rooms and a wall of light boxes. Everything fed passed the light boxes. The techs would hang films fresh from the developer and review their work. The light boxes were the beating heart of what we called the bunker.

The older techs say we lost something when we stopped developing film. The light boxes. By that I mean, we lost the heart of the department. Work became decentralized, which isn't all bad, but I think our pictures suffer for it.

The x-ray view boxes were like the department coffee pot. During downtime techs would stand around the light boxes and conversation would inevitably turn to the x-rays. People would congratulate you on a perfect lateral knee; offer tips on how to improve a barium enema; commiserate over missing a tricky axial shot.

Now, the darkroom has been converted to storage. The light boxes are relics, taking up space. Everything is done with computers, and those conversations about ways to improve our game? – during downtime now most techs have their heads in their phones. No one talks. Not like they used to. So I'm told.

A lot of this I've heard from Shelley. She remembers the days of film. Similar to the light boxes, she has a PACS computer by her desk. PACS is the picture archiving system, a secure network server of images, and Shelley keeps the PACS monitor open at the center of the bunker. She pulls up every single picture the day shift takes, looks at it, and lets the tech know what she thinks about their work – good or bad – when they pass through the bunker. Most the new techs hate it. The old techs get it.

Something about what Dorothy said made me wish we could go back to the days of film or at least the days of the light box. When I hold an x-ray film it makes me feel like I'm at a wedding or something - like there's hope.

X-ray films are solid, sure things. You take this weird theoretical phenomena, x-rays, pass them through a person's body; capture the remnant x-rays on a emulsion-gelatin of silver halide crystals; run the film through a processor; and you have this glowing work of art. I love that I can hold an x-ray film. I love that it's dark but glows.

Sometimes I wonder if – instead of rising up and destroying humanity – the computers will gradually erode away at our purpose until people simply have no imaginable use. I wonder if that isn't already the case, if the machines haven't robbed us of our wonder.

18

I don't think Shelly gave a crap about light boxes or lifelong learning. I think she liked busting people's chops and was willing to offer begrudging kudos on the good pics in exchange for the right to trash the bad ones. Anyways, that's where I found her, at the middle of the bunker, staring at a particularly awful portable chest x-ray.

She said, "Look at this."

The disgust in her voice was hot enough to cauterize flesh.

She said, "This is what passes for diagnostic imaging. I can't believe the radiologist read it. It's getting to where they're part of the problem."

I said, "What should the docs do?"

"Reject it. Track down the tech and tell them what an awful chest x-ray this is. Tell them in great detail why it's shitty, and demand that they drop whatever they're doing and go shoot another one, and that they better not make the same mistake in the future because people's lives depend on these pictures."

I could see the sense in that. It would take the docs away from their reading stations, but what are they, cyborgs? Will they die if they step away from their computers for five minutes and interact with humanity? Despite the short-term time lost, I can't imagine how feedback like that wouldn't benefit everyone – especially the patient – in the long run.

Shelly said, "That's what the docs used to do. Back when the light boxes were here. I will never forget Doc Gieseman's voice. He'd throw open that door and shout, 'Shelly, who took this goddamn portable chest?' Every tech in the department would pray to God it wasn't them, but man when he liked something you did, he'd let everyone know, 'That's how you do a fucking y-view.' You ask anyone who's been here long enough and they'll tell you about Doc Gieseman. Every one of them will say they're better techs for having known him. He got throat cancer. He chewed cigars, sitting in the reading room. The whole department went to his funeral. I mean the whole department. We carried pagers and everyone went. Those were different times."

I said, "About that. Is it true that Dorothy used to manage the department? I thought she was a receptionist."

Shelly turned and looked me up and down.

She said, "Did Dorothy Hicks manage the department? Hell, Dorothy Hicks built this department. You've been here what? — three years? How could you work here that long and not know that?"

"I'm not here much during the day. By the time I'm clocked in, she's out. Anyways, if she was so great, why's she a receptionist? Why isn't she still managing?"

Shelly laughed, "I'm sure she'd take over from Tim in the drop of a hat, but she can't. Doctors orders. This was, what? – ten years ago? Dorothy had a massive MI. Right there in the manager's office. They said if it happened anywhere else than inside the hospital, she'd be dead. Her admin called the code team and started chest compressions. They wheeled her into the ED on a department stretcher, and she was in surgery in thirty minutes flat. After that, Doc Abbot told her she couldn't manage anymore."

"But she couldn't stay away."

"Pretty much. Some folks, x-ray gets in the blood. Funny you asking about Dorothy."

"Yeah, why's that?"

"She was in here the other day asking about you."

19

Sometime that afternoon an email went out from Gary Bevoort, St. Rafa's CEO. He was stepping down from his position. In addition to his role as Chief Physician, Dr. Richard Dortman would be the interim CEO.

There was other stuff in the email. CEO stuff that no one except a CEO believes. Example: you can't manage what you can't measure. Now, there's a bedpan that needs changing. I can't measure effective radiation dose to the patient, but you better believe I manage it. Anything less than strictly managed radiation dose is negligent or, worse, malpractice.

No one could measure the impact of that email on staff morale, but we still had to manage patient care. People don't stop getting sick just because your hospital is in the middle of an organizational autopsy, which is what my swing shift felt like. Everybody seemed to be grimly dissecting the tissue of their own departments looking for the fatal disease.

We all know administrators don't "step down." Bevoort got canned. I'd bet my left ovary Dortman did it.

I was steamed. Walking down those long white halls, it was like you could see the compound fractures poking out of the hospital's walls. At any moment, the elevators in the main lobby would open up and flood the first floor with hemorrhaging blood.

The hospital was in traumatic shock. Folks who were usually focused and energetic were stumbling around in a doped haze. I felt angry at the patients for wandering through the doors needing to be patched up. Couldn't they see St. Rafa was circling the drain? I felt angry at myself for being so compromised I couldn't recall the basics of how to do the patching that I was certified competent to do.

20

It was only me and Dani at El Burrito Volador that night. He went straight to the tequila, ordering two shots before we'd sat down.

He said, "I refuse to drink tequila alone."

I said, "Ask the waitress. I'm not drinking with you. I've got eight more hours of fun ahead of me."

When the drinks arrived, Dani pushed a shot at me. I pushed it back.

He stopped my hand and said, "You're going to drink that shot."

I lifted the glass, "To your health."

While he tossed his down, I poured mine on the floor.

Wiping his lips on the back of his hand, Dani gave me a hard look. His muscles tensed.

I dropped the shot glass. It shattered. I had been going for effect but not full-on broken glass effect. Fortunately, there were only a few other people in the place. I was on that thin line between making a point and making a scene. It took everything in me not to start cleaning up.

Dani wrapped one fist in the other hand and popped each knuckle. He did the same with the other hand, tilting his head from side to side like a boxer before the bell.

He said, "This is exactly what Dr. Dipshit wants. Us fighting each other."

"Maybe so, maybe not," I said, staring him down. "I don't do things just because someone tells me to, and I don't drink before my shift."

Dani flinched first. He tried to pass it off with a smile, but his eyes betrayed him. For all his muscle and swagger, he wasn't a fighter.

He said, "Whatever floats your boat."

"Precisely. Now, help me clean up this mess."

This was a test. Would he sit back and watch me pick up the pieces or would he pitch in and help? The mess was technically mine, but I wanted to know if Dani could see that my mess was our mess. I needed to know if he was on my team.

Dani helped. Afterward, I bought him a beer, and the tension oozed away from our table, returning to that dark corner of the city where angst lives. I ordered a coffee and a burrito smothered in queso. Some folks have tequila. For me, it's queso.

The conversation returned to the STAT lumbar spine exam that started this whole situation. Neither Dani nor I had seen the study that shook up M so bad, but everything hinged on those images. The question was – could we see the pictures?

This was more difficult than it would seem. If we had been in the department at the time the images went to PACS, it would have made sense to review the pictures, but now that we were three days out, pulling the images up without the patient having some direct bearing on our work was a violation of the Health Information Privacy and Portablity Act or HIPAA.

HIPAA is pretty much whatever a facility makes it, and there are loopholes. Like for example education. You can claim you were reviewing old images for learning purposes, but anyone who pulled up the study would be flagged in the system, and Dortman was watching the system. People had lost their jobs for searching patient information on members of the Texas football team.

Dani said, "Say you walk into the department, review the pics, and there's something jacked up about the spine hardware, where would you draw the line between genuine mistake and intentional harm? Would you even be able to tell?"

He had a point. Negligence means neglecting reasonable care. Gross negligence or "reckless disregard for life or limb" is like next level unreasonableness. The point being it's all about reasonableness. It'd be hard to make a determination of reasonableness (or lack thereof) from a single radiograph.

One exception might be an abdomen film that made the rounds of few years ago demonstrating a patient's stomach with a large a metal bezoar composed of over one hundred random objects – nuts, bolts, scissors, tweezers – all swallowed during a prolonged episode of psychosis. The patient stated that he was swallowing the objects in order to treat tuberculosis. Do an online search for "metal in stomach" and you'll see radiographic evidence of unreasonableness. It's in the British Journal of Medicine.

There's other examples out there. Whole coffee table books dedicated to x-rays of everyday objects stuck in the rectums of everyday people. The point is unless Dr. Dortman intentionally inserted random metal objects into the patient or left a surgical sponge in her body, gross negligence would be tough to prove. M hadn't indicated that either situation was the case.

Dani said, "If there is something wrong, x-ray is pretty much the first place it would show up. There's a boatload of malpractice cases won off the x-rays."

Malpractice is the term applied to professional negligence. When you have a professional duty to care for a patient and you screw up, that's malpractice. It's all about what a reasonable professional would do in a similar circumstance.

Proof of malpractice requires establishing four things: duty to provide care; patient loss or injury; responsibility for the loss; and proof that the loss was a result of negligence or intentional harm. It would be darn near impossible to prove all four points from a picture, but Dani was right. X-ray was a start.

Something about the L-spine x-ray had upset M, and knowing that the x-ray tech was upset by what she saw was enough to convince Dortman he needed to track her down and threaten her.

I glanced out the window. The x-ray lightbox was dark in Dorothy Hick's garden. What had she said? I don't know policy? She was psychotic not delusional.

Speaking of delusions, the wheels were turning in Dani's head. His face becomes serious when he's thinking, which isn't often. Normally he wears a mask of humor. Everything is a joke, but I'm close enough to know the real Dani. He's almost the kind of guy I could like. Almost.

He said, "We definitely don't need to be pulling up that study under our own PACS logins. We need to figure out a work around for viewing the images on PACS to where they can't trace it back to us."

I said, "What you're talking about is illegal."

Dani pursed his lips and said, "Not exactly. The hospital is required to monitor who accesses what on the electronic medical record, but there are work arounds."

I have zero interest in Dani. I like him. If I was desperate or drunk, maybe, once, but that's not me. At least, I hope it's not, and I hope he has zero interest in me apart from the normal animal interest that every guy has in anything with legs.

I'm not a complete cynic like Alex, but I'm also familiar enough with physiology to have an inkling of the crippling effects of testosterone on otherwise healthy brain tissue. My dream guy is a little more serious, a lot less into Gucci Mane, and definitely not an x-ray tech. The idea of two people romantically involved and capable of seeing through each other sounds like a horror movie.

I said, "I don't like where this is headed."

Dani said, "We have a right to see the pictures because they have directly impacted our ability to care for patients. What we're debating is whether the powers that be need to know we're accessing the info—"

"If those powers are corrupt."

Dani nodded and drained his beer.

I said, "I still don't like where this is headed."

21

Sunday nights are often a horror show in the ED. People do desperate things to avoid work on Monday. Exhibit A: nicely bound books of everyday objects – shampoo bottles, cucumbers, light bulbs – in everyday rectums.

Monday nights, by contrast, are typically slow. People are resigned to fate, exhausted by the weekend, and defeated by the workday. You might get one attempted suicide, but those are late bloomers. If you're going to end it all, you do it before the workweek starts.

Once, as I helped clean up after a messy self-inflicted gunshot wound to the head, Nurse Trixie, one of my homegirls in the ED, said, "If someone wants to kill themselves, they should do it, and do it right. I don't see the point of keeping anyone alive who doesn't have the fight left in them. It's cruel to everyone."

Maybe she's right, but it sounds like cheating, like missing some essential part of being human. I suspect the guy who shot himself would side with me. Maybe I'll ask him someday. He survived. About five-percent of people put a bullet in their own head and live. The bones of the skull are weird. Bullets don't always do what you expect.

The point being, you develop some thick skin about desperation and despair after a few graves in the ED. So, I hung around with the ED crew that night. I tried to gauge their vibe on the hospital's new CEO, but the overall sense was apathy.

The nightshift at an emergency department is a pretty tough bunch of nuts. Like Trixie's real name isn't Trixie. She earned her nickname when it got out that she and Ron from respiratory therapy were hooking-up in the prayer room during their lunch breaks. Neither of them were fired. Sometimes the best job security is doing the work no one else wants.

The docs that night both looked unfortunately youthful – like still in high school. Behind their backs, the staff dubbed them "Barely Legal" and "Jailbait." The department could probably run itself without them.

The doctors kept busy with patient history and physicals, elaborating upon various brow-wrinkling poses so they would appear to be above needing to give orders.

There was a PACS viewing station behind the charge nurse desk. Anytime the docs weren't with a patient they hid behind the PACS computer. Jailbait was genuinely flustered by Trixie's none-too-subtle attempts at getting into his pants.

At one point, he called me over to the PACS workstation to ask my thoughts on a patient's CT. I had to confess my ignorance. Still, I love looking at CT images. I could meander through a brain study with the same mindless abandon that other folks browse Pinterest. He left me to scroll through the images.

This was my chance to pull up the L-spine exam. No one could trace it back to me, and Dani was right. I needed to see the pictures for myself.

I did a database query and found the study quickly enough. I hesitated before pulling up the images. This was too easy. Was I digging myself deeper? Was this something best left alone? What would I do if I saw something on the images? What if there was nothing wrong with the images? I took a deep breath and clicked the study.

There was only one picture: an anterior-posterior lumbar spine, AP L-spine for short. AP means the x-rays entered the patient's front and exited the back. This was an image of the patient's lower spine viewed as though they were standing in front of me. Their right was on my left and their left on my right.

A spinal decompression (or spinal fusion) surgery is like building a little metal suspension bridge along the spine. The metal bridge screws into the vertebral pedicles. The pedicles are two bony protrusions extending posteriorly from a vertebral body. It's important that the screws are placed at the center of the pedicles and securely anchored in the vertebral body. Between the two pedicles lies the spinal cord. Failure to place the screws in the pedicles can result in irritation of the spinal cord. Translation: intense pain. Worse. Paralysis.

48

On the x-ray image, the two lower screws appeared a little steep, like maybe they weren't completely inside the pedicles. It was difficult to say. The angles were symmetrical. The radiologist report didn't mention much more than an impression of surgical placement of hardware.

There was politics there – between the rads and the surgeons – the assumption being that the surgeons knew best what they were after with the placement of the various fasteners and hardware used in the operating room.

What I'm saying is nothing jumped out at me as evidence of intentional malpractice. It looked like a routine post-op image.

I closed the study and returned to the bunker feeling defeated. I don't know what I hoped to find in the exam. I should be glad the x-ray looked good. I'm sure the patient was glad. Instead, I felt lost. I didn't know who to trust anymore. When the day crew arrived, I biked home in silence.

Unfortunately, Alex was there with some guy. Gauging by the rhythm and pitch of her voice, they would be at it for at least another thirty minutes. Alex has sex in many different ways, but in the morning, it sounds like an aerobics class. Through the thin bedroom walls, I could hear her counting reps to Lady Gaga.

I grabbed my swimsuit and the keys to her Kia Soul and drove to Barton Springs. Austin sits on an ecotone. North of town is the Blackland Prairie; west is the Hill Country; south is the Gulf Coast and Rio Grande Valley. Barton Springs is the spiritual contact point of these different biomes.

The springs sit at the bottom of a shallow canyon. The land is hilly and rocky. The ground is grassy. Large live oaks grow on the lawn. Barton Springs is better than a trip to the beach. The water is clear, shining like an emerald. The temperature stays between 68 and 74 degrees year-round. Warm in the winter. Freezing in the burning summer sun. By unofficial law, it's pretty much open whenever. M and I once took our lunch break at 200 hours to go swimming under the light of the full moon. Far from being the only people there in the middle of the night, the place was almost busy.

I prefer swimming to running, but being on the ecotone divides the city, too. There's Austin north of the lake and Austin south. For whatever reason they feel distinct from each other – two different cities. I don't make the springs but once a week. Sometimes less.

Barton Springs is long. There's an eighth-mile marker for swimmers. I normally swim a mile. I was on my last lap when a cute guy walked across the lawn and spread his towel next to mine. I say he was cute, but I don't know for sure. He was wearing a swim cap and racing briefs. He had a serious face, kind of ugly. Like ugly-cute. Is that a thing? My goggles were fogged.

Alex says there's only three types of guys. You can tell the type by the way a man wears swim briefs. There's the self-conscious type. That's the majority of guys. They wear their briefs like they're stuck in a bad dream — gone to school in their underwear. Anyone swimming laps in bathing trunks fits in this category, too. There's the overconfident type. These are the guys who buy the briefs with the eight-ball in the front and pool rack in the back. Enough said. Finally, there's the utilitarian type. Their only thought is briefs are the right clothes for the job. Give me a utilitarian man any day.

He dove in, and I found myself swimming alongside him. The water felt tingly, full of potential. There's not a lot of guys my age swimming at Barton Springs at 700 hours. I held my breath and dove down, trying to look at him underwater. That didn't help. I never completely caught my breath afterward.

I don't remember how many more laps I made. I tried my best to impress him, but I was feeling waterlogged and woozy as I drug myself up the ladder. I collapsed on my towel. I must have passed out. When I woke-up, he and his towel were gone.

I drove home jamming Courtney Barnett – the kind of music Alex hates. I had a feeling I'd see the guy again, even though I hadn't exactly seen him the first time. I saw enough of him. Like I said, I prefer swimming to running.

22

Over the next few days, life became a tunnel of hospital and home. During my downtime, I read the St. Rafa's policy manual. Sad, I know, but I swore to myself that was as far as I'd go RE: picking up what Dorothy Hicks was putting down. She circled me like a flightless old buzzard. Random folks told me Dorothy Hicks asked about me: Trixie, Dani, Dr. Lasseter. I made a practice of avoiding her in the halls.

I didn't realize it was Halloween until I walked into the ED and saw Trixie dressed as a naughty nurse.

She's the kind of girl who can pull that crap off without getting sent home. Dirty blonde, mid-thirties. You'd think by the sound of her voice – gravely and low – she's a smoker but nope. She just has that sleazy, nightclub singer voice that guys like for some dumb reason. She drives a big black Ford F150 with a lift and bass speakers you can hear three blocks away.

Trixie blew me a kiss and said, "Get ready for the night from hell."

I rolled my eyes. I don't completely subscribe to the full moon and horseshoe set of hospital superstitions. Halloween is pretty much every night in the ED only with more costumes. What I'm saying is – seen from the patient's perspective – any night in the ED is a night from hell.

In the same vein, I was beginning to consider the possibility that the thing between M and Dortman had been blown out of proportion. It wouldn't be the first time M went high drama on something that was more melodrama. I was ready to give them both the benefit of the doubt and move forward. That is until Shelly stopped me on her way out the door.

She said, "I almost forgot. There's a surgery scheduled for 2300 tonight."

I said, "What the heck?"

She shrugged and said, "Dortman."

With that she left. There was nothing else to say. Not with all the security cameras and microphones in the place. Now, I am getting paranoid. I didn't curse, but I wanted to.

If the daytime surgery schedule runs late, that's one thing. Sure, it's a pain, but you cover it. Acute appendicitis, they're going to dial the on-call surgical team, but an elective surgery *scheduled* in the middle of the night is weird. As in patient with an extra head weird. I've never seen it before.

I looked at the OR list, and there was nothing all evening until – bam – lumbar fusion at 2300 hours. Trixie was right. The gates of hell were wide open. *Res ipsa loquitor.* That's legalese for stuff so obviously wrong even a lawyer can see it.

The first thing I did was call Timmy the Fearless on his cell. He was pissed in this completely passive aggressive way. Like instead of "hello," he said, "I'm trick-or-treating with my family."

I said, "And, I'm trick-or-treating with cannibals."

Tim said, "What are you talking about?"

I told him about the surgery. He tried to act unsurprised, but I could tell it was the first he'd heard about it.

He said, "Can you ask someone from the swing crew to work late?"

Coming from Timmy the Fearless, this wasn't a question. It was an order.

He said, "How about Dani?"

I said, "OK. And if Dani has places to go, people to see? –what's my back-up? Do we have a call tech?"

He said, "Me, I guess."

I said, "You guess? How close are we to getting M back?"

He made a noise.

I said, "*Are* we getting M back?"

Timmy said, "HR is reviewing her case as quickly as they can."

I said, "What about Dortman's case? How is it that he's still working and she's not?"

"There's not a case against Dortman."

My jaw dropped. I had assumed. Oh, assumption. What a tricky bitch goddess you are.

Timmy the Fearless said, "Listen, ask Dani. If he can't cover, call me."

I said, "Sounds like a plan, but you better answer when I call. Scratch that. I'm giving you an ultimatum. If I call and you don't answer, I'm biking to your house with a foghorn. I will wake up your whole block. I'm not going into this stuff alone night after night. I need back-up."

Tim said, "I will answer my phone. I promise."

I hung up.

23

Dani could cover until midnight, but he had a date at 100 hours. I didn't ask him what kind of date a person makes at 100 hours. I didn't want to know.

Frankly, I hated this option worse. It was the ambiguous, 'Yes I can cover, but I don't know if the time I can cover will cover everything that might happen in the time that needs covering.' It's like wearing an outfit that doesn't fit quite right and you have to keep readjusting to ensure you're not flashing everyone.

I texted Tim. He replied that he'd be on standby starting midnight. I don't want to be an angry person. I don't want to end up like Shelly, finding fault with everyone and everything all the time. Still, I couldn't help but feel angry at Dani and Tim for leaving me stranded right when I needed them.

There's probably more mature ways to handle anger, but I worked mine out by developing an elaborate sexual fantasy involving the guy swimming laps at Barton Springs. This was like a sex fantasy worthy of Disney animation with singing salamanders and bright bubbles gushing from the enchanted waters around us because we all know it is physically impossible to have sex in Barton Springs considering the water temperature. Come to think of it the water temperature is probably the one thing saving the springs from becoming another redneck glory hole like McKinnley Falls.

At 2200 hours, as I wheeled the C-arm into OR Room 6 for the fusion surgery, Aunt Flo came to visit. My uterus felt like it was full of cement. I didn't have anything in my messenger bag. I had to use one of those awful tampons the ED stocks for rape victims, the mentally ill, and anyone too out of sorts to remember their monthly visit. At that point, I included myself in the list of people pissing me off.

Dortman's nurse, Vanessa, was next on the list, telling me how to do my job. She had the almost orangish look of someone who spends too much time in a tanning bed. Anyone who fake bakes knows zip about safe use of electromagnetic radiation, but I didn't tell her that.

After scrubbing in, Dortman took one look at me and said, "You're new."

I said, "I've worked here five years."

He said, "First time I've seen you. Do you know what you're doing?"

"Yep."

He turned around and said, "Tie me up."

The fun began. The first part of the operation, they only need x-ray for localization. The operating team wants to make sure they're at the base of the spine before they start the incision. We use a big fluoroscope, an x-ray video camera, called a C-arm. The machine looks kind of 1980s sci-fi. It's a C-shaped thing about five-feet-wide with an x-ray tube on one side and an image receptor on the other. You put whatever you need x-rayed inside the "C" and you get live footage on the monitor.

C-arms are awesome, but like everything in x-ray they are clunky. That's why ballerinas make bad x-ray techs. Being a tech is more like driving a forklift. You have this big motorized chunk off the Large Hadron Collider that you have to bang around a little to make work. Folks in the OR tend to mistake our clunkiness with clumsiness because their own work – especially the spine surgery team – involves small, precision movements guided by microscopes and fancy robotic visualization systems.

I jostled and craned the C-arm into position, taking care to avoid the sterile field. X-ray equipment is probably the most contaminated stuff in the room apart from people's cell phones, and since everyone scrubbed in can't stare at their phones while you're clunking into position, they stare at you, which is fine, whatever. Judge me. I am x-ray. Hear me beep.

I shot a perfect lateral and wheeled the machine out of the way as the surgical team stepped from behind the lead barriers and swung the microscopes into position. I felt good. Shooting a solid lateral proved this wasn't my first rodeo.

As I removed my lead apron and thyroid shield, I hit record on my cellphone. I had the voice-recording app pulled up the whole time I'd been in the room. If he was going to assault or slander anyone, I wanted it on the record.

I said, "Doctor Dortman, I'm the only x-ray tech in the hospital after midnight. I'm carrying the department cell. I promise when y'all call I'll be here in under two minutes. May I have your permission to leave the OR?"

"Fine, but don't be fucking slow like that last bitch."

My face burned under the surgical mask. There it was, that infectious nastiness. There's nothing more virulent in the healthcare team than a bitter white male with an MD after his name.

I said, "I'm not sure who you mean."

Without glancing in my direction, he said, "Incision."

The circulating nurse charted the time: 00:01. All Saints Day.

24

As glad as I was to be away from Dortman, I knew I was probably safer staying in the OR and calling Tim to cover the ED. But if I claimed I was supposed to hang in the OR and Timmy the Fearless drug his sorry butt in to cover an ED with nothing happening and *then* found out Dortman gave me permission to float, there'd be trouble. Any way you sliced it, I was the chicken right before decapitation, dreaming of running.

The ED was quiet – like "too quiet" quiet, which is a real thing around hospitals. As thick as his calvarium may be, Dani knew he was leaving me in the lurch. He'd hung around the department to say his final farewell, which felt selfish like he wanted exoneration for deserting me in favor of a booty call.

There was a time – a very brief time – when I thought Dani and me could maybe possibly be an item. We're well passed that now. The man keeps a yo-yo in his pocket for down time. He had the good sense to keep the yo-yo in his pocket while he waited for me.

If I begged him to stay, he'd stay, but I didn't want to beg, and Dani didn't want to stay. I also didn't want to tell him "Go" – like I thought he should go because I didn't think he should go. I thought he should do what I would do and take one for the team. Tell his sexy witch the magic broom ride would have to wait. Instead, I stood there and watched him draw back into himself the way guys do when their feelings come too close to the surface.

Dani said, "You'll be fine."

And he turned and left.

Within fifteen minutes the ED lit up like Rockefeller Center on Black Friday.

The American Registry of Radiologic Technologists publishes a lot of stuff that – when you're a student in x-ray school – seems like cheap anesthesia. Read it for two minutes and you're out cold. I was genuinely shocked the first time I re-read the ARRT Standards of Ethics after working at St. Rafa for a few years. The words transformed before my eyes into this fiery manifesto, a furious cry for justice in the face of savagery and oppression.

The Standards of Ethics has two parts – the Code of Ethics, which is like the Ten Commandments of x-ray, and the Rules of Ethics, which is a laundry list of stuff that seems obviously wrong to most folks except for the chosen few who beg to differ. Example – fraudulent billing practices.

I found myself thinking a lot about the Standards of Ethics that night. I've shorten them for memorization: be a pro; give humanity dignity; play fair and impartial; know your machine; act in the patient's best interest; know the patient's history; minimize radiation dose; be ethical; maintain confidentiality; strive for improvement; and don't do drugs. I considered emailing the ARRT and asking if they'd add "don't be a selfish jackass who deserts your friends and fellow techs when they most need you so that you can hook up with single moms."

25

I stayed on top of the flood long enough for the ED to back flow into the waiting room, which was the best possible thing that could happen. The more I thought about it the less I wanted to call Timmy. I couldn't remember the last time I'd seen him wearing scrubs. He'd only get in the way.

Meanwhile, Dortman was taking his sweet time. Hardware placement for a fusion requires two hours tops. By 300 hours, I started feeling paranoid like – what if I missed the call? – would I get suspended? – would I even care if I got suspended? Should I move to Colorado and join the ski patrol? That's where my mind goes whenever life starts to get me down. Colorado.

At 3:45 the OR called. I was in the middle of wheeling an ED patient down the hall for a chest x-ray. I wheeled him right back to his room in the ED; asked Trixie to plug him into the monitor; and sprinted up three flights of stairs to the OR. I pulled my surgical mask on as I pushed through the doors, and I froze.

OR Room 6 was something out of a nightmare. I've seen surgery. I've seen blood, but this was next level. There was a red pool beneath the table. My C-arm was splattered with bits of gore. There were bone fragments pasted to the surgical lights by clots of leukocytes.

My arms shook. My hands went numb. The sounds in the room swarmed around my head. In a cardiogenic fog, I realize Dortman was singing along to Frank Sinatra as he hacked away at this person's spine. I hate Frank Sinatra.

I tried to make eye contact with the rest of the surgical team, but they looked professionally empty. They were watching this atrocity show, telling themselves, 'another day in paradise.' All except Vanessa. She stood watch like a bouncer at a tanning salon.

The operating room door swung closed behind me. Vanessa turned her gaze to me. The only way out of this was deeper in. I pulled on gloves along with my lead apron and cleaned the blood off the C-arm controls as I awaited the doctor's orders.

Dortman was drilling away intently with a power driver. He stopped from time-to-time to inspect his progress through medical loupes – surgical glasses with a headlight and magnifying lenses. He glanced up at me over the tops of the loupes.

Vanessa said, "X-ray."

I rolled and clunked my machine into place as the team walked behind the lead shields.

I remember thinking it was odd that Dortman and Vanessa were that much in tune. Surgical teams often arrive at that place where they can finish each other's sentences and marriages, but her calling his x-rays was telepathy if I ever saw it.

The image was a good lateral, but the screws were whack. All four of them spinning off in separate directions. Generally, screw placement lines up in neat little rows, following symmetrical spinal anatomy, the pedicles. The first thing I thought when I saw the picture was Dortman would be working on this patient when the day crew arrived.

He studied the image on the C-arm monitor. I'm not sure, but it looked like he was smiling under his mask. Difficult to say.

Dortman said, "Good. Great. That's all. Good work…"

He let the sentence hang. I realized he was asking my name.

I said, "Claire."

"OK," he laughed.

Vanessa joined in. I missed the joke. Awkward.

Dortman said, "No need to save that. Don't send it to PACS. We're done. Suture."

He pushed my machine out of the way with his bloody elbow and began sewing up the patient.

My head spun as I maneuvered the C-arm away from the surgical table. The machine was still draped, dripping gore on the blood-soaked floor. They were going to sew this person up with lose screws running every which way. It was just a matter of time until the fusion failed, and the patient would be right back where they started. Worse. They'd have a pile of metal scrap at the base of their spine.

Out of the corner of my eye, I noticed Vanessa studying me. I began cleaning my machine. I thought, I'll save the image, but the machine chimes when it saves. They would know. I could photograph it with my cell, but that risked a HIPAA violation. One thing I knew for sure, Dortman was wrong. According to policy, C-arm images still required a radiologist read and so needed to be sent to PACS. Most surgeons want a record of their work saved. Something to show the patient.

As I stepped to the monitor to hit save, Vanessa pulled the plug. She didn't say anything just stood watching me for a beat. She dropped the blood-smeared power cord on the floor and ambled back to the doctor's side of the operating table, rolling her hips as she walked, daring me to say something.

The images were lost forever. Meanwhile, Nurse Vanessa didn't bother putting on new gloves after dropping the power cord. Never mind that she was contaminating everything she touched. They had made me complicit in this mess. All in a day's work.

I left the C-arm. Exited the room. My surgical booties tracked blood down the OR hall. I was still wearing my surgical gown and lead apron. I ripped the shoe covers off, tossed them in the trash, and kept moving, tearing off my gloves, hat, and mask, stuffing them in the trash.

The Home Shopping Network was blaring on the breakroom TV. The coffee was burnt in the pot. I had a little cry, leaning against the sink. Why was Dortman doing this? How was he doing this? I was missing something. Some vital connection. No amount of snorting coke and banging nurses could explain what I witnessed in OR Room 6.

What about the anesthesiologist? – the charge nurse? We might be in the same room, but our jobs are very different. Only Dortman, Vanessa, and I saw the x-ray images. Maybe I witnessed something the anesthesiologist and charge nurse simply didn't see. Welcome to radiology.

I would bounce back. I would be fine, but the patient would never be the same, and the proof that his agony was deliberately planned and methodically implanted was gone. All that remained was a bloody streak down a dead power cord.

26

As I biked home, I stopped by the Torchy's on 51st and Berkman. The bells were ringing at Our Lady's Maronite Church. That's when I realized it was Sunday. Mother would be by in a couple of hours for brunch.

Climbing back on my bike, I pedaled home feeling sad and hungry. I slept for a little over an hour and drug myself into the shower. My hair was still wet when I heard her car horn.

I slipped into a blue shirtdress and flats, ran the blow dryer over my hair, and was out. The day was warm and sunny for early November. Mother gave me a peck on either cheek as I climbed into her Mercedes-Benz.

She said, "What do you feel like?"

With Mom it's never how do you feel or how are you. In Mother's world that information is unasked for and generally unwelcomed.

I said, "You decide."

She said, "Threadgills?"

I nodded. She turned up the volume on Sir Douglas Quintet as we sped down the frontage road to Koenig Lane.

At the brunch line, I piled my plate with migas, salsa, hash browns, garlic cheese grits, bacon, and an omelet stuffed with brisket, jalapeno, and cheddar cheese. Food coma time.

We bowed our heads, Mother said, "Grace," and the band played "Christ for President."

The Gospel Brunch at Threadgills was as close to church as anybody in the place was willing to come. The fact that some of us were upright and clothed at 1000 hours on a Sunday was a miracle.

Mother said, "What's new with you?"

I shrugged, "Not much. There's a doctor at the hospital who's trying to kill people."

"Sounds juicy," Mother said. "Is he single?"

It's always the same with Mother.

I said, "I don't know. Think I should ask?"

She gave me the stink eye. That's the sort of thing a young lady should never ask. You're supposed to find out by osmosis or something.

I said, "You did hear me say he's trying to kill people, right? I didn't know murderers were on your list of potential son-in-laws."

Mother laughed, "Oh Claire, how bad can he be? I imagine people dying comes with the territory. What kind of car does he drive?"

"I don't know."

64

"Is he good looking? Or is he one of those horrible angry little troll doctors? You know the type? The red-faced ones who drive Porsches and play golf?"

I shook my head.

She said, "Don't make that face. I know that face."

"What face?"

"Lord help me. It's Everyday Claire. That's what I call it. The resolute face of a young woman righting the wrongs of the world while ignoring the problems right under her nose. I thought Everyday Claire was a phase."

"Nope. I'm still Claire, every day."

"The worst was high school. My marriage falling apart. Your father and I seeing that awful counselor at the church. Meanwhile, you're obsessed with some boy at school you claimed raped a girl. I don't remember what all. That's what I mean. Everyday Claire. I thought you'd grown out of it, but I suppose it's a coping mechanism."

I held a finger up in the air as I chewed my food. Manners always wins with Mother. I knew better than to attack head on. It was also ill-advised to ignore Mother's accusation all together. She'd never forget this awful theory if she felt it had a grain of truth. I needed to know what she remembered about Suicide Steve.

I said, "I'm not sure what you mean. What boy?"

She said, "How should I know? I had enough on my plate dealing with your father. The point is, girlfriend, you and I both know x-ray's not all that we dreamed it would be—"

"Time out. I love my job."

Mother's face became a mask of forbearance.

She said, "Sure you do honey. It's a great job – if it weren't for all the sick people."

She laughed at her own joke, hiding her mouth behind her napkin. If it were anyone else, she'd say this was gauche – providing her own laugh track.

I ordered a second mimosa. The problem is I still want to please Mother. Even though I know she's impossible. Perhaps because she's impossible. She looks impossibly beautiful and imposing for however old she is. I have literally never learned her age. When Mother approves of something – even her passing approval of the band's cover of "Down in the Churchyard" by the Flying Burrito Brothers – I feel all is right in the world.

Her silver and turquoise bracelets caught the sunlight as she reached across the table for my hand. She didn't say anything. Mother could write a novel using only nonverbal communication. She blew air through pursed lips and made a lopsided smile.

The people at the table beside us were stealing glances, trying to determine if she was someone famous. I thought, Mother should be famous, and I found myself wondering for the thousandth time how she wound up with me for a daughter.

I said, "I love taking care of people. It makes me feel good. Maybe that's not for everyone. Some people go into medicine for the wrong reasons."

She said, "There's nothing wrong with money, dear."

"Right, but we live in the richest country in the world, Mother. There has to be a limit."

"You sound like your dad."

The anger was building in her face, reddening her cheeks, making her even more beautiful.

I said, "The point is this doctor shouldn't be practicing. He's making money off hurting people."

"Darling," she said. "I don't mean to be harsh, but don't you think this whole thing is a smoke screen? A diversion to distract you from your primary objective."

I had enough sense not to ask what my primary objective might be. It was simple: marry someone with money. In Mother's world, x-ray was a means to meet a marriageable doctor. I have long abandoned feeling burnt about this. I almost wonder if marrying into money isn't a sort of OCD thing with her.

I said, "Let's rewind. You said I did this before. I'd like proof. Do you have any of my old stuff? –from high school?"

She said, "I boxed up your yearbooks and diaries. Everything else went to the curb when we lost the house. Why?"

"Feeling nostalgic. Do you know where that box is?"

"In the attic somewhere. You're welcome to look, but you won't get me up there."

Mother is deathly afraid of spiders.

I said, "Tomorrow afternoon?"

She said, "Sure. And regardless of what you decide about Dr. McJackass, promise me this."

I tilted my head and said, "I'm listening."

"Don't do the thing until you see a ring."

27

I wanted to look for the box of yearbooks, to find a picture of Suicide Steve, his full name, anything, but when we left Threadgills, I was too sleepy to walk. Mother dropped me back at my place, and I fell into bed.

The swing shift was covered. I usually work the weekday nights and have my weekends free, but the department needed coverage on the graves. I woke around 2200 hours, showered, shaved, and pulled on some scrubs. Alex and Zoey were out.

I sat alone at the kitchen counter drinking a smoothie, pecking at Instagram on my tablet. It was pretty depressing – all the pix of friends partying, marrying, and playing with kids. I couldn't help but feel like I was missing out. I guess the word is lonely.

Maybe Mother is right. Shudder.

It all comes down to documentation. I was right to try to catch Dortman on tape, but from what I've seen on late night *Law and Order* marathons in the breakroom, the recording would probably be thrown out of court as inadmissible evidence.

Video would be the same. A video or live-feed posted online could possibly sway public opinion, but it could also land me in the federal pen or fined out of existence for breach of patient confidentiality. Plus, the likelihood that the general public understood neurosurgery well enough to know that something had gone criminally wrong was slim to none.

Dani and I needed to formally document grievances using either the hospital EMR – electronic medical record system – or the "confidential" ethics hotline. Neither option was efficient. It could take years, and it was possible little-to-nothing would change: a slap on the wrist; anger management classes; temporary suspension for investigation.

Hospitals are desperate for neurosurgeons. St. Rafa was no exception. The board of directors wasn't about to fire a spine doc for anything short of running through the main atrium with their scrubs on fire, dragging a bloody vertebral column. Never mind that. Dortman was interim CEO. He'd veto anything sent through the ethics hotline. That left us with the EMR.

The problem with the EMR is it's traceable. That's usually a good thing. You want to track who viewed the patient's chart and when. What doctor made which order and who completed the order. The EMR is generally the last place to note anything other than what happened at a given time. Notes are short and to the point. We have whole classes at orientation dedicated to proper communication on the EMR. The basic message: the less you write the better.

I could note on the requisition that the surgical nurse unplugged the C-arm, causing a loss of exam data. That wouldn't implicate Dortman directly, but it was something. The question became was it worth the risk? Also, the requisition had already been processed. The order for the surgical x-ray guidance was in billing by now. If I added something after the fact, it might only build a case against me.

No risk ever feels like it's worth the risk. That's why it's called risk.

28

Sometimes I wish I could see things the same as Mother. Reduce life down to money and romance – consumerism, in a word. I wish I could be a whore for stuff, and work it until I land a rich, happy man-whore.

We could wear *Life is Good®* t-shirts and tool around in a ski boat on Lake Travis.

Life presses in, and it's not all good. Like I can't remember a time when there wasn't a war somewhere. There's American citizens who have never learned how to read – not because they can't but because no one ever taught them. And, St. Rafa daily fills with the traumatized and lost. People terrified, suffering, and stressed out of their minds.

I wish I could Mother my way through it all. It would be great to simply not care. Caring is overwhelming. Caring never does enough. Maybe some people can turn it on and off. That's not me.

I want to learn a new way of caring. One that doesn't threaten to consume my soul. I don't know if I even have a soul anymore. What's a soul? – some kind of reservoir for personal suffering? Cheerful thought.

When I walk into a patient's room, even if I'm only going to see them for the fifteen minutes it takes to do their x-ray, I want to be holding something more than the doctor's orders. There has to be a hope that goes beyond prognosis. I can't imagine what it looks like. I don't know the words to describe it.

When someone is looking for answers and coming up empty, miserable and dying, even worse, begging to die, is it possible to move beyond needing to answer? – to simply be their answer? And if so at what cost?

None of that went in the letter I typed up that morning, but it explains why I wrote it. It had one sentence: "Dr. Dortman intentionally messed up your lumbar spine surgery last night." I printed it off, stuck the letter in an envelope, and biked to St. Rafa, arriving a half hour before my shift.

I went to the intensive care. I can't give the patient's real name. I'll call him Ron. He wasn't much older than me. His wife was there beside him, and I could see the fear wild and unchecked in her eyes. In both their eyes. I introduced myself.

I said, "I ran the x-ray machine during your surgery last night."

Ron's face was covered in perspiration. The monitor chimed. His heart rate was elevated.

I had already run out of things to say. I sat with him and his wife. She asked me a few questions. I don't remember what. I left the envelope in her lap.

On my way to the time clock, I ducked into the ladies' room to have a little cry. I washed my face, slapped myself three or four times. I needed to feel something. The floors and walls were beginning to numb into nothingness. I clocked in late. Timmy would be ticked. I didn't care.

29

As I rounded the corner into the bunker, Shelley said, "Keep walking. Tim wants to see you."

She didn't look up from the exam work list.

I said, "What? I'm like five minutes late tops."

"And he was here waiting for you at five minutes til. Had his phone out. I think he was tracking the time clock remotely or something. I didn't ask. He wasn't chatty."

Shelley and I both knew this was out of character for Timmy the Fearless. When Tim was in the bunker, you could hear him halfway to the ED, talking sports or reenacting his favorite TV commercials. I have always felt confused when people talk about their favorite commercials – as if ad executives deserve more headspace than they already own.

I think it's a nervous thing. How chatty Timmy gets in the bunker. He knows his leadership style doesn't count for much in the trenches.

"He said, 'Tell Claire I want to see her in my office,'" Shelley explained. "That was 15:01."

She was a master of saying a lot without saying much. Basically, Timmy the Fearless wanted everyone to know he had declared war. He was gunning for me.

I said, "Wonder what's eating him?"

Shelley shrugged. It would appear she subscribed to the ostrich school of workplace politics. Everything's fine down here in the sand.

I locked my messenger bag in a locker in the breakroom and headed to the cafeteria. I don't drink Coca-Cola. The stuff is pancreatic cancer in a can. I don't drink it, except when I'm fighting. I find the sugary taste of cocaine-flavored soda water offers the perfect counterpoint to wanting to choke the life out of someone.

Gail, Timmy's administrative assistant, looks strangely like her boss. She tried to stop me at her desk, but I strode passed, right into his office, and plunked down in a chair.

Timmy was on the phone. He pursed his lips and furrowed his brow, glowering at me. He tried to wave me back, out of his office, but I stayed where I was, sipping my Coca-Cola and pulling up the recording app on my phone.

Tim said, "She's here. Right now. Yes. Yes, she's in my office. No. I don't know. I will. I promise I will deal with it. Thank you. OK. Good-bye."

72

He hung up the phone.

I hit record on my app and said, "Who was that on the phone?"

Timmy swallowed and said, "Close the door."

He doesn't do confrontation well.

I said, "I prefer it open. Do you mind if I record this conversation?"

"Yes, I mind."

He rose from his desk and, walking behind me, closed the door. I shivered involuntarily. I get the heebie-jeebies when people walk behind me. I tried not to let it shake my composure. Took another sip of Coca-Cola.

He said, "Did you turn off the recorder?"

"No."

He returned to his chair, eyeing the cell phone resting on my thigh. I so wanted to push him and his office chair through the floor-to-ceiling window behind him. Outside, the sky was gray.

Timmy the Fearless swallowed.

I asked a second time, "Who was that on the phone?"

He said, "You know who it was."

"All I know is Shelley said you wanted to see me in your office. Now, you're being all secretive. What's up?"

Tim looked at the clock on the wall.

He said, "I'm asking you to turn the recording off for your own sake. I'm on your team."

"Why don't you tell me who you were talking to on the phone?"

He said, "You're late for an assigned shift. Consider this your verbal warning. If it happens again it's a written warning, suspension, and conduct review. A third time and you're fired automatically."

I said, "Granted, I was five minutes late clocking in. Two minutes passed an official tardy. I know the policy. What's this really about?"

"Why were you late?"

"That's none of your business."

"I received a phone call from a concerned staff member here at the hospital who claims you were fraternizing with a patient."

I laughed.

Tim said, "That's nothing to laugh at, Claire."

"I can do what I want on my own time."

"Not if what you want is here at the hospital."

"If you don't like me visiting patients in my off time, go ahead and fire me."

"Trust me. Getting fired is the least of your worries."

I paused. That was all my ammo. I had burned through it pretty quick.

Tim said, "Fraternizing is the kind of thing the company could take to court. It's one thing to find yourself without a job, but winding up jobless and the defendant in a corporate law suit is a different story."

"Are you threatening me?"

"No. I'm trying to help you see reason. I'm on your side, Claire."

He was wearing down my natural resistance to the disease spreading through the hospital. I felt like a susceptible host.

The word "nosocomial" sprang to mind. Hospital acquired infections plague roughly two million patients annually in the US. According to the CDC, about ninety thousand patients die each year from preventable nosocomial infections. Many of the microbes were custom made by medicine – like methicillin-resistant staphylococcus aureus (MRSA) and vancomycin-resistant enterococci (VRE).

The main path of spread is healthcare workers. Specifically, our hands. It's morbidly ironic that the same hands used for healing and care can be the agents of disease and death.

I was angry that Tim had blasted through my resolve so easily. Then again, I should have known it was futile. Pathogens don't fight fair.

I said, "OK. You win. I'm going out there and shooting some x-rays, but you can forget about me covering any more graves. I'll work through my schedule—"

Tim broke in: "That's the other thing. We don't need you on graves anymore. After tonight, travelling techs will cover the vacancies."

My mouth fell open.

I said, "What about M?"

He shook his head, "You'll be the first to know the minute I hear anything new. These things take time, Claire. That's why HR approved the travelers. You don't mind showing them the ropes do you?"

He offered me a patronizing smile. I sipped my Coca-Cola, imagining him up there in the patient's bed with his spine looking like a junk drawer. No, I didn't want that. I just wanted Timmy the Fearless to have a spine, but vertebrate life simply wasn't his scene.

Travelers, though? Nothing against them personally. What tech hasn't dreamed of traveling? Going exciting new places. Seeing the sights. Pulling six figures all expenses paid. The problem is, sometimes, travelling techs are the mercenaries and strikebreakers of radiography. They're called in to beat the local workforce into submission, to keep the engines of empire running while management quells the rebellion.

You have to wonder why rad techs have never unionized – as much day-to-day garbage as many of us are forced to swallow. Like this steaming pile that Timmy the Fearless shoveled onto my plate. He totally preempted my move to use the grave coverage for leverage. The answer: travelers. Administrators aren't above using techs against techs. Divide and conquer.

I turned the recording off and deleted the file. Timmy was right. For my own sake, I wouldn't want to play it back. All the recording held was the quiet, polite sounds of unconditional surrender.

30

I'm not sure what I imagined when I pictured the travelling tech lifestyle. Tanning on the beach while taking x-rays? These guys were both big, short-necked types. One had a wide chest. He was an ex-marine. The other had a big belly. He hailed from Chicago. That was as much personal history as I garnered from them.

Not to be mean, but their origins didn't seem entirely human. It was like they had evolved from office furniture. They were gray-skinned, hairless beings of an entirely different species. Interstellar truck drivers or something.

I couldn't keep their names straight. They clearly didn't care what I called them. They were the first travelling techs I ever met. St. Rafa never needed mercenaries in the past.

They worked. I'll say that. They didn't sit still. Even the one with a belly was a model of efficiency. Too efficient. Like instead of people, human beings, they were x-raying the inventory in a vast warehouse of used body parts.

By the end of my shift, I was bone tired. My workout with Alex in the morning felt like a slog. She gave me a ride home, and I fell into bed. I didn't set an alarm, didn't care if I ever woke up. I was awake anyways at 1400 hours. My body wouldn't let me sleep.

Mother texted to ask if I planned on coming by the house. Neither of my roommates were around. I burned some cash on a Car2Go. It was either that or Uber, and I didn't feel like chatting.

Mother married Collier long after either of them were interested in having kids. He has a fifteen-year-old son, Travis, who lives with them. Travis is a hardcore, semi-pro gamer. Super into virtual reality. He spends a lot of time in his bedroom. It's like Mother lives with a younger version of Dad.

She's a good step-mother. That's coming from Travis. They have a system. System being the closest thing to a relationship Travis is interested in. There's a reason he stays at his Dad's place over his Mom's, and it's not that he gets away with more. He has boundaries. Mother has boundaries, too.

Travis and Mother were making dinner together when I rolled up. I knew that was their "together time." So, I headed up to the attic.

77

I felt sad seeing Mother cooking with this boy who is basically a stranger to me. I see Travis at holidays and birthdays, but it hit me that in the four or five years they've lived together he's cooked with Mother more than I ever did. Occasionally, we made cookies from a tube or breakfast. That was it.

Sitting in the attic, I couldn't think of a single recipe Mother taught me. I felt miserable. I found a box labeled "books" and opened it to a collection of science fiction. I immediately started to cry. These were Dad's – from back when he dreamed of being a writer.

Dad used to tell the best stories. That's what I remember about meals growing up. He'd sit at the kitchen counter while Mother cooked, and we'd talk about our day: what was the best part? – the worst? – the hardest thing you did? – what did you learn? As we ate, Dad would weave the events of the day into a story.

Stories were everything he lived for. Stories were what kept their marriage alive. Dad was working on a novel in a coffee shop when they met. Mother's always had a thing for artistic types. Their first date wasn't even a date. More like a long conversation that turned into burgers and fries at P. Terry's. I can't imagine meeting someone that way now.

One thing led to another and a year later they were married. A year after that I came into the picture. By the time I was five I knew Dad would soon finish his book. Sometime around seven or eight-years-old, it became a point of friction. When he would finish. By my tenth birthday, he announced it was complete. By my fifteenth birthday, it was clear the project was a failure. That's when the video games took over. I saw Dad less and less.

It struck me as odd that Mother kept this box of science fiction books. As far as I knew, there wasn't anything else of his in her house. I read a few titles: *Double Star; A Canticle for Liebowitz; The Waystation*. I hadn't heard of any of them. They were old. Covered in plastic covers like collectibles, but I couldn't imagine they'd be worth much. The largest one was something called *Stranger in a Strange Land*. They were all first editions.

The books must have been important to both my parents. Something they shared. Everything else of Dad's wound up in his car or on the curb. I felt so lonely stumbling across this collection. I didn't doubt that Dad had read each one of these books. He read constantly, and for some reason he saved them. More than that Mother saved them.

I hauled the box down from the attic. Dinner was in the oven. Travis was in his virtual reality. Mother was in her's, sitting on the back porch with a glass of wine, listening to Steely Dan. She offered me a drink. I declined.

I said, "What are these books about?"

She glanced inside the box and said, "Honey, those are Hugo winners. Your Father collected them."

I could tell there was more. I set the box down. We stared at the scrub oaks in the backyard.

She said, "He used to read them to me. Some of them were pretty good. Anyways, he didn't want them, and I couldn't bring myself to toss them out."

She pronounced a laugh and said, "You take them. Give one of 'em a read. Maybe you'll have something to talk about next time he calls."

That was her attempt at a joke. We both know Dad never calls. That isn't him.

I said, "OK. Thanks."

She said, "Did you find the yearbooks?"

I remembered why I had gone to the attic in the first place. My heart prolapsed below my diaphragm. That's how it felt. I didn't want to remember why I had gone to the attic. Deep in my gut, I knew what I would find, but I was no closer to understanding any of it.

I shook my head, "No."

She said, "Come on. I'll help ya."

By help Mother meant stand at the foot of the stairs and yell directions at me. I found the box of yearbooks and stayed for dinner. Mother drove me home.

She said, "You know I miss your Dad. At least the way he was when we met. I really thought he was going places."

I said, "What changed?"

She said, "Love's a funny thing. It's there one day. The next it's gone. It doesn't matter how much you want it back. When it's gone, it's gone for good."

31

Talk about an emotional hangover after Mother dropped me off. That was the most we ever discussed Dad. I completely forgot about the yearbooks. I locked myself in my bedroom and tried to cry. The tears never came.

I grabbed a book from Dad's box, *A Canticle for Liebowitz*. The cover art looked out of place in the pile of spaceships and aliens. It was a monk standing among ruins in the desert looking up at the sky.

Something about the cover spoke to me. I imagined the hospital in ruins, the city returned to wilderness, years after a deadly pandemic. I couldn't imagine a better place to while away the end of the world than inside the bunker in the radiology department. I suppose there's something monkish about x-rays. I decided to give *Liebowitz* a try.

I was asleep by the end of the first chapter, but something about the story kept me tossing and turning through the night. I dreamed Dad and I were living in a post-apocalyptic monastery. Shame and loneliness were there to meet me in the morning.

When faced with the past, some people drink themselves to amnesia. Others get so high it looks like an all-time low. There's a healthy number of individuals who copulate until life is one big orgasm. Not me. I'm a runner.

I was in my running clothes and out the door before sun up. I hit the road bearing south to 51st Street. I ran west on 51st over the interstate to Hyde Park, and south across the University, the Capitol, downtown. I crossed the river on the pedestrian bridge at Seaholm and ran east along the trails until I came to Airport Boulevard and Highway 183.

I'm not sure where I went from there. I forgot myself. I must have run north. Maybe west on 969. The numbness that met me was total. I felt free from myself.

I collapsed on old Highway 20 in Manor outside the fire department. One of the fire fighters saw me lying on the side of the road, an older guy. Maybe the chief.

He hauled me into the station. They were about to put me in an ambulance, but I had just enough strength to protest, to claim I was training for an ultramarathon (a lie) and that I had run further than I ever had in my life (true). One of the firemen drove me back to my house. I was grateful he wasn't the talkative type.

My Garmin said I clocked 38 miles. I had an hour before I needed to be at work. I crawled into the shower, cleaned up my scrapes and bruises, and pulled on a fresh pair of scrubs. Alex drove me to St. Rafa.

Parking at the main entrance, she inspected her long blonde hair for split ends and said, "I worry about you."

I said, "You and me both."

I punched the clock at two minutes to the hour feeling like one gigantic bruise, regretting everything.

32

As I limped into the bunker, Dani was working the controls in Exam Room 1. A patient stood at the wall bucky for a PA chest x-ray. The bucky holds the image receptor, ionization chambers, and an oscillating filtration device called a grid. You can think about that the next time you hug the board for a chest x-ray. You're hugging a giant radiation detector.

I leaned against the radiation barrier by the control console.

Dani glanced at me, did a double take, and said, "Girl, you look ratchet."

"Thanks, I think."

He rested a hand on my shoulders and said, "That's not a compliment."

I hadn't looked at my hair. Salt trails burned my cheeks. I was chafed. You know you look bad when a party animal says you look bad. Note to self: look up "ratchet" in the Urban Dictionary.

Dani continued eying me. I pushed his face away, but I didn't move his arm off my shoulder. It felt good there, and I experienced a weird pull toward him. Call it desperation.

He said, "Next time you get that wrecked call me."

The patient said, "I wasn't in a wreck. I have bronchitis."

Dani started the rotor.

He said, "Take in a deep breath. Hold it."

The radiation alarm beeped. The x-ray image popped up on the monitor.

"You can breathe," Dani said as he sauntered out to position the patient for a lateral view.

Proper breathing instructions for a chest x-ray require full inspiration. You guide the patient through two inspirations and shoot the picture on the second breath. Dani cut a corner firing on the first inspiration.

X-ray tech laziness bothers me more than people who say techs are lazy. I trust my abilities as an x-ray tech, and I want others to trust those abilities, too. Sometimes, as a profession, x-ray techs are their own worst enemy. What I'm saying is I still felt burnt about getting ditched on Halloween.

Returning to the control console, Dani said, "Seriously, call me."

I said, "What happened to exposing chest x-rays on the second inspiration?"

"Not necessary if the patient takes a full breath on the first inspiration."

I low-key wanted Dani's arm slung back over my shoulder, but I didn't want to tell him that, and I definitely didn't want to put it there myself.

"Watch," he said. To the patient, he said, "Take in a deep breath. Hold it."

Dani made the exposure.

"See. It's good. Ten ribs."

That's the measure of a full inspiration: ten ribs above the diaphragm. It's difficult to see on the lateral.

I clicked on the PA.

I said, "You counted the ribs?"

"Yep."

"You're quick."

Dani smirked and said, "And you're faded. What did you do last night?"

"Got in bed and read a book."

"Must have been a hell of a book. Will you take this kind gentleman back to the ED?"

As I walked into the exam room, the patient exhaled dramatically and said, "I can't hold my breath that long you jackass. I told you. I have bronchitis."

33

Dortman had another late fusion surgery – scheduled to start at 2100 hours. Dani and Shelley were discussing this when I returned to the department from the ED. Arguing more like. They were both pretty hot. What's happening to this place? Common decency is an endangered species.

When he's angry, Dani's hands become animated. He stroked his chin with one hand as he waved a finger in the air with the other. The way to calm him down is literally to take him by the hand.

I rested my hand on his and said, "It'll be fine. I'll handle the surgery. You take the ED. The travelers arrive at 22:30."

He said, "Have you seen the geniuses Timmy hired to cover for M? It's like Tweedle Dee and Tweedle Dum joined the Aryan Brotherhood."

Shelley looked at him out of the corner of her eye like I didn't hear you say that. Dani forgets the day and night crews have different modes of communication.

I said, "What he's trying to say is we miss M. Have you heard anything about when she might return?"

Shelley shrugged and shook her head, taking her cue to exit.

Once she was out of the bunker, Dani turned to me and said, "I don't want you working with that creep."

"You didn't mind leaving me with him the other night."

Dani slumped into a chair. His face was a mask of seriousness.

He said, "That was different."

I rolled my eyes. Dani smiled despite himself. He almost spoke but stopped. Guilty.

He said, "Let me take on Dr. Douchebag tonight."

I shook my head and said, "He's mine. I've got a game plan. We're going to take this mother down."

We both knew it was just something to say – to cut the tension – but at the same time I hoped that by being the better technologist I could catch Dortman. I could see through him. I could expose his scheme to the world. Whatever that scheme was.

First, I needed coffee. I fired up the pot in the breakroom and downed about eight cups. My kidneys hated me, but I've never knocked out exams quicker in my life.

The ED heated up. I was a blur of hands, x-ray tubes, and lead markers. I almost achieved that same empty space I enter while running – no thoughts, pure movement – the one thing that stopped me from full nirvana was the patients. These were people. I couldn't go complete nonattachment here. There had to be a lifeline. They needed to know I cared.

The C-arm was locked and loaded in OR Room 6 thirty minutes before the surgery. I wanted to take Dortman to the cleaner while simultaneously minimizing contact. I was thinking about whatever taint he'd spread to M. I was thinking I could be the clean tech. That that would be enough.

The surgery went off like before only with less blood loss. Dortman took his sweet time and the hardware placement looked janky. At least he was consistent. The final image on this surgery looked as screwed up as the last operation.

I hit the image save button at the same time I hit the x-ray button. The save button makes a notification tone different from the radiation safety beep, but by hitting the buttons at the same time the tones were close together. They almost blended into a single sound.

Dortman moved in to sew up the patient.

He said, "No need to save an image or send to PACS. That's all. Suture."

As I powered down the machine, I smiled behind my mask. I had won the day.

That's what I thought as I wheeled the C-arm into storage, jacked into the network, and powered up the monitor to send the image to PACS.

I didn't hear the door behind me. Dortman was wearing surgical booties. He moved without a sound.

He rested a hand on my shoulder, and I spun around.

"Didn't mean to scare you."

His voice was neutral.

"Right," I said.

I tried moving toward the door. Dortman blocked my way.

He leaned closer, examining me. His eyes were dead, glassy things. I thought about what M said, about him being on drugs.

"She's just not that smart," he said, staring straight through me.

I fought the urge to flinch, to back down.

He said, "I told you sending the pictures to PACS is unnecessary."

"Not according to policy."

"Policy changed."

Dortman pulled the C-arm computer tower over, toppling it onto its side. The monitors shattered, shooting sparks. A wisp of smoke rose from the wreckage.

He did all this with complete control and efficiency. By the time I moved to stop the computer's fall, the damage was done. Dortman stalked toward the door. My heart boomed like a bass speaker in my ears.

I was a solid synapse of rage. I curled my fingers around the hemostats in my pocket. With enough force, the tiny clamps could stab. I could hit him in the neck, sever the jugular. He might die. Might not, but he wouldn't be intentionally botching any more surgeries. I was already answering the homicide detectives' questions in my head as I step toward him.

Something stopped me. Call it a soft spot, confusion, good upbringing, my better angels – whatever constraints of primate consensus and cotillion classes keep us from going for the jugular over every disagreement. My hand relaxed its grip on the hemostats. It was a physical sensation, the restraint, like a hand on my chest, pushing me back from the brink.

Dortman paused at the storage room door. His hand rested on the handle. His back toward me. Look, he seemed to say, here's your chance.

The moment passed. The door swung open. Vanessa was standing in the hall, overly-tanned arms folded over her augmented breasts.

Turning to me, Dortman said, "Don't worry about the incident report. I'll have my nurse file it."

The door swung shut.

I remember afterword, after I puked in the sink in the fluoro bathroom, after a good ten-minute panic attack. I remember wondering how someone with so much self-control could bungle surgery so thoroughly.

Unless it wasn't bungled at all.

34

Dani drove me home. I'm skipping stuff. Things ran together. Rewind. There was an incident report, but I don't remember what I wrote. There was the shattered glass from the C-arm monitors. Dani and I cleaned that up. I vaguely remember a brief conversation with the travelling techs when they showed up for the grave.

The silence in Dani's car was awkward, but I couldn't bring myself to talk.

Finally, there was that awful haunted sensation that followed us down the streets of the Upper East Side. It was like I had witnessed a murder. I couldn't get the dead monitor out of my head. The lights and buildings slid by the car windows, and I could see my machine there on the storage room floor, shattered glass everywhere.

She was my favorite C-arm. Tori. That's what I called her. It's silly, I know, but I have names for some of my machines. It's not a thing. I don't talk to them or make name tags, but yeah. You work with a machine long enough, and you come to know its personality, its idiosyncrasies. Quirks that go beyond the programming. I swear some machines don't like certain techs.

Tori had worked well passed her service contract. There was no way to repair the damage done. What I saw broken on the storage room floor wasn't just a junker piece of medical equipment, it was a member of the team.

I don't remember saying good-bye to Dani. I don't recall walking through the front door of my house. I couldn't say whether Alex and Zoey were home or not. All I know is I went straight to my bedroom, poured the box of yearbooks on the bed, and searched the index for Dortman.

He was there. My sophomore year. Steve Richard Dortman. He had the same carefully disheveled hair. The same phony smiling good looks. The same dead eyes. Suicide Steve. Peggy Nash was there, too. The yearbook must have been sent to publication before her expulsion. Now that I saw him. I couldn't unsee him. It was like that dead smiling face was staring at me from every high school memory.

The revelation didn't bring me any closer to understanding Dortman's motives. It moved me deeper into myself. I had run from him before. He was the reason I had broken things off with Beth, Peggy's younger sister. I had still liked Beth, but I couldn't stand to see what Peggy's suicide did to her. I was too young then, and now I felt too old.

I pushed the book away in disgust and opened the pages of my junior yearbook. There was a full-page ad for Peggy Nash. The sort of thing families buy to celebrate their graduating seniors. This one was different. Sure, the page was filled with pictures of Peggy, Beth, and the Nash family, but it read, "In Memory of Peggy and her child."

35

I will thankfully never suffer insomnia. I can run all day nonstop, but when my thoughts start to race, I'm tired within an hour. As I lay in bed, yearbooks in a heap on the floor, remembering Beth, I weighed my options. Call the cops? No evidence. Hospital ethics hotline? Probably feeds right to Dortman's office. Quit and wander the earth handing out flowers and words of encouragement? I'd never forgive myself for bailing on the patients at St. Rafa.

I'm not a super spiritual person, but I prayed then. It seemed like the only thing I could do. I prayed for Beth, wherever she is. I prayed for Ron and his wife and M and all the patients Dortman had hurt. I was asleep before "Amen."

My legs felt wooden and numb the next morning. I sat on the back patio, surrounded by bamboo, and read *Canticle for Liebowitz*. I'm not sure how, but I was hooked. The book was not so much a story as a meditation on all things A-bomb. It helped that Dad had read it before me. I almost felt like he was there with me.

As I read, I puzzled through what to do about Dortman. I couldn't bring the situation to the forefront of my thoughts. I didn't want to talk about it with Zoey or Alex or Dani or Mother or anyone really. If I thought about it too much, I knew I'd no show at work. My legs were too jacked to run. So, I read.

Around 1000 hours, Alex came home from the gym and asked if Zoey and I wanted to go to Barton Springs. It was November 3rd, but the high was 80. The three of us piled into her Kia and cruised down Lamar to Zilker Park.

I made sure we were close to where the guy had dropped his towel last time I was at the springs. He wasn't there. I tried to swim a couple laps with Alex, but my body protested. I crawled back to my towel and read while Zoey trolled fashion videos on her smartphone.

She wore a black square neck high-waist designer swimsuit that was probably too expensive to swim in. Her hair was cut in an inverted bob and layered with gray. Around her neck, hung an evil-looking raven skull pendant.

I said, "Where did you get that necklace?"

"You like it? I picked it up in New York last month."

I didn't realize Zoey had travelled to New York. I felt completely out of touch.

The guy showed up as Alex climbed out of the pool. I groaned inwardly and muttered, "Please don't see him. Please don't see him."

Thankfully, she was sacked out on her towel, pulling her goggles and swim cap off when he walked by. This was my shot.

He was there, five feet from my towel, gym bag in hand. I don't know what made me want him so bad. My insides were a jumble of feelings about Beth, which didn't even make sense because I had dated two other girls and three guys since high school.

Zoey exchanged a knowing look with me. Was I that obvious? Alex smiled from underneath her towel.

She mouthed, "Go get him, girl."

I loudly said, "Do either of you have sunscreen?"

Alex and Zoey chimed, "No."

He either didn't hear or didn't take the hint. So, I turned and asked him if he had any sunscreen.

His eyes met mine, and I swear it was like a nuclear bomb went off inside my skull. I couldn't have passed a basic mental orientation assessment. Didn't know my name, where I was, time of day. It was his eyes. They were the same shape as Beth's eyes – hooded and wide set.

He said something and rifled through his gym bag. He was sitting right beside me, and swim briefs leave nothing to the imagination. I tried not to stare, but I couldn't think of my next move.

The sunscreen he offered me was oily generic stuff. Zoey gasped.

I said, "Thanks."

I spread some of it over my legs, which looked awful, slightly swollen, covered with stubble, bruised, and scraped, but I wasn't putting this stuff anywhere I didn't mind getting zits. He was watching.

He said, "Do you play soccer?"
I shook my head and said, "No, why?"

He said, "Your legs are all banged up. I thought maybe. Lacrosse?"

I studied him closely. He smiled neutrally. I couldn't tell if he was poking fun. I wanted to punch him.

I said, "I run ultra-marathons. Did 38-miles yesterday and had a little tumble."

He whistled.

I said, "What about you?"

"What?"

How difficult was he going to make this? He looked me in the eyes, and again I was completely disoriented.

He shrugged, "Not much. I work. I swim. I'm new to town."

That was good. We're getting somewhere.

I said, "When did you arrive?"

"Just over a three months."

"You like it?"

He shrugged and said, "Hard to say. I miss Arkadelphia."

"Arkadelphia? Where's that?"

"Arkansas?"

He looked surprised that I'd never heard of the place.

'What does Arkadelphia mean?' I wanted to ask. 'City of Brotherly Ark?' How could anyone miss Arkadelphia? Unless there was someone else.

I said, "What brought you to Austin?"

"School," he said.

He went silent. He was drawing into himself. I tried not to feel stung, to find something dumb about him, dumber than Arkadelphia, and focus on that. But, he couldn't help where he was born, and there was nothing dumb about him. He was smart and good-looking in this Robert Pattinson kind of way and nice enough to lend me his awful sunscreen. He was like a daywalking vampire – disgustingly perfect.

He said, "And work. I'm a patient account specialist."

I said, "That's cool."

Wait. Calm down, Claire. Since when was account specialist cool?

He said, "It's something to do. I'm saving for med school. Listen, I need to get my laps in before that storm rolls in—"

"There's a storm?" I said.

My brain stopped braining.

He said, "Yep. So, if you don't mind, drop the sunscreen by my gym bag when you're done."

Pulling on his goggles, he dove into the pool and swam away. He might as well have stomped on my sternum, driving the xiphoid process straight into my heart.

Zoey said, "Ultra-marathons? Is that even a thing?"

I said, "You're not helping."

Alex said, "Arkadelphia? Please. What a rube."

I said, "I hate men."

Alex snatched the sunscreen out of my hand, "This shit is going in the trash."

She jumped up, grabbed her towel, and ran toward the exit. I limped after her as fast as I could. Zoey threw an arm over my shoulder and pulled me in close.

She said, "If you love her, let her go. If she loves you, she'll come back."

Struggling to disentangle myself, I said, "Damn it, Zo."

From the top of the hill, Alex held the sunscreen high over her head and screamed, "To hell with Arkadelphia."

She spiked the sunscreen into the trash. I buried my head on Zoey's shoulder and laughed as we ran after her.

36

Alex wanted to hit up the food trucks on South 1st. I had time enough before work. I also had a bad feeling. Call it a premonition. The trailer park was atop a hill. The sky to the south was dark. Clouds gathered. A storm.

Zoey said, "It'll be fine. You bike. You forget having a car means you don't have to worry about the weather."

The rain hit before our food was up. It hardly mattered. We were wearing bathing suits and sarongs. The water was warm, a Gulf storm, but it shot down from the sky chaotically like jets from a million writhing fire hoses. The world was dark and loud.

We huddled together under a metal-roofed shelter. The strings of patio lights looked sullen. We were soaking wet. Fortunately, we thought to leave our towels under the shelter when we ran to pick-up our food from the truck. We draped the towels over our shoulders and legs and sat skin-to-skin to fight off the cold. A comfortable silence settled over us.

Sighing, Zoey said, "It's been too long."

Alex nodded, biting into a Bombay masala sandwich, "I can't remember. When was the last time we were all out together? – Austin City Limits?"

I shook my head, "No, I was at St. Rafa."

"You were at the hospital? – All ACL?"

I shrugged and nodded.

Zoey said, "You work way way way too much."

Alex said, "That shit needs to stop. What's that even about? Is it money? Are you trying to land a doctor? What's so major that you're at that stupid place 24-7?"

"Saving lives."

Zoey rolled her eyes.

Alex said, "Is that what you tell yourself? – saving lives?"

It's an old hospital joke. Something to say when you're covered in a stranger's precious bodily fluids and you pass a co-worker in the hall. Impossible to explain to my roommates.

Zoey shifted away from me. I don't know if it was conscious. She moved less than an inch. We were under the same towel but no longer touching. It felt like an impossible distance.

Alex said, "What about your life? Hell, what about our lives? Do we matter to you?"

I said, "Of course you matter. Don't even."

"Why don't you make us a priority?" she said. "Why aren't we doing this every week? – like five times a week? When was the last time we worked-out together?"

"I've been tired."

"Because you work too much."

Zoey said, "And, you're bringing your work home. Do you want to tell us what you did the other day that required an escort from the Manor Fire Department?"

Alex said, "Wait. What?"

"I ran a little too far and needed a ride. And, yes, I'm sorting through some stuff, but it's not work. It's personal. Listen—"

I wasn't sure what to say. I couldn't take the tag team much longer. They'd have me promising something awful – like a roommate road trip to San Diego – within the next five minutes. I love Zoey and Alex, but two hours in the car with them is my absolute limit. They have a long list of obnoxious driving habits: attempting to rap – a lot, conference calling a string of old boyfriends to brag about whatever, that Kiki dance.

The rain drummed on the roof. Thunder rolled down 1st Street.

Zoey said, "We're listening."

I said, "Y'all know me too well, and you're right. I'm going through some stuff. It's nothing between us. I love my girls, but I need space to clear my head."

Alex said, "Fair enough. But, you should know, we're people too. If you keep distancing yourself from people – even people who love you – you drift apart. That's human nature."

37

It rained through the afternoon into evening. Things stayed quiet at St. Rafa. Rain keeps the hypochondriacs and looky-loos at home.

M and I had been texting for the last few days: Missed you at the Halloween Party; Jamie Lee Curtis meme; Check out the band *How to Disappear Completely*. That kind of thing.

She hadn't heard word one from St. Rafa HR. She didn't even know why she'd been suspended. We made a date for Burrito Volador the next night.

At 2200 hours an order dropped for a portable lumbar spine exam in the ICU.

Dani said, "That can only mean one thing. Dr. Dickface is at it again."

I nodded. I didn't recognize the patient's name. It wasn't one of the surgeries I had assisted. I figured the day crew covered it.

Another order dropped for a body-gram from the ED, x-rays of everything from c-spine to foot. History: MVC. Motor vehicle crash. Used to be MVA, motor vehicle accident until the lawyers decided not all crashes are accidents.

We flipped a coin. Dani landed the body-gram. I rolled out with the portable.

I'm not friendly with the ICU nurses at St. Rafa. The ICU nurses aren't friendly with anyone – even other ICU nurses. I know their names, talk to them about patients, but there's only so much you can do. And, I get it. They see some rough stuff. The kind of stuff that makes chit-chat seem blasphemous.

The thing is I noticed that Vanessa, Dr. Dortman's nurse, entered the portable x-ray order, and Vanessa isn't an ICU nurse. It was a little mystery. Why was Vanessa – a surgical nurse – ordering for an ICU patient?

I asked the charge nurse who the patient's ICU nurse was.

Without looking up from her computer, she said, "It's on the order."

"The order says Vanessa."

The charge nurse looked up from her computer. She studied me for a moment. By the look of it, she had been a nurse for a while. She was a pro. It was evident in the way she sat. The way she wore her scrubs. She understood my confusion. Shared it even. She wanted to say something, but she didn't, couldn't.

I said, "I feel like I'm missing something. When was the patient's surgery done?"

She said, "At 300 hours."

"Today?"

She nodded.

I said, "OK."

Because that was all I needed to know. Dortman was doing spinal fusions in the dead of night using some kind of ghost crew and an expendable traveling x-ray tech to man the C-arm.

I wheeled down the hall to the patient's room. Behind the curtain was a quiet scene from hell. The woman was wide-awake and delirious in pain. Sweat covered her body. Her sheets were soaked. She mumbled to herself, clutching the button for the morphine drip.

I said, "Ms. Albernathy?"

Her eyes flicked in my direction, but she didn't move her head. A small keening cry emerged from her lips. When she spoke, her voice was childlike.

She said, "Please don't move me. Don't move me. Please don't."

I checked her armband and said, "Ms. Albernathy, my name is Claire. I'm here to do a portable x-ray of your lumbar spine. It's one quick picture. You don't have to leave your bed. I'll be as gentle as I can, but I have to place a hard plate under your back."

She continued to beg me not to move her as I pulled on nitrile gloves and slipped the image receptor and grid into a disposable plastic sleeve, placing everything inside a pillowcase.

"Please don't. Please don't move me."

I watched as she pushed the button for morphine over and over. The machine couldn't give more. She'd hit the limit.

There was no easy way to shoot this picture. I swung the tube into position, pulled on my lead apron, and gently dropped the side rail of the patient's bed.

I explained what I was going to do: lift her slightly using the bed sheet, slide the board under her back, and quickly shoot the picture. I don't know if she understood. At times, she didn't seem aware there was someone else in the room.

On the count of three, I pulled up on the bed sheet and slid the image receptor into place. The moment I lowered her onto the receptor, she screamed so loud I fell back a step. I hit the rotor for the machine before I made the door. Shot the picture and pulled the receptor free in under fifteen seconds. Her face was swamped in tears and sweat. What had Dortman done to her?

I docked the x-ray tube, hung up my lead apron on the portable, and parked the machine outside the patient's room. I was pretty sure I had the picture, but it pays to be safe. I wiped down the image receptor and the machine with germicide.

St. Rafa has direct digital imaging in the ED, but the machine dedicated for the ICU is still computed radiography, meaning the image receptor is developed at a reading station. I was waiting for the image to pop up when Vanessa appeared, trailing a scent tanning oil.

She said, "That's the L-spine I ordered?"

I said, "This is the exam that was requested on Dr. Dortman's patient, Ms. Albernathy."

As we studied the image together, I slipped my phone out and hit record on the audio app. I did it quick like I was checking a text. The image was good. The hardware placement was awful.

Vanessa said, "Excuse me."

She attempted to nudge me aside. I held my ground.

She compressed her lips into an insincere smile and said, "Dr. Dortman asked me to text him a picture."

I stepped to the side but kept my hand on the computer's mouse. There was something weird going on, and I wasn't ready to relinquish control of the computer.

Holding her phone camera up to the monitor screen, Vanessa snapped a picture of the x-ray image.

She said, "Thanks. OK, so Dr. Dortman has ordered that you delete the image. No radiologist read is necessary."

"Vanessa," I said. "That's not how this works. Once the image is acquired, it's the property of the radiology department."

"Wrong. That's Dr. Dortman's patient. You have to follow his orders regarding his patient."

"Not exactly. That is a radiographic image of Dr. Dortman's patient, and that image falls under the direction of the radiologist."

She said, "Bitch, if you send that picture—"

I hit send and stepped away from the machine. Vanessa dialed Dortman. I wanted to punch her so bad my hands shook as I drove the portable away.

Back in the bunker, I turned off the recording app. I doubted anything Vanessa said was incriminating or even permissible in court, but it was something. Maybe enough to change HR's mind about M.

When I went to close the portable examination order, the requisition was cancelled. I pulled up PACS. The image was gone. What had they done? How had they done it? The implications were huge. If he could vanish an order and an image that quickly, Dortman controlled everything.

The blood drained from my face. I dropped into a chair and buried my face in my hands. I wanted to scream.

I was on my feet in a flash, headed for the time clock. I was done. The hour had come for the nuclear option: hit the door and keep walking.

I remembered Dani, pinned down in the ED. If I quit, he was screwed. The patients were screwed. I owed it to them to stay, to put in my two weeks. I picked up an emesis bag on the way to the ED x-ray room. I felt that sick, but I knew I'd feel worse if I bailed. As much as I'd like to be, I'm not a quitter.

38

I woke the next morning feeling free, feeling like maybe we should take that girls trip to San Diego, do something to celebrate putting in my two-week notice. I threw on a black and white striped tee and red shorts and biked to the original Kerbey Lane Café. I ordered

Fried Avocado Eggs Francisco with extra queso for breakfast. I brought *Liebowitz* with me and sat reading and drinking coffee for over an hour.

Afterward I rode to St. Rafa to personally deliver my notice to Timmy the Fearless. I typed it up the previous night. It was short and to the point. I could email or text, but I wanted to see his face when he read it.

I locked up my bike at the rack and turned around to find Dorothy Hicks standing there, studying me.

She said, "I had a feeling you'd drop in today. Can I have a minute of your time?"

Before I could answer, she grabbed my elbow with one of her wrinkly talons and led me down a sidewalk away from the hospital entrance.

"Where are we going?" I said.

Ignoring my question, Dorothy lifted the sleeve of my tee shirt and inspected my tattoo.

"Anna Bertha Roentgen? Suits you."

I said, "What's this about?"

"There's a blind spot on the other side of that tree."

"Blind spot?"

"From the cameras and microphones and such. How'd you think I found you so quick?"

"You've been watching me?"

I was creeped-out. She laughed.

"Be glad I'm watching you because I'm not the only one. In fact, I'm watching because he's watching."

I said, "Dortman?"

She tapped her nose.

"We don't have much time. So, give it here."

I said, "Give what here?"

"Your notice. Assuming that's why you dropped by four hours before your shift on a nice sunny day. I saw how it hit you when Dortman disappeared that exam. Call it intuition, I had a feeling you'd come up here today to hand in your two-weeks—"

"You saw Dortman disappear the exam? Do you have proof?"

Dorothy swatted my arm. "Of course I have proof, but do you think a little data tampering is enough to stop someone like Dortman?"

"Wait," I said. "What do you mean?"

My head was spinning. Dorothy Hicks was old school Texas: talk fast, think faster, and pack big guns. Like Angelina Eberly, the hero of Austin, who tried to blow-up Sam Houston with a six-pound cannon. Cannon Lady. That's what everybody calls her statue on Congress Avenue.

Dorothy said, "Try to pay attention. The point is I know you. I know you're not a quitter, and I knew you wouldn't deny yourself the satisfaction of seeing Timmy's face when he reads your notice, but that's not all I know. So, give it here."

I raised my eyebrows, smiled, and turned to leave. She grabbed my arm and pulled me back.

"Ow," I said.

The old bat was stronger than she looked. I stumbled against the tree.

Waving a crooked finger in my face, she said, "You listen to me, young lady. If you quit, they win, but if you stay—"

"Nothing will change."

She shook her head, "It will. It takes time. And energy. You have them scared, but you have to keep the pressure up. Now's not the time to quit. It's not the time to fight either. Not yet. But, we have to be ready to move when they slip up."

"It's sweet you think you can fix this place, but you're in over your head."

She looked at me sideways and said, "Honey, we're finally swimming at depth."

Dorothy released her grip on my arm and held her wrinkly hand out in front of me.

"Give it here."

I don't know why I did it. Must have been something in the old lady's eyes. There was a fire, a fierce affection in her gaze. I wanted to live at that level of intensity.

When I handed Dorothy the envelope, she didn't open it. She didn't even look at it. She kept her eyes fixed on mine as she tore it into tiny pieces.

She said, "Ask yourself who do you trust. Who can you depend on when the whip comes down?"

'Trust?' I wanted to say, 'Not you,' but again something checked me. Dorothy wasn't safe. She wasn't a happy person. The biggest smile couldn't hide her bitterness, but Dorothy Hicks was built like a primary barrier – solid lead dressed in poured concrete.

She said, "Beat it. Not a word of this to anyone. You understand? When the time comes, we'll be in touch."

39

Weird became the new normal that night at St. Rafa. Dortman fired the radiologists. It was more corporate and bureaucratic than him holding the reading room door open and saying, 'Get the hell out,' but yeah. It left everybody speechless. I mean everybody. Not just the imaging techs.

Wherever Dani and I went, a hush preceded us: 'Shh, here come those poor x-ray techs. They lost their doctors and now they've nowhere to go.'

It was like we had Ebola plus a noise sensitivity. If I sound jaded, it got old fast.

In that single act, Dortman sent the message loud and proud – 'Nothing is sacred. No one is indispensable. It's everyone for themselves, yo.'

That's not the weird part. Sure, it required some adjustment to send our images to an off-site "nighthawk" service for interpretation, but the contracts were in place. The transition was seamless. That's teleradiology – radiologists in Australia interpreting the images of diseased America.

No, the weird part was how quickly everybody adapted to the new, more cutthroat normal. Maybe people are herd animals, sheep, mindless followers, but we're like flesh-eating sheep. Ready to devour each other wool-and-all if anyone strays from the herd. I don't know what I'm saying. I didn't sleep much, and I don't know how we're going to do interventional procedures without radiologists.

One thing's for sure. I drank too much coffee. Call it a nervous habit. When stuff goes bad and I can't run, I start thinking if only I were more awake. Maybe I could be so awake that I wake up from this nightmare.

The second big blow was M. HR dropped the hatchet earlier that day. She waited until Dani and I were seated at El Burrito Volador to break the news.

She brought her partner, Janet, along. They were both stoned – glassy-eyed and holding hands, which seemed out of character for Janet. Being stoned I mean. She's a kindergarten teacher, a wide-eyed innocent from Lincoln, Nebraska. I don't know how Janet wound up with a partner who falls asleep every night watching splatter films. M looked strangely happy. Maybe downers have like the reverse effect on gloomy people.

Dani and I had to act incensed that M hadn't told us she'd been fired right away. Secretly, I was glad she waited. I probably would have hit the hospital's backdoor and kept walking if she'd texted while I was on the clock. The one thing that carried me through my shift was thinking how I could trust M. Having her back in the department felt essential to whatever crazy plans Dorothy had.

I kept thinking about Dorothy's question. Who do I trust?

I wasn't sure about Dani. Would he really be there if everything blew up in my face? – would I? As it stood, we could commiserate together, drown our sorrows in queso. And yes, I know, two orders of queso in one day is a quick way to a coronary.

M said, "I figured as much last week when they blackballed me."

"What do you mean?" Dani said, studying his own muscles.

"I had an interview with Mobile-X. I've always thought mobile work could be cool. Anyways, I aced the interview. The manager's like 'You're hired. When can you start? –tomorrow?' I say, 'Sure.' Tomorrow rolls around. No call. Day two. Nothing. Day three, I call her. She says, 'I don't think it's going to work out.' Blackballed. I can't work at St. Rafa, and now Dortman is making it so I can't work anywhere."

Janet said, "Maybe you should get out of x-ray all together. Children need teachers."

I could see M being a good teacher. She's patient and organized and smart. M could be anything - in this multi-purposed, skinny-assed vampire kind of way.

She shook her long, straight black hair and said, "Maybe someday, boo, but not yet. I don't want to admit defeat to that asswipe."

Janet said, "Think about it. Now, if you'll excuse me, I need to powder my nose."

As Janet exited, M leaned over the table conspiratorially.

She said, "Not a word of this to her, but someone left an eyeball on my bedroom windowsill."

I said, "What are you talking about?"

"I woke up the other day to all these flies buzzing right outside my window, and when I open the blinds there's an eyeball setting there. Right outside where I sleep."

Dani said, "I've been to your house. You sure you didn't leave it there?"

M glared at him and said, "Yes, I'm sure."

Janet returned. Dani ordered shots all around, and we drank to M. The fleshy burn of tequila, the numbness, it spoke to something.

This was more than parting. This was the loss of a false future. A lie we had all once believed – that we would always have each other. We saw our sweet lie, saw our self-deception, and wanted the lie more than the truth, but most of all, we wanted to catch Dortman.

Maybe that's a measure of trust, surviving a lie together. If so, these were people I could trust.

40

M gave me her proximity badge to return to security. She didn't want to go into the hospital again. I couldn't blame her.

The following day, I biked to St. Rafa around 1300 hours thinking I'd drop off the badge and head to a coffee shop. I enjoyed reading at Kerbey Lane. Plus, I finished *Liebowitz*, which felt like an accomplishment. I don't mean finishing a book. I mean clearing the junk out of my mind enough to finish a book.

Reading presented a different way of seeing the world, more thoughtful. That's what I accomplished. Contemplation in the middle of chaos.

I settled on another of Dad's books: *Left Hand of Darkness*. It sounded like a story about problems, and whatever problem-solving skills I have must come from Dad. My problem-evading skills come from Mother.

The security department was hidden. I found it eventually – an unmarked door with an intercom and a security camera. The officer on duty buzzed me in.

The department was a single largish room. Against one wall were lockers and gear storage. The long wall held two command posts with monitors showing surveillance video. The other two walls had cubicles, the badge computer, and a counter by the entrance. It's the least *hospitally* place in the hospital. Feels like a low budget movie set for a police precinct.

As the officer completed the paperwork, I glanced over at the security monitors. On one screen Dr.

Dortman was standing in the conference room pointing at revenue figures projected for next year. The numbers increased on a very steep slope.

I couldn't imagine how those increases in profit could happen so quickly. It didn't look like sustainable growth. That was the catch phrase of the last CEO.

My phone chimed with an email from Ronald Bowser. I didn't recognize the name, but it was a St. Rafa employee email address.

It read: "Want to hear what he's saying?"

The security officer was the only person in the room, and he was busy with paperwork. A surveillance camera hung above the door. Could someone see me through the camera and know I was looking at Dortman? My blood pressure dropped. What else was Ronald Bowser watching?

I looked back at my phone. The email was gone. Not retracted. Vanished.

The officer said, "That's all. You're good to go."

I stood there a beat too long, trying to sort myself out. My alarm must have been apparent because the security officer glanced at me and did a double take.

He said, "You OK?"

I nodded and shuffled toward the door grateful he didn't follow.

41

Caffeine clears my head. Something about the drug sets the neurons firing at the right rate to power through any mental logjam. If I hit a particularly big hurdle – like some pervert cyber-stalking me through the hospital security system while I'm preoccupied with stopping a psychotic surgeon – I prefer taking my medicine via soy latte.

There's always a long line of caffeine addicts at the coffee shop by the hospital's main entrance. I joined them, taking comfort in our numbers, certain that Ronald Bowser was ogling me through the cameras filling the building.

Hospitals do a lot to control access to information. There's no law requiring a certain system, but most hospitals use electronic charts to control access to patient data and a vast network of surveillance cameras and proximity card locks to control access to the building.

The main focus is the data. Only those individuals connected with a patient's treatment can access the patient's health data.

The control of access to the hospital information system is the usual – username and password. Once you're in, you can search any patient's record past, present, or future.

Access of patient data is generally observed retroactively through random data audits. The network administrators follow the user's data trail to ensure they haven't been looking at anything other than what was required to treat their assigned patients.

There's tons of users and pathways to monitor. The chances that an employee – granted an official user name and password – could be in any part of the system and find a blind spot in the network surveillance are pretty high.

That doesn't explain how Ronald Bowser accessed the security cameras or how he made an email disappear, but it illustrates the difficulties of preventing hackers within the system.

Conclusion: Ronald Bowser was a hospital employee, but there was no way "Ronald Bowser" was the culprit's real name. That reduced the list of suspects down to a thousand individuals, give or take.

Over the next three years, if I asked three co-workers every day whether they were watching me through the hospital security cameras, I would either find Bowser or be admitted to the state psychiatric hospital. All this was brought into laser focus by the sweet caffeine of the soy latte.

I recalled the message: "Bet you'd like to know what he's saying."

Assuming Bowser wasn't Dortman or Vanessa, he could still be working for them. Was it possible Bowser was on my side?

The other day Dorothy knew about blind spots in the hospital surveillance. The most practical way she could know that is if she'd worked with someone else. Someone with an eye on the cameras.

I walked out the main hospital doors and stood in the blind spot, hoping for a clue. I got nothing, but it helped knowing I wasn't being watched while I finished my latte.

At the radiology department front desk, the receptionist said Dorothy was off work. I asked for the employee directory. Lo and behold, Ronald Bowser was a real person. He worked in the morgue.

42

No one goes to the morgue for fun. Or, I mean, anyone who enjoys hanging in the morgue, I hope, also enjoys scheduled medications. The morgue even creeps M out, and she lives in a haunted house.

St. Rafa's morgue was in the basement. It's between shipping/receiving and the door for the hospital dumpsters. Hospitals don't do death. It's nothing you want advertised. Not in this day and age. Because Americans don't do death. Death is someone else's problem. The caffeine started working against me. I hadn't even made it to the morgue, and I was planning my own funeral.

Without proximity card access, the hospital basement was a long white hall. Pipes ran along the ceiling. It was hot and humid, and it smelled like biohazardous waste wrapped in red plastic biohazardous waste bags. I had been to the basement a handful of times – never to the morgue – to pick-up packages from shipping/receiving.

I guess I always knew I'd wind-up at these cold, metal double doors, but I didn't want to imagine the situation that brought me here. Death is supposed to be unusual, right? That's what I was taught.

The non-descript metal doors to the morgue suggested the opposite – that death was the most humdrum, everyday thing imaginable. My roommates would tell me to see a therapist if I told them where I spent my morning.

There was a doorbell. I rang it. No response. I rang it again. Still nothing. The quiet was creepy. A security camera angled out from the wall peering straight at me. I willed myself not to look up at it.

After the third ring, I tried the proximity card reader. The electric locks popped, and the doors opened inward on automatic motors. Odd. I was certain my proximity card didn't have clearance for the morgue.

I stepped inside. The doors closed behind me.

The room was large, brightly-lit, and cold. I expected odors of disease and decay, but the place was lemon fresh with disinfectant.

The opposite wall had a mortuary refrigerator. To my left, at the far end of the room, an autopsy table with surgical lights stood behind ward curtains. The curtains were open. The table was empty. The department appeared deserted. The only presence was the security camera pointed at me from above a metal door in the cinderblock wall to my right.

Whatever resolve I had failed me. I don't know if it was the human body refrigerator or the shiny steel table or the sweet lemon-scented freshness of the room, but my skeleton was about to tear itself out of my skin. I couldn't take it. I definitely wasn't about to step over to the room's one metal door and confront whoever or whatever stood behind it. I needed a can of mace or holy water or something.

As I turned to leave, that single, metal door slowly opened. I froze. A face appeared. The room beyond was dark. The face remained half-hidden in shadow. It was smiling in an awful dreamlike way. The large teeth glistened white against the darkness. The face was low, about the level of the door handle.

I backed away.

The face moved unnaturally. The person attached to this awful, smiling face was seated in a rolling chair. She was large. Her skin was grayish black, ashy with the cold. Her hair was white and crew cut. In her left ear, she wore a Bluetooth earpiece with a microphone.

She said, "Yes?"

I swallowed and managed to say, "I'm looking for Ronald Bowser."

Her awful smile slowly increased in size. Her movements were slow, lethargic. I had the presence of mind to hit record on my phone's audio recorder.

She said, "I am Ronald Bowser."

"You?"

"Call me Ronnie."

That creepy smile spread halfway around her skull.

I said, "Why are you stalking me?"

The smile transformed into a deep scowl.

"No one is stalking you."

The face backed away. The door began to close.

I strode toward her, audio recording, and said, "What do you want?"

I braced my foot against the door. Ronald Bowser moved with surprising speed: snatching the smartphone from my hand, stopping the recording, and deleting the file before I could protest.

She said, "There will be no personal recording here. Hospital policy."

I grabbed my phone and said, "But it's OK for you to record me?"

The smile returned to her face. It seemed her resting position. A mask of sorts. It wasn't a happy smile.

She said, "You still haven't answered my question."

My eyes adjusted to the dark room. Computer screens and security monitors filled one wall. The other held supply bins for surgical instruments and protective equipment. There was also a sort of makeshift altar to angels. An odd assortment of ceramic angels piled together on a narrow shelf.

She said, "Do you?"

"Do I what?"

"Want to hear what Dortman was saying?"

"You recorded him?"

Ronald Bowser raised and lowered her shoulders. I guess it was a shrug.

I said, "Show me everything you've got."

She turned her smiling face up toward me.

"That will take a while."

43

We ended with Dr. Dortman's boardroom address. The broad outline was that he felt all doctors at St. Rafa should aggressively pursue out of pocket procedures. These included a variety of elective surgeries that insurance will not cover, meaning patients pay cash up front.

When the recording stopped, I said, "I doubt elective surgery could drive those kinds of numbers."

Ronald nodded, "It can't. It's a smoke screen. Something to keep the board happy while Dortman makes his move."

"What's the real action?"

Ronald Bowser studied me. She rose to her feet. Standing required effort. It wasn't that she was overweight. Several times, I noticed her wince as though in pain. She stopped to brace herself against a door at the back of the storage room.

I said, "Are you OK?"

She didn't respond. She swiped her badge at a proximity reader and pushed the door open.

She tapped the Bluetooth earpiece she wore and said, "You need one of these."

"What for?"

"You can get lost down here. Put this on."

She pulled the earpiece from her ear and passed it my way. I'm sure I made a face as I placed the earpiece in my ear.

I said, "Where are you sending me?"

Ronnie said, "I don't know. I was told to show you the footage. That's all."

"Who told you?"

"If you want answers, it's down this hall. If you want safety, turn around, and walk away. Don't tell anyone what you saw. They won't believe you anyway."

44

The hallway was a service sub-corridor. It wasn't on any map of the facility I knew. The walls and ceiling were a maze of pipes, conduits, and ducts.

The lighting was red, the emergency backup lighting that runs even if the power to the hospital is cut. I felt like I was travelling through the hidden arteries of the facility.

I told Ronnie what I was seeing, and she gave me directions. She must have a photographic memory. She knew every detail of the sub-corridor. I came to a ladder, and Ronnie told me to climb to the next level, the first floor of the hospital.

The passageway became more complex. Hallways branched and divided to the left and right. I knew I was close to the radiography department when I heard the MRI machine through the sub-corridor walls.

Magnetic resonance imaging or MRI is the weirdest of all the medical imaging technologies. Using induction coils, the machine produces a magnetic field thousands of times more powerful than the earth's magnetic field. When a patient is placed inside the coil all the protons in every atom in their body line up with the magnetic field lines.

The MRI machine produces loud radiofrequency pulses – almost like the radiofrequencies used by a microwave oven. It sounds like bad techno. The pulses are attuned to hydrogen protons. They knock the protons out of alignment with the machine's magnetic field. In the process of re-aligning themselves, the hydrogen protons produce a net magnetic field of their own – like an echo of the radiofrequency. The machine detects the proton signal using a very sensitive smaller coil around the part of the body to be imaged.

I've come to the conclusion that MRI technology is evidence that aliens exist and Area 51 is a cover-up. Shifting magnetic fields and singing protons are not the kinds of things human beings think up, and I could hear the cooling pumps and radiofrequency pulses of the MRI scanner nearby.

Ronnie said, "I'm going to lose your signal at the next corner. So, listen up. Take a left and another left. You'll find a panel in the wall half way down. Unfasten the panel and crawl through."

"Then what?"

"They'll show you what to do."

"Who will?"

"Don't worry. You can trust them."

45

The panel opened to one of the MRI changing rooms. It was empty. On the bench was a hospital gown and a list of instructions. I removed all my clothes except my underwear and slipped on the gown. Everything else – my phone, bra, the earpiece, and keys – I placed in a locker. No one met me outside the changing room. The instructions told me to walk to the third scan room.

The door was open. I lay down on the scan table. The room lights went dark. Someone entered. I couldn't see their face. It was a woman.

She placed a coil over my head and draped a blanket over my body. She gave me clickers to hold in either hand. I felt like I was trapped inside a very awkward video game. She moved me into scanning position inside the magnet.

MRI does not use ionizing radiation. Safe use of the technology focuses on avoiding ferromagnetic materials inside the examination room and the small risk of overheating the patient with the radiofrequency waves. There's not the scary (but super small) risk of cancer caused by x-ray usage.

Knowing this did little to diminish the sudden spike in terror I felt with my head strapped to the table inside a futuristic cage thing as my body moved into the rumbling bright tube of the MRI gantry. I wanted to claw my way out screaming.

A woman's voice came over the intercom.

She said, "Thank you for volunteering as a test subject in our fMRI polygraph trial."

That answered one question. How the tech could justify performing this exam without doctor's orders. It was a trial protocol for fMRI (aka functional MRI imaging). She was going to measure the physiological response of my brain to questions.

MRI can get away with using human volunteers for experiments and protocol development. In x-ray and CT we use phantoms, specially designed objects, to test protocols and evaluate quality measures.

Through the intercom, the tech said, "Use the clickers to reply to the questions. Right clicker means 'yes' and left means 'no.' Do you understand?"

Right clicker – yes.

"Good. I am required to inform you that you are under no obligation to answer any of the following questions. The test begins now."

Radiofrequencies bombarded my head, rattling my skull.

She said, "Have you ever told a lie?"

Yes. Right clicker.

The radiofrequencies ground into my head again.

The tech said, "Have you ever stolen anything?"

I really didn't want to answer this one, but yes, in the middle of my parent's divorce, I stole twenty dollars from Mother to buy gasoline. I never told her I took the money, and I don't think she ever realized the money was missing. Two years later I put the money back in her wallet because I was sick of feeling like a thief.

Right clicker.

"Have you ever used a false name, date of birth, or place of birth for any reason?"

Nope. I've always been proud of who I am and where I'm from. Left clicker.

"Have you ever moved out of any place you have lived due to eviction, foreclosure, or arguments with your spouse, family members, roommates, neighbors, or landlords?"

I moved out of Mother's house, but it wasn't because of arguments.

Nope – left clicker.

"Did you ever cheat on any exam, tests, assignments, projects, or papers in high school or college?"

That's easy. I was always too paranoid that I wouldn't learn whatever I was supposed to learn if I cheated. Left clicker.

"Have you ever been fired from any job?"

I was fired after working the holidays at the Texas Candle Company. They used me for selling their blue bonnet and mesquite candles and left me high and dry. I haven't liked scented candles since. Right clicker.

"Have you ever deliberately violated any serious employment rules or regulations?"

Left clicker. The same for: "Have you ever committed any criminal acts against any of your employers or coworkers?" and "Have you ever declared bankruptcy?"

I was beginning to feel pretty good about myself. I mean things can always be worse, and being reminded of that between radiofrequency barrages was oddly satisfying. In spite of the noise, I was beginning to feel a little drowsy. Like falling asleep on an airplane.

"Have you ever operated a vehicle after consuming any intoxicating substance to the point of impairment?"

A car? No. I use a ride-hailing app. My bike? Yes. Drunk bike riding is perhaps my one and only genuine vice. Is a bike a vehicle?

Whatever. Right clicker.

"Have you ever received any traffic tickets as a result of a traffic accident?"

Left clicker. While I was under her insurance, Mother swore she'd sell my car if I ever got so much as a speeding ticket. It's one of the reasons I prefer riding my bike. That plus Austin traffic makes it so that I can get where I'm going faster on a bike most the time.

"Have you ever blacked out or passed out from drinking?"

Regrettably yes. One time. On my 21st birthday. I blame Zoey. She thinks it's funny to feed people drinks and watch what happens. Never again. Right clicker.

After that was all left clicker. I mean the tech asked about all the bad stuff. Not that passing out drunk is good, but there's levels to bad, right?

For example, the next questions were about illegal drugs. I've only ever smoked pot twice – both times at a concert with the Old Flame. That's what Zoey and I call my ex-boyfriend, Nat. The Old Flame. It suits him.

Next came questions about stuff like arrests; domestic violence; child abuse; use of weapons; sex with family members; sex with prostitutes; sex with animals; burglary and robbery; blackmail; impersonating a police officer; assault and battery; kidnapping; murder; manslaughter…

All I know is I don't look good in orange.

The whole ask-a-super-intense-question-and-bombard-your-brain-with-sound-waves thing started to wear. I guess I had an anxiety attack. It felt like anaphylactic shock. Like my throat closed up and I went blind. It must have been vasovagal. Something about the whole situation rubbed me the wrong way, and my blood pressure tanked.

The next thing I knew I was smelling ammonia and studying the ceiling lights outside the exam room. Dorothy Hicks stared down at me. I wanted to curl up in a ball under my blanket. I wanted Mommy and Daddy. All I had was this withered-up crazy woman leering at me.

I said, "Stick a fork in me. I'm done."

Dorothy flashed a crooked smile and said, "OK kid, you passed. Get dressed. We got work to do."

She helped me to my feet and into the dressing room. I heard the techs walking the next patient into the exam room while I pulled on my clothes. Everything felt less real, like all the atoms in the universe had slid apart, making everything a little more nothing.

The MRI must have sprained my brain. If I was ever going to develop mutant superpowers, this was it. Yet again, I reaffirmed my sense of wonder at all the weird crap we put people through in hospitals.

46

The last thing in my MRI locker was Ronald Bowser's Bluetooth earpiece. The thought of a return trip to the morgue was as appealing as a trip to the state mental health hospital. Maybe Dorothy would return it for me.

When I picked the stupid thing up, it vibrated. A call. Scared me half out of my scrubs. I didn't trust the thing. There was no telling how it worked. It wasn't synced with my phone. Plus, there was ear wax. No telling whose.

I cleaned the earpiece with the hand sanitizer from the wall dispenser and shoved it into my ear.

A notification voice said, "Incoming call from Donnie Darko. Answer or push to voicemail?"

I said, "Answer."

The line clicked, I said, "Really? Donnie Darko?"

Ronald Bowser said, "What? It's my favorite movie."

"Don't ever forget to take your medications."

"I do what the voices tell me. So, you made it?"

"Yep."

"Maybe you got what it takes after all. I told Dorothy she'd never get me inside that thing. Anyways, listen. You hang on to the earpiece. Keep it with you at all times. I mean sleep with the thing. If you're at the hospital, it will sync with the hospital intercom system. I've set up a secure line. Completely untraceable. If you're away from the hospital, it will sync with your phone. The phone connection is not secure. It's basically a Bluetooth earbud. You understand? Do not use it or your cellphone to discuss dootily squat. While you're here you can say whatever to me or Dorothy on that thing and it's locked down tight. Oh, and Dorothy will give you the facility master key, but we can't give you a key card for the proximity locks. That would raise too many red flags. You just say, 'Donnie Darko,' and the earpiece will ring me. I can open any proximity lock in the hospital for you. Completely untraceable."

The thought of having open access to any door in the hospital was exhilarating. I felt like I owned the place.

Ronald Bowser continued, "Don't go getting any big ideas. Keys and proximity locks are for emergency use only. If you start wandering in and out of doors, it will blow your cover. FYI I can see people going in and out of the sub-corridor, but I can't see anything inside the sub-corridor. If you're in there, I'm pretty much blind."

I said, "Roger that, what's the plan?"

"Beats me. I figured you already knew."

"Don't have a clue."

I glanced down at my watch. 15:06. My blood pressure dropped so fast I had to brace myself against the wall.

"Gotta go," I said. "Late for work."

Ronald rang off as I ran down the hall for the time clock.

47

Timmy the Fearless was waiting for me. He had my written warning in hand.

He said, "Keep walking. You're suspended."

Ignoring the piece of paper, I sidestepped him to clock in.

Vanessa slid around the corner and sauntered toward us.

"I wouldn't do that if I were you."

She was dressed in tight, white scrubs. Her low v-neck top revealed more augmented anatomy than was medically necessary. The other day Trixie told me Vanessa failed her first attempt on the nursing registry exam. Had to retake it. Too much time in the tanning bed kills brain cells.

I looked hard at Vanessa, and then studied Timmy. What were these two doing together? Timmy's eyes flicked toward Vanessa. He gulped.

I said, "Oh my stars, Tim, really?"

Oozing guilt from every pore, he said, "What?"

"Her? You've got a wife. Kids."

Vanessa pretended not to hear.

She said, "I happened to be walking down the hall and couldn't help but overhear Tim give you notice of your suspension. I know this is disappointing, but I'm sure your department manager has your interests and the interests of the hospital in mind."

Vanessa snapped the written notice from Tim's hand and shoved it into my chest. I glared at her as I took the paper.

Tim looked pathetic, but stabbing people in the back is pathetic. It was everything I could do to keep the tears from my eyes.

I took a deep breath and said, "OK, have it your way."

Dorothy Hicks rounded the corner.

She said, "Here's where you're hiding, Timmy. I've been looking all over for you. Oh, and Vidalia, right? Nice of you to drop by."

Vanessa looked stricken. The color drained from her fake-baked face. She took a step back.

Dorothy said, "What's this?"

She took the paper from me, read it over slowly, clicking her tongue.

Dorothy said, "Oh, no-no-no. This won't do, Timmy. What on earth are you thinking? Claire is one of the best techs we've got."

Tim glanced at Vanessa. Her lip rose in disgust.

He said, "I agree that when she's here Claire is one of the best techs we've got, but she has exhibited a trend of tardiness of late that creates real risks for her co-workers and patients."

Dorothy put a finger on her lip.

She said, "You may want to review your records on that. You see. Claire already clocked in today at exactly 15:02, didn't you girl? And you can imagine the sort of field-day lawyers would have if you serve her a written notice for tardiness and suspend her when poor Claire wasn't actually tardy. That's the sort of managerial error that gets people fired. No warning. No notice."

I think Vanessa's poison sacks ruptured internally. Her body went flaccid and boneless. Timmy tried to form a response, but his mouth wasn't working right.

Dorothy held the notice up for all to see. She looked as though she was going to tear the page in half. Instead she stopped, folded it neatly, and handed it to me.

She said, "You may want to hold onto that."

I'd sooner swallow a scorpion, but I didn't say that. I tucked the notice into my scrub pocket as Dorothy looped her arm through mine and led me away.

She said, "I want to show you something."

48

Dorothy Hicks led me out to the main lobby and up the elevator to the third floor, the same floor as

Dortman's office. I thought that's where we were going, but she turned in the hall before his office door. We stood at a big window looking over East Austin. Dorothy took a deep breath and slowly let it out.

She said, "See that little white house on the other side of the flyover? -Behind Burrito Volador?"

A smile rose and fell on her wrinkled face. She looked very old and very tired.

"That's my house. If you ever need anything or if life gets to be too much, look for the house with the angel in the garden. You can come any time of the day or night."

Dorothy pressed something into my hand. Two keys.

I said, "What's this?"

"One is the master key to the hospital. The other is a key to my house. They're yours."

"Why are you doing this?"

Dorothy shrugged and said, "I don't know. Maybe I'm an old fool. I see something in you, girl. I'm hoping – with the right kind of direction – you can steer this place on a better course."

I said, "Has St. Rafa changed that much? I know the stuff with Dortman is bad, but –"

"He's made it as far as he has because there's enough people around who think medicine is a business like anything else. They're complicit. It's all about money."

Dorothy shook her head.

She said, "The nuns would have thrown them all out on their ears."

I said, "There were nuns?"

"Oh yes, and they were some tough mothers. Merciless if you were negligent. Dortman wouldn't have survived two days with the sisters."

"What changed?"

"The nuns sold the place in the late eighties. St. Rafa became part of a larger healthcare network. Apart from little adjustments in the way job satisfaction scores were handled not a lot changed on the surface, but beneath the surface was a whole other story. I never understood how much those vicious old bats held back the forces of darkness."

She paused, laughed at herself.

Dorothy said, "I bet you think I'm being overdramatic, but I watched a good thing go bad. Now it's filled with corruption, pettiness, malpractice – all for the sake of money. It's like a disease, an epidemic. And it happened on my watch."

The realization hit me. She knows what Dortman's up to. She's seen the spread of his infection firsthand. She knows the incidence rates, the epidemiology.

I said, "How did Dortman make it this far?"

She said, "He has drive. The whole family is like that. His dad was a surgeon, a workaholic. Worked himself straight into the grave, but not before beating the same unchecked ambition into his son. The god complex is real, girl. There's a cult of people who follow it religiously. They tend to hang out around hospitals. Vanessa is a prime example."

Dorothy peered into my eyes.

She said, "You're not like that though."

Dorothy turned away from the window. I followed her to the service elevator and down to the main level.

We walked the back hallway through the radiology department into the radiologist reading room.

It was dark and cave-like, lit by a screensaver of fish swimming around a single computer monitor. The reading room was always dark. The atmosphere close. The temperature cool. Still, it had changed. The room felt dead. The radiologists were gone. The workers had begun removing furniture in preparation for converting it to storage or whatever Dortman had planned.

Where in the past the reading room always held the quiet murmur of the radiologists dictating findings from the patient studies, now silence permeated the room. This was the heart of the department, and the heart was gone, outsourced.

Behind the sheetrock, the walls were secondary radiation barriers, 1/32 inch of lead equivalent. None of the hospital noises – the wailing from the ED, the bustle of technologists in the exam rooms – penetrated this inner sanctum. Without the radiologists, it felt like a tomb.

Dorothy went to one of the reading stations and pushed the monitor out of the way. Behind it the wall held a small alcove, and inside the hidden nook was a statue of an angel with a flaming sword held in his right hand over his head. Beneath the angel's foot, pinned to the ground, was a writhing dragon. The monster was caught paralyzed in the instant before the killing blow. Its wicked eyes were fixed on the shield in the angel's left hand. On it was emblazoned something in Latin.

Dorothy said, "Quis ut Deus. It means, 'Who is like God?' It's a literal translation of the name Michael.

This is a statue of St. Michael the Archangel, the patron saint of radiologists."

I said, "I never knew it was there."

She shook her head and said, "I've seen a lot of changes in radiology, and I've been against all of them. Knowing that statue hid there helped keep me sane. There's a war going on between medicine and health. It's not a new war. It's been going on for a long time. Dortman was a casualty in the war."

"More like a traitor."

Dorothy winced. She almost spoke but stopped herself.

I said, "How long have you known him?"

She said, "I first became acquainted with Richard Dortman in high school. I had a son in his class."

"You knew him when he was at FCA? You know about Peggy Nash?"

She nodded. "That poor darling. I also knew Dortman's father. He was a surgeon here at St. Raphael. His family worshiped medicine. We all did back then, but we didn't understand anything about health."

She was hedging, evading my questions.

I pressed harder, "What does that have to do with stopping Dortman?"

"By the time I realized what was happening, it was too late."

Rage stabbed me repeatedly in the chest and abdomen. My heartrate and blood pressure surged. I was ready for a fight.

I said, "It wasn't too late to call the cops. If you want to talk healing, talk about what happened to Peggy and her family. Why did all the parents – everyone at that stupid school – let him get away with it?"

Dorothy said, "There were a number of us who tried to stop him, but there wasn't any evidence. Peggy was afraid to come forward immediately after it happened—"

"—because of all those awful evangelical rules. I know. Suicide Steve used to joke about it."

Dorothy winced, drew a deep breath, and said, "Jokes don't hold up in court, hon. Around that time, I had my heart attack. Then the divorce. When I heard Dortman was accepted to Baylor Medical, I swore I'd do everything I could to stop him, but I knew it wasn't something I could do alone. I've been waiting for someone to help, someone like you."

I said, "Why do I get the feeling there's something you're not telling me?"

Dorothy drew another deep, ragged breath. She looked pale and fragile.

I said, "Do you feel OK?"

She reached into the alcove and retrieved the statue of St. Michael the Archangel.

She said, "If they find it, they'll toss it in the dumpster. It was mine to begin with. It's yours now."

The statue was surprisingly heavy, carved from marble. I had no clue what I would do with it. I'm not an angel statue kind of girl. It wouldn't fit in my bike messenger bag. An awkward silence passed between us. The rage drained out of me.

I said, "Thank you."

She rolled her eyes and said, "I know you don't want it, but it's yours. Maybe it will all make sense someday."

I said, "OK, what next?"

Dorothy lowered herself into a chair and said, "I've taken up enough of your time."

"I'm lost. You put me on a snipe hunt to the hospital morgue, stuck me inside an MRI machine long enough to microwave my brain, and threatened my manager with legal action in order to give me an angel statue and the key to your house. Now, you're telling me that's it? There's nothing else to do? You have enough evidence against Dortman already. Do what you should have done when he was in high school – call the cops."

Dorothy looked near collapse, but the glare she turned toward me was fierce and defiant.

She said, "The police won't find anything because they don't know what to look for. People like you and me are the only ones who can see there's a problem. When everybody else looks at Dortman, they see a doctor obsessed with medicine, and somehow in our twisted society that's a good thing. End of story. It takes a special set of eyes to see what happens when someone is obsessed with medicine but completely opposed to health."

"I don't follow. Medicine and health are the same thing."

"Wrong again, hon. Medicine is a tool, a knife. It can cut out a tumor, saving a life, or slice through the carotid arteries and kill. Medicine isn't an end in itself. It comes at a cost. Health is a relationship – mind, body, and spirit. It's a community. Health is inside us and all around us. Health is an end in itself. Human beings might survive using tools but we live in relationships. Health wins over medicine every time."

Dorothy's head sagged. Whatever secret she was keeping bottled up inside was killing her, but she couldn't let it out. We didn't have that level of bond. Not yet.

I put my hand on her shoulder and said, "I don't think I can actually help. There's something you're not saying."

Dorothy nodded and said, "Give an old woman some time with her memories. There's time. I'll tell you in time."

She waved her hand at the door to the bunker and said, "For now, you can help me by helping the patients. Go on. They need you."

49

I thought about what Dorothy said as I worked. Medicine as a means to health and health as an end in itself. The idea took some weight off my shoulders. When I rolled into a patient's room, I had something more important than an x-ray machine. I had myself. Healing begins in relationship. That's nice.

Too bad Dorothy was lying through her shiny, white dentures. Even if it was true, it was a diversion from the facts. She knew something about Dr. Dortman, and she wasn't talking.

Dani and I ate in the hospital cafeteria, which always feels like an admission of defeat. The dining experience is a step above prison gruel and a step below airplane food. The mood somewhere between intense shame for being so weak and worthless as to require sustenance and self-loathing for being willing to eat the slop in front of you. I simply couldn't spare a single neuron to decide on something like dinner.

I tried to explain to Dani, but he didn't get it.

I said, "We can't have medicine without health, but medicine can improve health."

I talked about how Dr. Dortman was focused on improving the hospital's bottom line by using medicine without health.

When I finished, Dani held out a hand and said, "Give me the drugs."

I said, "You don't understand. Medicine is a tool. Health is a relationship."

"Girlfriend, we all need a little healing from time-to-time. You feel me?"

"I can't tell you anything."

Dani rested his hand on mine and peered into my eyes.

He said, "Maybe we need a little healing, you and me. What do you say? Will you heal me? If I heal you?"

I withdrew my hand and raised it in a fist.

"I'm about to put you in the hospital."

Dani extended his muscular arms and said, "I'm already in the hospital, baby."

I let my gaze drift around the cafeteria. Near us sat a dad of five clearly down a mom, struggling to replace her with French fries and cheeseburgers. A thin, stoned girl barely wearing a hospital gown slumped in a wheelchair behind Dani. She was hooked up to an IV pump, staring in disbelief at the tatted guy across the table from her who seemed to be attempting to freestyle rap. A large table across the room swarmed with nurses, feeding on patient gossip like hyenas.

I was among my people: the sick, the sacked, and the sickened. That's when I saw him, kicked back in a chair eating an apple and reading something on his phone. The guy from Barton Springs.

Dani caught me staring.

He said, "Hello."

Dani did a doubletake.

"You know that guy?"

I said, "Uh-uh. Nope. Moving on."

Dani said, "Claire, a minute ago you looked like you were straining to push out a turd inside your brain—"

"Good gravy. Do think before you say anything?"

He said, "Now you got googly eyes. You're going to talk to him."

"Talk? Words? Who needs words? That's my philosophy."

"My philosophy is people gotta bang. He needs to bang. You need to bang. You dig him. Y'all bang. World's problems solved."

Dani popped up, wandered over to the dude's table, and dropped into a seat. I couldn't hear what they were saying, but I saw the guy laugh. Dani waved me over.

I strained to smile – ditching my half-eaten sandwich and texting Dani, "I hate u" – as I bounced over to the table.

His name was Adam, and he was working as a patient survey specialist – whatever that is – while he completed an undergrad in biology at UT. Of course, Dani connected with him on the fact that bro was from Arkadelphia. They were talking about a rapper named Big Dank from Little Rock when I slid into a chair.

Dani said, "This is Claire. We work x-ray."

Adam smiled and gave me a nod. He was even more handsome dressed business casual. There was something about his facial bones that really appealed to the x-ray tech in me, perfect radiographic proportion. I wanted desperately to perform a tangential projection of both his zygomatic arches.

He said, "I saw you at that big swimming hole."

"Barton Springs."

He said, "That's the place. I don't get out much."

Dani dropped a hand on his shoulder, "And homey rolls with Big Dank? We got to fix that."

Adam shook his head, "I don't think so. I used to party. Not anymore."

Dani pushed him and said, "Uh-uh, Big Dank. We got to fix that."

They both looked at me.

I said, "I don't know. Is it broken? Is not partying something that needs fixing? Maybe partying what's actually broken and not partying is the fix. Because like I always say, if it ain't broke don't fix it, right?"

"Right," said Adam, suddenly captivated by a sign instructing guests to return dining trays to the wash line.

Dani stared at me bug eyed and mouthed, "Get it together, bitch."

Rising to his feet, Dani said, "I'm gonna grab a grape soda. Y'all want anything?"

He sauntered off, making a show of walking slow, waving to people, shaking hands with an old lady, chatting with the cafeteria workers.

Adam said, "Your friend is very outgoing."

I nodded, "Never met a stranger."

"I wish I could do that. It's not my style."

"Me neither. I'm not even interested in trying. Dani does enough of it for the both of us."

It's funny, but I missed Dani. Was I really just a bro to him? Was there nothing between us that might slow his role as my wingman?

Adam looked at me for a moment, searching something out in my eyes. His hooded, deep-set gaze passed through me like a bolt of high voltage electricity, pinning me to the cafeteria chair.

When he looked away, I nearly collapsed. I hadn't felt this hopeless around a guy since junior high. What is this? - Lust? – A pituitary disorder? Was this how Alex felt with guys? Was I turning into Alex?

Adam said, "How long have you worked in x-ray?"

He could have asked me about the filing status of my W-2 forms and it would have been the sweetest, most soul-searching question I'd ever been asked. I hated feeling this way. I couldn't afford to fall in love. Not now.

Love turns the brain to guacamole, and I needed every neuron processing faster than the new iPhone. I was almost mad at him. I knew I'd be playing this conversation over and over in my head for days to come.

I said, "Doesn't matter."

It came out harsher than I meant it.

I tried to recover. "I mean, it's just a job, right?"

Wrong. X-ray was my life. Even now I was palpating the epicondyles of my left elbow, feeling the smooth motion of the olecranon process beneath the skin.

He said, "I've always thought x-ray is fascinating."

Again with the lingering, electrifying gaze. If he kept up the fascinating stuff, I was going to collapse on the cafeteria floor, requiring CPR.

It's the surface tension, I told myself. You have to break through the surface. What's the closest thing to your heart? Tell him something deep. See what he does.

"You know what's fascinating," I said. "There's a doctor here who is intentionally injuring patients."

Woah, Claire. Hold up. Is that seriously the closest thing to your heart? Alex and Zoey were totally right. There' something wrong with you.

Adam leaned closer and said, "What do you mean?"

"His name is Dr. Dortman, and he hates me right now."

"You seem nice to me."

I shook my head and said, "You probably think I'm crazy but whatever. You need to know that up front."

Adam said, "I don't think you're crazy. You might be the smartest person in this hospital."

He definitely thought I was crazy.

"Listen, Claire. I've suspected the same thing. You should see some of the patient survey data. Can I get your number? We can text? Maybe grab some coffee?"

Dani returned. It was time to head back. I swapped numbers with Adam, but I knew it was hopeless. Goodbye, you ridiculously hot client survey specialist, I thought. Maybe now I can get my brain back online.

50

A few days passed. I saw Dorothy here and there. Dortman performed a series of flawless surgeries, which was creepy in its own way. Knowing the guy wasn't incompetent. He could do the job if and when he wanted to.

The department was busy. They finished converting the reading room into a storage closet. It was weird how little changed — losing the rads to teleradiology. For all their nifty new technology, the radiologists finally managed to make themselves obsolete. I missed them.

I put the statue of St. Michael the Archangel on top of a cinderblock among the bamboo in the backyard. I could see it from the window above the sink.

What Dorothy said – about medicine as a tool and health as a relationship – stayed with me. It explained so much. Every conflict, from tiny differences of opinion to the silent war with Dortman, existed in that tension. I still couldn't bring myself to believe her. I don't like manipulative people.

Trying to explain the difference between medicine and health to Dani had been a fool's errand. Maybe that's what Dorothy saw in me – someone who could understand that distinction. It might not seem like much, but it's something. The question became when would she tell me the rest of the story? And, how much could I trust her until then? How much could I ever trust her?

One evening, Dorothy called me on the Bluetooth earpiece.

She said, "I meant to tell you, we have a little get together every year on November 8. You should drop by if you're free."

I said, "Sounds interesting," as noncommittally as possible.

November 8, 1895 was the day Wilhelm Conrad Roentgen discovered x-rays. Of course, Nikola Tesla claimed to have found them before that, but he didn't write it down. Lesson one from x-ray history: document, document, document.

Truth is, with everything else going on, I completely forgot about the International Day of Radiology. In x-ray school, we threw keggers. "Drinking with Roentgen" was the general theme. We'd toast to Wilhelm Conrad and Anna Bertha and recite the dirty limerick: "On November 8, 1895, Ms. Roentgen was glad to still be alive…"

It seemed wrong to let the day pass without lifting a glass to Roentgen, but Dani had a "date" with his mystery lady, and M had tickets for the Laura Dern-A-Thon at the Alamo Ritz. If I went, I was going unaccompanied.

After I clocked out, I pedaled over to Dorothy's. I didn't bother changing out of my scrubs or bringing wine. This was an appearance: a hi-how-are-you, one drink, a half-hidden yawn, and a work excuse before heading home.

Except for the strings of lights hanging above the path through the garden the place didn't look like there was a party going on. The lights were out in the cottage's front room. I heard piano music – a polka, I think – at the back of the house. Through the beveled glass of the front door, I saw a red light glowing beneath the hall door inside.

The cottage was old but meticulously crafted. Each detail – from the door handle to the carefully constructed eaves – was built by skilled craftsmen. The garden also was immaculately tended. The big palm plants and plum trees formed a sound barrier. I could see the interstate flyover through the branches above, looming like a space-age cathedral, but the noise of the cars and the endless day of the halogen lights was muted by the garden and the piano.

I knocked. The music stopped. The hall door open. Red light framed a man in a cowboy hat. He sauntered to the front door. I nearly turned around and hightailed it out of there. I've seen enough drunken cowboys in the ED. Beneath all the swagger they're the worst drama queens of the lot.

I was stopped by his face – seen in the muted red light. It was uncannily familiar.

He swung the door open and said, "You must be Claire. I'm Selman Brookes."

As we shook hands, my mouth dropped open. *The* Selman Brookes? I had never seen a photograph, but I had seen his caricature a thousand times. Selman Brookes wrote *the* book on x-ray image production and radiation physics. He was half the reason I passed the radiography registry. This was as close as I'd ever come to meeting a genuine x-ray celebrity – as dumb as that may sound.

Selman slapped my shoulder and said, "Get on in here and get your hand x-rayed."

He turned and strode into the house. The fumes coming off him were like kerosene. What did he mean? – hand x-ray?

I followed him into a small dining room. Two of the walls were lined with old wavy glass windows facing the garden. An antique dining table stood at the center of the room, and on the table were two small x-ray machines.

The first machine was a table-top portable, AC powered, 110 volts. It was plugged into the wall. The machine looked like a robot from a 1970s science fiction movie. Two blocky legs extended to the table. The collimator formed its body. The x-ray tube and operator console formed the robot's clunky, outsized head. Dad would have loved it.

The other x-ray machine was terrifying. A Crookes tube wired to a car battery. The tube was unshielded. If you turned it on, x-rays would shoot out in all directions. Uninsulated copper wires ran from the battery to the tube with a simple switch between. The machine was primed to burst into a flaming electric ball of radioactive death the second it was energized. Hard to believe this was what x-ray technologists used to play with.

Selman caught me gawking at the Crookes tube.

He said, "Trust me you don't want to be x-rayed by her. The exposure time for a hand is close to ten minutes. That's right, ten minutes. I tell ya. Your skin starts to tingle before the Crooke's tube is done with you."

I swallowed and stared at him. Was he talking about x-raying me?

Selman said, "That's why we all pitched in and bought this thing."

He patted the robotic tabletop machine.

Dorothy stepped into the room.

She said, "I see you've met the instigator. Don't let him bully you into anything."

Selman pushed the cowboy hat back on his head.

He said, "Ms. Hicks, you have offended my honor. I cajole. I most certainly do not bully."

Dorothy said, "What difference does it make what you call it? This sweet young lady has no interest in puerile stunts."

I said, "What does he mean?"

Dorothy said, "He wants to take your hand x-ray."

Selman said, "Think of it as a reenactment of that great day when Roentgen first x-rayed his wife's hand."

I said, "Isn't that illegal? —to just x-ray people for the sake of x-raying them?"

"Good question," Dorothy said.

She arched her eyebrow at Selman.

He said, "Define illegal."

"As in against the law."

"What law?"

"I don't know what law. I just know we shouldn't take an x-ray without a doctor's order."

He said, "You want a doctor's order? I can get a doctor's order."

Dorothy said, "Oh no, you don't. You will not drunk dial any of your poor friends from my house."

Selman staggered back a step theatrically.

He said, "Drunk? Madam, I am not drunk—"

"You ain't sober either."

Selman turned to me and said, "Did Roentgen think of the laws of the land when he made his great discovery? No! He thought only of the laws of science."

Sitting down near the table-top portable machine, I said, "What the heck. I'll do it."

Selman draped a lead apron over my body. He gave me a thyroid shield and lead glasses.

I set my left hand on the table then noticed the ring on my pointer finger. I removed it and set the ring on the table. I didn't want the ring to show up on the image. Anything that could obscure a diagnosis is called an artifact.

Selman picked up the ring and placed it on my ring finger.

He said, "For the sake of history."

The first x-ray demonstrated Anna Bertha's wedding band superimposing her fourth proximal phalanx, the birth of both x-ray imaging and image artifacts.

Selman placed a cassette under my hand.

I said, "Is that film?"

"Nothing digital here."

He grabbed the exposure button, took two steps back, and shot the picture.

51

The bathroom was the darkroom. A red bulb glowed in the fixture above the sink. The antique clawfoot bathtub held three pans: developer, fixer, and water. A tomato-shaped egg timer set in the soap dish. The ceiling fan blew the air out of the room. It still smelled of chemicals.

Once inside, Selman ran masking tape around the edges of the door, sealing out any light. Layers of heavy black paper covered the window.

Handing the film-screen cassette to me, he said, "Your turn."

He demonstrated how the latches worked. It was clunky. The cassette was heavier than computed radiography cassettes. The back panel was lead, the front, carbon fiber or something equally radiolucent. The design wouldn't stop the x-rays from entering the cassette, but the photons would be attenuated by the lead backing before exiting.

Inside the cassette, sandwiched together around the film were two intensifying screens, which glowed when struck by x-rays, shortening exposure time.

Selman gave me a pair of dishwashing gloves.

He said, "The chemicals are probably worse than the x-rays. They definitely cost more."

I slipped on the gloves, pulled the film from the cassette, and dropped it in the developer. He started the egg timer.

While we waited, Selman said, "So, are you going to help Dorothy take down Dr. Dortman?"

I said, "What? No. How do you know about that?"

Selman gave me an exaggerated wink. The egg timer chimed.

I pulled the film from the developer and slipped it into the fixer pan. I had never actually hand-processed film, but film development had been a required part of my studies. It's kind of magical to watch the image emerge from beneath the surface of the fluid.

Resetting the tomato-shaped timer, Selman said, "Dorothy really needs your help."

I said, "Right. We met like five minutes ago, and now you know all about me."

Selman pushed the cowboy hat back on his head. He looked completely alien, dressed like a cowboy, holding a ticking tomato, bathed in red light.

I thought, I don't have to justify myself to this clown.

The timer chimed. I pulled the film from the fixer and dropped it into the water.

52

Where other little, old ladies would have a trellis or a metal star of Texas affixed to the exterior wall by the patio, Dorothy Hicks had a radiographic light box. It was above a potting table littered with garden tools. On the light box were hung film after film of left-hand x-rays.

Written on each image was the individual's name and the date. Always November 8. Only the year changed.

Some of the panels were dark.

Selman said, "Those are the techs who've accelerated off to that big anode in the sky."

He sloshed wine into the flowerbed.

Joining us, Dorothy offered me a cocktail that smelled strongly of herbs.

She said, "Underberg. It's a digestif bitter from Rheinberg. I don't know what Roentgen drank. Perhaps, he abstained all together—"

"Impossible," Selman said. "He was German."

"Prussian, actually," Dorothy said. "Anyways, Underberg seemed appropriate to the occasion."

Selman said, "Probably because it tastes like medicine."

Dorothy said, "I honestly don't know whether it's best to take it all at once or sip it slowly."

I said, "You guys really know how to sell this stuff."

Selman held up his glass and said, "To Wilhelm Conrad Roentgen."

Dorothy added, "And Anna Bertha Ludwig."

We clinked glasses, and I tossed back the drink. The bitter liquor hit me in the nasopharynx. It tasted like rose petals and licorice.

I said, "That is certainly different."

Selman slapped me on the back and said, "I'll get you a Schneider Weisse to wash it down."

I had no clue what that meant.

"Please, no," I said. "I can't stay too long."

Dorothy said, "Nonsense, you haven't even tried Lisbeth's homemade spaetzle. Selman made beschwipster huhn. I knew I shouldn't have started with the digestif."

I felt my resolve gradually eroding beneath the influence of the aromatic drink. I had never tried German food. Dorothy loaded up a plate, and we sat together at a picnic table by the x-ray light box on the patio.

Dorothy introduced Lisbeth, of the homemade spaetzle fame, as a "clown from that circus in Albuquerque." I think she meant the American Society of Radiologic Technologists, but I was too embarrassed to ask.

Lisbeth seemed like a quiet spiritual person. The type of woman who would make a good hospital chaplain. The spaetzle was amazing. More of a noodle than a dumpling, it was cooked in a cream sauce and perfectly complimented by the beshwipster huhn (aka chicken) and Schneider Weisse (aka the most amazing beer I've ever drank). I began to relax.

Ronald Bowser was there, too. She seemed a lot less scary outside of the morgue. At some point, the weird computer hacker had dyed her hair pink, which looked electrifying against her brown skin. She was busy chatting with a very thin, very tan man with a red bindi on his forehead. He wore a gray golf jacket and gray Oxford shirt.

Dorothy said, "That's Samish. Our resident philosopher of digital imaging. I'm afraid, now that Ronnie has him, you'll never get a chance to meet."

The four of us sat for moment in contented silence. Selman stood, walked through the open French doors into the house, and sat at the piano. He played Mozart's piano sonata no. 16 in C Major. I recognized it from countless registry study sessions.

Dorothy reached out and placed her hand on mine.

She said, "Claire, all of this, this is what medicine should be. Good friends, science, culture, good food, and genuine caring. Half of St. Rafa used to attend our little celebration of Roentgen. The house and garden would be full."

Lisabeth said, "Selman would play the most wonderful improvisations. Litz. He used to play Litz. Now, we're just old timers with our memories."

Dorothy said, "You can bring it back."

I withdrew my hand and said, "I don't know what you want from me. I'm an x-ray tech. You said it yourself. There's a whole sea change going on. I didn't make these problems. I inherited them, and I can't even begin to understand how to fix them."

"So, pass them on to the next group of x-ray techs?"

"Why not? That's what your generation did."

Dorothy sighed and said, "Oh, no. I fought. I fought it every inch of the way, but—"

"But nothing changed."

"No. Believe me a lot changed. So much changed. Only it changed in ways I didn't expect."

I said, "Then it's pointless to even try."

The old woman shook her head. "No, we have to try harder. We have to strive further. Think about Mozart, about Crookes, about Roentgen. What if they had been content with the world as it was given to them. Where would we be? Listen, it's a fight, sure. Sometimes it seems impossible, but you have been given a sword, an edge. It's that pioneering spirit. I see Roentgen's spirit in you. You don't recognize how powerful a weapon it is."

I pushed my plate away and downed the beer.

"I'm a kid with an associate degree from the local community college."

Dorothy said, "Roentgen was a high school drop out."

I stood and said, "I'm sorry. It's a job. You know? Anyway, I need to go home and get some rest."

Dorothy rose to her feet. The look she leveled at me nearly caused me to topple backward off the bench. In the silence that followed, her fierce expression mellowed.

She said, "Stay here tonight. I promise I won't bring St. Rafa up again. Lisabeth hasn't had a chance to enlist you for her little popularity contest, and Selman puts together the most amazing German breakfast. If you get tired, you can sleep in the guestroom. Please, stay."

As she said this, Dorothy seemed more scared than angry. Like the fierceness I'd seen was directed elsewhere. There again was that nagging sense of something left unsaid. What did Dorothy know that she wasn't saying?

I said, "I have some things I need to do at home tomorrow. You know."

Trying to keep this polite.

"Stay, please," Dorothy said. "It's not safe."

The cagy stuff was starting to grate.

I said, "What is that? Are you threatening me? Is this some sort of game you like to play with people?"

Ronald Bowser emerged from the shadows of the garden. She cleared her throat and exchanged a look with the old woman.

Dorothy said, "This isn't a game."

So much for being polite.

I shouted, "What isn't a game, Dorothy? What? You think I can't tell you're hiding something?"

Dorothy started to speak, but I cut her off.

"You know what?" I said. "I'm done. Whatever it is you're cooking up, count me out. That's final."

I dropped the Bluetooth earpiece and keys on the table. My face felt hot as I strode toward the French doors.

Selman continued playing Mozart. He nodded at me as I said a hurried good-bye.

He said, "I didn't see it at first, but you're a young Dorothy Hicks. You got that same fight."

I nearly slapped his face.

53

I pedaled furiously home, averaging eighteen miles per hour. Running every red light, cutting every corner, I made my street in less than ten minutes. The ride typically takes twice that.

Inside my chest was a super-heated tungsten filament of rage. I slowed to a stop at my house. A red

E-class Mercedes-Benz was parked on the street out front. Either there was a new dope dealer on the block or Alex had moved up a tax bracket with her tastes in fellas.

Regardless, I was too worked up to sleep. I kicked off, pedaling up and down the hills around Dottie Jordan Park. The live oaks, twisting in the moonlight, streamed by like cursive writing.

It was nearly 200 hours, and I was alone in the world. I sprinted up and down the hills until my legs began to shake with the effort. Then I slowly wound my way home.

Thankfully, the house was dark when I rolled up. The red Mercedes was still parked on the road. The license read "SUICIDE" — definitely not Alex, I decided. That had Montopolis Bloods written all over it.

I let myself in and quietly made for the shower. I was drying off my hair when I heard the bathroom door through the towel. I figured it was Alex or Zoey sleepily shuffling toward the toilet. Without looking, I pressed myself against the wall to allow them to squeeze by. I didn't even think about how naked I was. The house's single bathroom had long since become something of a high school locker room for privacy.

Whoever it was stood there. A memory of the red Mercedes parked out front flashed through my mind, and my blood pressure tanked. That's when I caught the scent of cologne. I wrapped myself in the towel before I turned to find Dr. Richard Dortman leaning against the doorframe, looking sheepish, dressed only in red boxer briefs.

With a scream, I swung at him. He grabbed my forearm.

Dortman said, "Woah, woah. I didn't hear you."

Down the hall I heard Alex and Zoey stirring in their sleep.

I screamed, "Let me go."

My voice sounded delirious and crazed.

Dortman said, "Not until you calm down. It was an honest mistake."

His voice was so phony and smooth. My mind raced, calculating all the ways he must have worked to engineer this moment, hunting me down, stalking my roommates, seducing Alex. I hadn't seen it coming.

I tried to break his leg, kicking down at his knee.

Dortman sidestepped and pulled his hands up over my head, wrapping his arms around me, pressing my back against his chest.

Blind with panic, I screamed and thrashed until I heard Alex's voice and felt my roommate's hand on my shoulder.

She said, "Claire, calm down."

Zoey said, "What are you doing to her?"

Dortman said, "Nothing. I swear. I didn't hear her in the bathroom. When I accidentally walked in, she attacked me."

I screamed, "That's a lie."

Alex said, "Claire, if Richie lets go, will you promise to calm down?"

I nodded. I didn't know what else to do. He slowly released his grip. I ripped myself away as fast as I could, diving into my bedroom, locking the door. I pulled on a t-shirt and jeans and dialed 911 before Alex knocked at my door.

"I'm on the phone with the cops," I said. "I want him out of here now."

The house was closing in on me. I heard Dortman dressing to leave. Heard him kiss Alex, heard her apologize, right outside my bedroom door. I dry heaved as I listened to the dispatch read back my complaint. Dortman sped off before the police cruiser pulled up.

54

I gave my report to the officer. I knew I didn't have a case, but she was kind enough to listen. She asked to talk to Alex. I dropped onto the couch feeling half-vivisected. When the officer left, it was with a stern warning to Alex.

As soon as the police cruiser pulled away, it was Alex's turned to go berserk.

She screamed, "What the fuck, Claire?"

Alex threw a pillow at me and another. Zoey stepped between us. Alex took a deep breath and paced the living room.

She said, "Are you seriously going to press charges?"

Her hands were up in her hair, pulling on the long blonde strands.

Zoey said, "This is why we don't let guys sleep over. That's a house rule."

Alex said, "That wasn't just any guy. That guy is my ticket to ride. He's rich. A doctor. Likes to travel. Good looking. The total package. And now because she doesn't know how to lock the bathroom door—"

I said, "He's using you."

"As long as he's shelling out, who cares? He paid off my fucking car note."

Zoey said, "He paid your car note?"

"It's not like that. I've been seeing him almost a month. It's getting pretty serious. Y'all have to see his place on Lake Travis."

Zoey glanced at me. Impressed.

Alex nodded, "That's right. Plus, we mesh. He wanted to sleep over so we could all get breakfast. I picked tonight because we're all free in morning."

I said, "It's a put on, Alex. That guy is a rapist."

"Listen Claire, it was a genuine mistake. Richie's a big pushover. He's always groggy when he wakes up. He was as confused and startled as you."

"You sure about that? He jumped in that car of his real quick once I was on the phone with the police."

"Who wouldn't?"

"Alex," I said. "I know Steven Richard Dortman. He might seem nice, but that man is a monster. Ask him about Peggy Nash. Ask him why his vanity plate says, 'SUICIDE'—"

"Duh, I did, he said it's because he lives a life to die for. It's a joke."

Zoey said, "Kind of a sick joke."

"OK little miss sunshine."

I said, "He raped a girl in my high school, Alex, and after she died from complications with the baby, he bragged about it. Called himself Suicide Steve."

Zoey shivered, "That was Suicide Steve?"

I nodded. We both turned to look at Alex.

She said, "Boys will be boys. Anyways, where's the proof? I'd have put out for him in high school. Hell, in junior high. You're trying to tell me she didn't want it?

If a guy that sexy and rich wants you, bring on the rough stuff—"

"Remember my friend M? –Dr. Dortman's the reason she got fired. He's doing these creepy surgeries in the middle of the night. He's butchering people's spines. He threatened my life, Alex. Do you seriously think it's a coincidence he's dating you?"

Alex's eyes narrowed. "What are you saying?"

"Richard Dortman is the worst doctor in the history of medicine. He's a monster, and now he's dating the roommate of the one x-ray tech who has some dirt on him and isn't afraid to speak up."

Alex laughed.

She said, "I'm sorry. Was that a joke? Are you really that paranoid? Oh my god. You're serious."

Zoey said, "OK. Listen y'all. This isn't all that different from the time I was dating Billy."

Alex said, "Tiny Tarantino?"

Billy was a film student.

I said, "No comparison."

Zoey said, "Remember how we all went to see that horror film he made, and Alex you said it was torture porn, and Claire you got creeped out when he tried to convince you to take him on a tour of the hospital? Right? Y'all need to agree to disagree. Alex, you'll grow out of him. Claire, you're paranoid, but you bitches love each other. That's what's important."

I opened my mouth to say something, but couldn't drum up the words. There was nothing to say. Alex was too worked up. I'd never seen her so angry. If she was blind to Dortman's disguise, anything I'd say would be twisted around and used against me later.

With a single maneuver, Dortman had destroyed my home. He poisoned the trust that made our sisterhood work. I couldn't live here anymore. He would turn Alex and Zoey against me. There was nothing I could do to stop it. This was personal.

Alex was too tired to fight clean. If provoked again, she would start swinging. I was too angry at Dortman to care what she thought. I wanted out. The quickest, least painful out. And, I knew Zoey wouldn't let it drop until we made up. It was false – so phony – the hollow hugs and apologies we exchanged.

I said goodnight and locked myself in my room. I didn't recognize the wild-eyed stranger in the mirror on the bedroom door, but she had my tattoo. *Ich habe meinen Tod gesehen.* I have seen my death. Is this how Anna Bertha felt on the great day of her husband's discovery? Horrified by someone she loved?

The numbness started in my chest and spread through my whole body. I couldn't feel my phone, couldn't remember dialing Dorothy Hicks, couldn't hear more than a whisper though I pressed the phone to my ear so hard something popped inside my temporal bone. It felt like doing CPR. You don't think. You just do. The training becomes every move. Your body is a protocol.

Whatever Dorothy said didn't matter. She wasn't the one who changed. That was me.

I said, "I'm in."

55

I packed clothes in my messenger bag, grabbed my toiletries, *Left Hand of Darkness,* and one other book at random from Dad's box of Hugo winners. I left a note on the kitchen counter: "Need time to think through stuff. Love, Claire."

The rising sun sliced through the bamboo, casting light on the statue of St. Michael the Archangel as I climbed on my bike and slipped silently around the corner of the house. I didn't look back. I was asleep on the handlebars, wheeling through the early morning traffic, cranking *The Beths* on a Bluetooth speaker lashed to the front cargo rack.

When I rolled up to Dorothy's house, the x-ray equipment was tossed aside and a feast was spread across the dining room table. I spied it through the windows as I pedaled along the garden path.

The smell of coffee spilled from the open kitchen window. Dorothy was there as I rounded the corner to the back patio. I nearly fell off my bike from exhaustion.

I said, "Did you know?"

Dorothy shook her head and said, "Not exactly. We suspected he would try something. It was just a matter of time."

My vision went watery. I wiped my eyes with my hands.

Dorothy hugged me and said, "The good news is you're right on time for breakfast."

I laughed in spite of myself, and she led me into the house. Selman, Lisbeth, and Ronnie offered hugs and high-fives as they guided me to a seat at the head of the table.

With the air of a general directing troops across a battlefield, Selman gave us a tour of the table. There was English cheddar, French goat cheese covered with ash, Camembert, Comte, smoked Ammerlander cheese, real butter, raw milk, fresh squeezed orange juice, homemade blackberry jam, strawberry-rhubarb jam, elderberry jam, local honey, cherry tomatoes, hardboiled eggs, liverwurst (no thanks), schlackwurst (like salami), some kind of smoked ham I didn't catch the name of, pumpernickel and multigrain breads, and baskets and baskets of fresh rolls, sticky buns, and pastries. I was in heaven.

Everyone turned to Dorothy who sat opposite me at the other end of the table.

She pointed out the window into the garden where the statue of St. Raphael the Archangel stood. The angel looked like a ten-year-old boy. Two wings folded neatly across his back. He held a staff in his right hand and a fish in his left.

Dorothy said, "It seems more apt than ever that the sisters were inspired to name our troubled hospital after St. Raphael the Archangel. His name means 'God please heal.' In scripture, St. Raphael drives away the demon Lust and heals blindness using the heart, liver, and gallbladder of a fish. As Tobit proclaims, 'The Lord afflicts and shows mercy, casts down to the depths of Hades and brings up from the great abyss. What is there that can snatch from his hand?' That same question today is my prayer."

She invited us to bow our heads and offered thanks for the meal. I felt numb and exhausted. The prayer was a platitude, a little sentimental something for those times when nothing else works. Prayer doesn't work either, but it doesn't hurt. That's what I thought as Dorothy prayed. I was amazed how much better I felt when I mumbled, "Amen."

We passed our plates around the table and served each other from the selections before us. A cabinet record player stood against the wall. Selman dropped a record on the turntable and experimental rock poured quietly from the speakers. I glanced at the album cover. *Monster Movie?* The sound was bluesy and druggy and mellow.

Selman said, "It's a German band, Can."

New to me. So much of this was new in a good way, in a way that said yes to the world and yes to life even if it's a struggle. I don't remember the conversation. I didn't say much. Didn't feel like I had to. I relaxed and enjoyed the food, the music, the flow of conversation, sunlight in the garden, everything. I forgot my roommates, forgot St. Rafa, forgot Dortman. Almost.

I don't remember falling asleep at the breakfast table. I only recall Dorothy massaging my shoulders until I was awake. She guided me to a daybed in a cool, dimly lit room where I climbed beneath the covers and slept so deeply and completely that waking up felt like being reborn into a new life, a new world, a world full of promise and mystery.

56

I lay in the day bed half-reading *The Left Hand of Darkness* trying not to think about the burning bag of biohazardous waste my life had become. Dorothy knocked on the room's French doors. I told her to enter, and she sat in the pneumoencephalography apparatus that was the room's one chair. I set the book on the antique Mayo tray, which posed for a night stand. The décor was shabby chic meets surgical suite with a touch of the Cold War. Hanging in the corner above an old sterilization cabinet was a vintage movie poster for *The Horror of Party Beach*: "Weird Atomic Beasts Who Live Off Human Blood!!!"

"Ursela Le Guin," Dorothy said, nodding approval at my reading choice.

I said, "What's the plan?"

"You're scheduled for the swing shift. Didn't want you to oversleep. Ronnie can't pull that timeclock slight-of-hand again. They'll be watching."

"Sure, but what's the plan? What next?"

Dorothy said, "You tell me."

"Is this a test?"

"There isn't a moment of life that isn't a test. So, yes, it's a test, but it's also a genuine question."

I'm sure my face betrayed confusion.

"But," I said. "This is your show."

Dorothy said, "Oh, no. My show ended last night the moment your show began. My plan was to find someone younger who could see the problem and give that person what they need to fix it."

"Let me get this straight. The problem started under your watch, and you want me to fix it?"

"Are you saying I'm lazy?"

I shrugged.

Dorothy said, "I've worked my shriveled ass off, and it's not as though I didn't inherit a few problems from the folks who came before me."

She nodded toward the poster for *The Horror of Party Beach*.

"That's the way of the world."

I said, "I don't have the authority you have. The power."

"Power is as power does. If you act like you have power, people give you more. That's how you got here—"

"Holed up in a strangers house, hiding from a homicidal surgeon, afraid to go to work? This is power?"

The part of the mandible people rub in thought is called the mental point (aka symphysis). Dorothy rubbed her mental point.

She said, "Sometimes I think power is best in the beginning. Before it realizes its own strength."

I said, "You haven't thought this through, have you?"

"Nope, you're the one with the plan."

The part of the mandible on the side that you ram a fist into when someone's not thinking is called the ramus.

I said, "Did I miss something? I don't have a plan."

Dorothy said, "Then it's your job to figure one out."

"My job? What do you call that job?"

"You've got to learn that for yourself."

"You're not going to teach me."

Dorothy said, "You catch on quick. If there's a teacher here, it's—"

"Dortman."

She nodded. "There's a reason he's in your life. There's something vital you need to learn from him. Something only he can teach you, and teach it to where you never forget. Pain and humiliation. That's your lesson."

I said, "I hate school."

Dorothy patted my leg and stood.

"I have something for you," she said.

Stepping over to the closet, she retrieved a hanger from the dry cleaners and tore away the plastic. A lab coat.

She said, "Let's see if it fits."

I stood, and she helped me into the coat. I inspected myself in the cheval mirror. The coat's cut was a little old school, but fashion moves slow in the world of lab coats. The difference didn't stand out in a bad way. It fit perfectly in the shoulders and sleeves, which was the important thing, and wearing it gave me a little something extra. Maybe it was just extra pockets, but extra pockets are helpful around a hospital.

Dorothy stood at my shoulder.

Adjusting the collar, she said, "You like it? It's yours. My first lab coat. I bought it when I earned my bachelor's degree."

"Thank you," I said and turned to look at her. "Why are you doing all this?"

She shrugged. "Selman thinks you and I are alike. I don't see it personally. You're stronger and more focused than I ever was. Also, by the time I was your age I was married."

"Thanks, mom."

She shook her head, "I didn't say happily married. It would take me a decade to figure out how miserable I was. By then we had a child."

"Had?"

Her face darkened. She said, "He's dead."

"I'm sorry."

"Never apologize for someone's loss, honey. This life is a losing game. Losing is the only way to know we've played well."

"Maybe that's true. I'm still sorry you had to go through that pain."

She said, "It's crazy how much pain and fear you can squelch by staying busy. I remember back in the 70s and 80s they promised computers would make life easier. We'd have more time to relax, they said. Now, the moment we stop running around, checking off reminders and updating our status, is the same moment we realize how much we're hurting, how terrified we are of the future. Maybe technology makes life easier, but we've only used that ease to make ourselves busier."

"You still haven't answered my question," I said. "Why are you doing this for me?"

Dorothy smoothed the sleeve of the lab coat.

She said, "I'm not interested in letting computers make my life easier. I'm interested in people, and people make life complicated. If I'm honest, maybe I'm living vicariously through you but not in a controlling way. I don't care what you do. Whatever you do, you'll do the right thing."

"No pressure or anything."

She shrugged, "A little pressure makes us perform. Anyway, there's no sense in moving out of your place. Not yet. I have a feeling Dortman's reign of terror is approaching its inevitable end, and then you can patch things up with your roommates. In the meantime, stay here as long as you like."

I said, "What makes you think Dortman is anywhere near his end?"

"I'm an old woman, Claire. When you get to be my age you've seen enough folks like Dortman. They don't last longer than a mule fart. Get your posse together and saddle up your horses. When he goes down, you better be ready to ride."

"Why?"

She laughed, "Girl, don't you know ass cheeks come in pairs? There's another Dortman waiting in the wings. With folks like him, their rise is as inevitable as their fall, and there's always another one right behind them."

57

I didn't believe for a millisecond that Dortman's fall was inevitable, but Dorothy was right about needing a team. Dortman had a team. I thought about Vanessa and Tim and wondered who else was in his pocket? – who could I trust?

The problem is I don't team well. At least that's what I determined in the shower. I pulled on a clean pair of scrubs and wandered around the little house.

The place was a museum: antique radioactivity signs; health physics notices from Oak Ridge; a whole china cabinet of fiesta dinnerware complete with a Geiger Muller counter; and framed movie posters for *X: The Man with the X-ray Eye; Panic in Year Zero;* and a host of other b-grade movies that all seemed to star Ray Milland and promise the End of the World in bold, electrifying fonts. There were Crookes tubes galore. A shoe fluoroscope stood by the piano, and a cabinet of radiation-themed toys hung on the wall by the kitchen counter.

Dorothy puttered in the garden. I decided to leave early for St. Rafa. When I hit the door, she waved me over.

I said, "I can't think of anyone I trust enough to have on my team."

Dorothy said, "Trust isn't an entry qualification. Trust happens after you've been through some ups and downs. At the start, use motivation."

She grabbed a piece of junk mail from the recycling bin and outlined the Hicks Guide to Motivation: 1) tell people what they want 2) write down three things they have to do to get what they want 3) help them 4) let them sink or swim.

I said, "Don't the third and fourth points contradict?"

She said, "Yep. That's how you get inside their heads. Keep 'em guessing."

"Sounds more like controlling people than motivating."

Dorothy said, "We'll leave that debate to the lawyers. As I see it, people are lazy good-for-nothings. They will slave – throw out their backs – to justify being lazy good-for-nothings, but when the slaving is done their essential nature is unchanged."

"I've worked hard to get where I am."

"Good for you, but you're as lazy as the rest. Prove me wrong."

I stared at her for a moment, turned, and walked away, winding down the path through the garden. Passing the statue of St. Raphael, I said a little prayer. It went like this: "Keep that woman out of my head."

58

As I reached the street, a Cadillac hearse cruised up, subwoofer bass blasting from the back. The tinted passenger window rolled down. There sat Dani, straight-faced, wearing pimp shades. I didn't recognize the guy at the steering wheel.

I said something. I don't remember what. My brain was overloaded, and Triple 6 Mafia was turned up too loud.

When he didn't respond, I grabbed Dani's arm and said, "What is this?"

He couldn't keep a straight face.
"It's a fucking limo, girl."

Ignoring the three cars behind him, the driver climbed out of the hearse; walked around to my side; and opened the door. The car's interior was remodeled with a leather couch, wet bar, TV, and running lights. Ronald Bowser lounged on the couch with a guy holding an expensive laptop. He was the driver's twin. Both of them Hispanic, sporting identical shadow fade haircuts, and pale. Yes, you can be Mexican and pale. *Guero* isn't just an old Beck album.

To Dani, I said, "What are you doing here?"

Dorothy stole up beside me.

She said, "This is your team."

Dani said, "And this is a motherfucking war cabinet on wheels."

Ronnie said, "They call it *El Coche de la Muerte*. Allow me to introduce the Cortina brothers, Nepo and Pepe."

Dorothy and I piled inside the hearse. Nepo, the one with the expensive laptop, shook my hand. Pepe, the driver, turned the music down and lowered the partition window as he cruised south on the I-35 access road.

Ronnie said, "I've known the Cortina family since back in the day. They don't do anything unless it's done Gucci. Pepe does all things cars. Nepo does all things money."

Nepo said, "I understand that St. Rafael Hospital is being mismanaged. Get me access to the financials, and I'll locate any accounting errors. Ronnie will cover the costs. She gets the family discount."

He spoke in a clipped, precise way. Not the talkative type.

Dorothy said, "I have it all right here."

She handed him a black USB stick.

Nepo said, "Perfect. I will get to work on this."

To me, Ronnie said, "I hired the limo-"

"Hearse."

"Whatever. It's ours all the nights you work for the next thirty days. If you need a pick-up or a safe meeting place, call us."

Safe? This thing was serious creepypasta. I prayed the Cortina brothers used hospital-grade sterilizers in their chop shop.

The hearse turned east on Holly Street. We stopped at a house with a white picket fence made of plastic bones – femurs and skulls. M would never believe me. Nepo climbed out. Pepe pulled back onto the access road heading north.

I said, "I'm lost, Dorothy. You told me you don't have a plan."

She shrugged and said, "I wasn't lying. I don't have a plan for you and Dani, but it's always good to have an ace up the sleeve. Anyways, I don't think Nepo's going to find anything. Doesn't hurt to check, and I like the idea of having a limo-"

"Hearse."

"Girl," she said. "Pepe can park at the morgue entrance, which isn't covered by the surveillance cameras. A hearse might stick out in traffic, but it's invisible at the back entrance of a hospital."

She had a point.

I said, "You think Dortman might run?" Dorothy winked, "You'd be surprised what rats like him will do once they're cornered. You better believe he has an exit plan. He has all sorts of ideas."

Ronnie said, "You know he's a licensed helicopter pilot, right? He's always bragging about it in the board room."

"Y'all ever heard of a daemon?" Dorothy asked.

Ronnie said, "You mean like a computer program that runs in the background?"

Dorothy shook her head. "It's similar. Imagine there's a thing pulling the strings behind your thoughts. A sort of spirit that feeds you certain ideas. That's a daemon. It can teach you things. Some nice things and some not-so-nice things."

Goosebumps rose on my arm. Dorothy was talking about the parasitic process I had seen, the thing that caused Dortman's disease to spread.

She said, "Dortman has some really sick ideas, but trust me when I say there's something sicker behind those ideas. That thing – that daemon – could undermine the entire healthcare system."

59

Pepo dropped us off at the morgue entrance. Timmy the Fearless was waiting at the time clock. I checked my watch. Five minutes to spare.

I punched the clock and turned to regard him. Dani stood at my shoulder. I was glad to have him there.

Tim said, "About the other day, I'm sorry. It was a genuine mistake. I don't know how I missed your punch. Must have been a computer error?"

He studied me. It wasn't a rhetorical question. This wasn't an apology; it was an interrogation.

I kept my face neutral and said, "Apology accepted."

Tim smiled. He had his moves planned out.

He said, "To prove there's no hard feelings I have a one-time offer. How would you like to cross-train in CT?"

Tim glanced at Dani. The smile never wavered.

Truly greedy people, the ones who'd happily sell their own children to advertise baby food, specialize in making you feel like a million bucks. You know you've met a completely mercenary class-A douchebag when the person can smile – relaxed and sincere, happy even – while they toss you in the soiled linens and send you to the cleaners.

That joyful, simple, thoroughly avaricious smile was the smile Timmy the Fearless smiled at me then.

I didn't believe his offer was real, but I've always wanted to cross-train in computed tomography. I was a perfect fit. CT is fast-paced and exciting. I had applied to cross-train twice before and lost to more senior technologists. Now he was handing it to me? – why?

I said, "I hadn't heard about any openings in CT."

Tim said, "Walk with me."

Dani peeled off to the bunker as I fell into step beside our fearless manager. If I ever wondered how Tim landed in management, my doubts were answered in the conversation that followed. It was simple: the man could wheedle and connive at a heroic level.

The best connivers are the ones who can convince you their ideas are your ideas. That's what Tim attempted to do with CT.

I agreed to "strongly consider" cross-training.

He said, "I need an answer before 1700 hours."

That's when I understood. This was divide and conquer. Take the troublemaker out, or failing that, take her out of x-ray. In CT, I would be less likely to cross paths with Dortman. Plus, I'd be separated from Dani.

I disentangled myself from Timmy's used car salesman tactics by wandering back toward the bunker and grabbing the first order that dropped. A two-view chest in the ED. I called Ronnie on the earpiece on my way out of the department.

She said, "I heard it all. Take the sub-corridor. There's an entrance by the lockers in the breakroom. You can walk and talk without anyone overhearing."

I found the door by the lockers like she said. I'd never noticed it before. A rack clogged with forgotten coats hung on the door camouflaging its presence. It opened with the master key.

The sub-corridor paralleled the department hallway to the ED.

Walking down the narrow, red-lit passage, I said, "Am I right to think this CT thing is an attempt to get me out of the way with minimum drama?"

Dorothy came on the line.

She said, "That's exactly what it is. The question is do we play into their hands?"

I hadn't thought about that.

I said, "How would that work?"

She said, "We'd need someone to stay inside the department. That's Dani. We'd also need someone outside the department – outside the hospital – who understands the situation in radiology."

"M."

Dorothy said, "You're sure about her?"

"I trust M as much as anyone else on the team."

"OK," she said. "You just got promoted to CT."

60

The CT department at St. Rafa was two scanners in two separate examination rooms with a shared control room. I swiped the proximity card at the reader, but the door popped open before I grabbed the handle. Standing there, blocking the entrance was Sam Filcher, the swing shift CT lead tech.

Filcher was a fifty-something white dude with an asthenic body habitus. That's Latin for scrawny ass. He also had an off-putting black leather fanny pack dangling from his emaciated hips. It looked like a necrotic scrotum. Pretending to ignore me, Filcher slowly reached into his awful little pack and retrieved an e-cigarette.

I said, "Hi, I'm the new—"

Filcher cut me off.

"I know," he said.

He drew a long drag off the e-cigarette and exhaled nicotine vapor in my face. It smelled like banana nut bread and rage. This wasn't the right time to mention he and his fanny pack were breaking five different hospital policies.

"Timmy called," Filcher said. "We don't need you, OK? I'm sure you did someone special some kind of favor, but that stuff doesn't fly in my department. If you can't cut it in CT, you'll be lucky if you're still working in healthcare when I'm through with you. Understand?"

I said, "Nice to meet you, too," and shouldered passed him.

Who was he kidding? I thought, how hard can CT be? The machine does most the work.

The other techs were more cheerful than Filcher. Within a few minutes, I attached myself to a woman named Becky. She was about my height, mid-fifties, high-energy. Her hair was blonde streaked with highlights and cut in a long bob.

Pointing to the CT scan table, she said, "There will be no births, deaths, or conceptions on this table."

I said, "Agreed."

"And remember it can always, always get worse."

She was demonstrating the use of the power injector when an order dropped. We rolled out for the ED.

On the way, Becky said, "The CT machine runs itself. The key to the job is playing detective. We're about to give the patient a radiation dose equal to one hundred chest x-rays. We need some solid history for the radiologist, and if we're using contrast, we have to do a med rec."

After introducing herself to the patient, Becky began asking a long list of questions about health history and current medications. She made notes on a tablet computer with access to the EMR.

For CT exams, the questions focus on known risks for adverse contrast reactions or drug interactions.

Intravenous iodinated contrast agents (aka IV contrast) are made of iodine covalently bonded to carbon molecules, mimicking organic compounds. This much I know from x-ray tech school. It's not the type of thing you explain to a patient before injecting the stuff into their body.

Questions answered, Becky pulled the vitals monitor off its bracket, set it at the foot of the patient's gurney, and rolled out for the CT scanner. The exam was a CT angiogram (CTA) of the chest to rule out pulmonary embolism (PE).

Iodine is the secret ingredient in contrast. It has an atomic number of 53, making it the heaviest essential mineral nutrient. Infomercial version: Contrast stops x-rays, but won't slow you down! Fine print: Iodine contrast increases radiation dose and risk of thyroid storm, nephrotoxicity, anaphylactic shock, and death.

Because we love iodine contrast so much, we don't read folks the fine print. We say "morbidity and mortality." It sounds nicer. Ultra-fine print: there's a crap ton of things in CT that may result in death, but it may be the only way to figure out if you're going to live.

According to Becky, the important word is "may."

Sitting behind the scan computer, she said, "That's why we get paid the big bucks. Do the CT without killing the patient. No pressure."

Patients normally think about the CT scanner as a big plastic donut. They confuse it with MRI, which is an even bigger, more plasticky donut. What they don't realize is underneath CT's sugar-glazed surface is a giant robot armed with a high-powered radiation source spinning around a narrow opening at roughly one hundred rotations per minute. It's basically a massive smoothie blender that emits radiation. As techs, we prefer patients don't know about the giant robot because the resulting anxiety would only increase mortality and morbidity associated with the exam.

Becky pulled up the patient's labs on her computer. She documented the creatinine level (not creatine – that's the stuff of roid ragers and baseball players). Creatinine is a waste product of digestion. It circulates in the blood until picked-up by the kidneys and excreted. Think of it as proto-piss, flowing in yellowish rivulets through your blood stream.

High levels of creatinine are associated with impaired kidney function. The patient's kidneys need to be fully functional before we inject iodine contrast because the kidneys filter out crap like iodine contrast. The most common side effect of an IV contrast injection is feeling like your bladder is about to explode. In the wonderful world of CT, we call that a golden shower. Congratulations, you have a healthy urinary system.

Becky rattled off more questions related to kidney function, diabetes medications, and allergies. She tested the IV with a bolus of saline and hooked the patient up to the power injector. A CT power injector is a robotic syringe on wheels. It holds over a tenth of a liter and it can push fast. You guessed it! Just another thing in CT that can kill you. No one in the hospital pushes junk through IVs faster than CT.

Taking a seat at the control console, Becky said, "The power injector could shotgun a beer intravenous in under twenty seconds."

I said, "They ought to rent them out on Dirty Sixth."—referring to Austin's neon-lit party district.

"By the way," Becky said. "Ignore Filcher. He's bent because Tim didn't ask him about you. He'll get used to the idea. He's a good guy, but male menopause is for real."

I understood Filcher's frustration. I remembered having the travelling techs forced on us. Timmy the Fearless hated confrontation; so he made big decisions without input from people in the trenches.

Filcher was right. They didn't need another CT tech. There wasn't even room for another chair. I stood and watched Becky work the controls for the power injector and the CT scanner.

She sent the patient through the gantry twice for two images that resembled x-rays – AP and lateral. She drew a box over the area of interest for the angiogram. It covered the chest through the adrenals. She also set a bolus tracker at the level of the patient's pulmonary arteries.

Hitting the intercom for the gantry, she said, "Now, you're going to get a warm feeling like you just wet your pants. It didn't really happen. That's the contrast."

Becky triggered the power injector and the scanner's countdown simultaneously. The machine took a series of axial images of the Y-shaped bifurcation of the pulmonary arteries as the contrast began to perfuse. Suddenly, the arteries lit up bright white. The contrast bolus. The scanner shot the patient through the gantry, and the exam was done. The computer began reconstructing the images for viewing.

Becky bounced into the exam room to check on the patient. For all the prep time, the actual exam was over in under a minute. The whole thing made me dizzy. I sat staring at the images as they flipped across the monitor. Hundreds of pictures – what would take an entire x-ray department a week – one tech and her robot friends pulled off in a matter of seconds. Maybe Filcher was right. Maybe I was in over my head.

61

Ronnie called on the earpiece during the second half of my shift.

"We got video," she said.

"Video?" I said. "What do you mean?"

"Come see. Five minutes. That's all I need."

CT was slow. I was in the exam room, playing with the table controls. The techs lounged in the control room debating smoker versus fryer for Thanksgiving turkey. I told Becky I needed to powder my nose.

As I exited the CT department, Ronnie said, "Use the sub-corridor."

I took the door hidden behind the coat rack in the radiology breakroom. Ronnie rattled off directions to the morgue down the sub-corridor. I arrived at her computerized angel altar.

She pointed at a monitor. The image was black and white. The sound was fuzzy. It took me a minute before I understood what I was seeing. Live feed from OR Room 6. Dortman's room.

Ronnie said, "Dani put a peephole camera on top of a cabinet."

I said, "His idea?"

Ronnie nodded. "Yep. He had the camera, too."

"I didn't want to know that."

"The software alerts me when people enter the room. It auto-captures video."

"And?"

She glanced at me and said, "That's it."

It wasn't much, but it was something.

62

Arriving back in CT, an order dropped for a contrast abdomen pelvis from the ED.

Becky said, "We're slow. Want to give it a shot?"

Earlier in the shift, I performed a few non-contrast brain studies, but a trained monkey could do a non-contrast CT brain. Lay the patient on the table. The machine does the rest. An abdomen pelvis with contrast was more challenging.

I said, "Sure."

Becky said, "That's the spirit."

The patient was a muscular guy, tattooed and wearing a faded Slayer tee. His name was Niles. The nurse had already started him drinking the gastrografin and lemonade cocktail used for oral contrast.

Niles skipped the chit-chat to say, "Does this shit get you drunk?"

I said, "Nope. It helps us figure out why you're sick."

"Waste of fucking money. You'd think by now we'd have stuff that would get you blotto. Damn nurse won't give me any pain meds."

"Where are you hurting?"

"Are you people stupid? I've said the same damn thing like five times."

I waited.

He said, "In my gut."

"Which side?"

"My fucking right. Feels like someone's stuck a knife in me."

Right lower quadrant pain is a classic symptom of acute appendicitis. I went through the questionnaire. Niles bitched the whole time. I couldn't tell if he was angry or hurting or both.

I said, "We need to wait about an hour before we can do the exam."

He said, "What? I have to be at work in thirty minutes."

"Then you'll need to phone in. You're sick."

He cussed and moaned as he pulled his phone from the pocket of his black jeans. Becky and I headed back to CT.

She said, "Gosh, he's a nervous Nelly."

I said, "What gives you that impression?"

"Everything. Dresses like he's in a metal band, avoids eye contact, cusses too much."

"I figured he was pissed."

"Maybe. I think it's a put on. Little Niles is scared."

I didn't see it. Not until an hour later when I had Niles lying supine on the CT exam table. I started the IV contrast injection, and he puked all over the gantry. Lemonade-scented vomit. It splashed across my arms and scrubs. I barely kept myself from returning the favor.

Becky stepped in as I backed away. She had a washcloth and emesis bag for Niles. He started to rise off the exam table.

She said, "Lay down. Don't move or we'll have to start this whole thing over."

He said, "I'm freaking out. This is too much. I can't take it. I'm covered in vomit."
She grabbed his hand and press a wet washcloth to his forehead.

Becky said, "Squeeze my hand."

The timer was still running on the scanner. The gantry started spinning.

I was frozen. Vomit dripped from my arms.

Becky said, "Grab a towel. Clean yourself up. Then clean off the inside of the gantry."

I hurried to comply. There was twenty seconds until the scan. Neither of us was shielded. Niles had his hand locked on Becky's. He was breathing rapidly.

She said, "Toss me a lead apron and clear out."

Becky held the lead up one-armed like Dracula's cape as I hit the door. Filcher was sitting at the controls.

He offered a sadistic grin and said, "Your first hurly splash. Welcome to CT. Go get cleaned up."

My face felt feverish with shame as I hit the door and strode down the halls to the OR locker room. I slipped off my shoes, dropped my cellphone, earpiece, and badge on a bench, and stepped into the shower still wearing my clothes. I was so angry and disgusted I didn't care the water was ice cold.

I washed my scrubs with the cheap body wash in the dispenser. Slipping out of my clothes, I wrung everything out and dropped the pile on a towel. I stepped back into the shower.

The water was warm. I turned it up as hot as I could and scrubbed every inch of my body until my skin felt raw. I imagined all my revulsion and shame washing down the drain, imagined myself brand new, a fetus bathed in warm amniotic fluid.

Toweling off, I slipped into some standard issue OR scrubs. I was standing near the industrial-size laundry chute, a towel over my head, drying my hair, when I heard someone step into the room. Just as I looked up, the person grabbed me in a headlock and forced me backward.

I tried to fight. The towel blocked my vision. I caught a glimpse of standard issue scrubs and fake-baked skin before toppling backward. Banging the back of my skull against the edge of the chute, I fell through darkness. Frantic, I braced my arms and legs against the metal walls, slowing my descent.

The walls vanished, and I landed on my back in a bin full of dirty scrubs and wet towels. Something popped in my chest. The fall knocked the air out of my lungs. Tears leapt to my eyes as I struggled to catch my breath. I rose and immediately fell, toppling out of a laundry bin.

63

The room was small, pitch dark, and hot. It stank of cheap detergent and filth. I heard movement in the next room, footsteps. I was on my feet, but my lungs strained to fill. My brain was numb with shock. I passed a hand over the back of my skull. It came back sticky with blood.

The fall played in a loop in my mind. My hands shook.

The shadows of two feet appeared beneath the door.

I braced myself against the wall and clutched the laundry bin. It was on wheels. When the door opened, if it opened, I would shove it at whoever was there with everything I had.

Someone whispered, "Claire, are you in there?"

I said, "Ronnie?"

My voice sounded strange in my own ears, tearful and childish. The air was weak in my lungs.

Ronnie threw open the door, and I limped toward her. Her eyes were wild.

She said, "We got to get out of here."

I draped my arm over her shoulder, but when her arm wrapped behind my back, I felt a stab of pain.

I drew a sharp breath.

Ronnie said, "We're walking. Let's walk."

She led me out of the small dark room into a large room, brightly lit, the environmental services central supply. The place was deserted. We exited into the basement central hall.

I said, "Take me to the ED."

She said, "OK. Good. What do we tell them?"

"The truth. Someone pushed me down the laundry chute."

My skull vibrated. The hall swung sideways, but the pain in my ribs kept me focused. I could see the elevator door ahead of us.

"Phone Dani," I said. "Tell him to get my stuff from the locker room. Tell him to be careful. She might still be up there."

Ronnie said, "I could only hear through the earpiece. You saw who did it?"

"I have a good idea, but I need you to verify. Can you go back over the surveillance footage?"

Ronnie nodded. We stepped into the elevator. She hit the button for the first floor.

I said, "Do that as soon as you drop me at the ED. Before they scrub it. You've got your phone, right?"

The elevator chimed, and we stepped into the back hallway. I made a short video in which I stated the time and date and showed the extent of my injuries. Then I sent Ronnie back to the computer and walked the rest of the way to the ED solo.

I got the charge nurse's attention and said, "I fell in the course of my duties. I have a laceration on the back of my skull, and I believe I fractured a rib."

She said, "What?"

I said some other stuff. My eyesight went blurry. Someone started messing with the lights. The last thing I remember was a clean stretcher. I was moving toward it as it receded into the distance. Then I fell into a shiny, headachy darkness.

When I awoke, I was laying on the CT exam table, and Becky was staring down at me. I saw Filcher to. He was on his cellphone in the CT control room. He had his hand over the mouthpiece. When he saw me looking at him, he turned and disappeared around the corner.

All this seemed hilariously ironic. The tech was the patient. I never realized before but in the supine position you can see a considerable distance up people's nostrils.

The CT confirmed what I already knew. My brain had all the conductivity of green jello. Most likely a mild concussion. Plus, I needed ten stitches and a new punk rock hairdo with a shaved patch and a bandage around my skull. The ribs fortunately were just bruised. Dani did my x-rays.

The ED is a common signpost along the road of life for the point of no-return. Once you've been pushed down a laundry chute, you lose all interest in business as usual. Then the employee health nurse made me pee in a cup.

Ronnie appeared in my exam room door. She didn't wait for the nurse to clear the door before she said, "You'll never guess."

I said, "Vanessa."

Ronnie clapped her big hands together. "We got the bitch."

64

I was acquainted with Dr. Lasseter. Had seen his name on countless orders. Our conversations were brief and work-focused, but I believed he was one of the good guys, a kind and intelligent doctor who cared about his patients.

Lasseter had a curly crop of reddish-brown hair streaked with gray. His face was tan and leathery. He'd grown up on a ranch in the hill country and still worked the land. He was missing the distal phalanx of his fifth right digit from an incident roping a cow for branding. I had heard the story second hand from Nurse Trixie.

Closing the exam room door, Dr. Lasseter glanced at the vitals monitor and inspected both my eyes with the ophthalmoscope, assessing for asymmetrical pupil dilation, a sign of a cerebral hemorrhage. He tested my reflexes and muscles spasticity.

All these evaluations were done when I was admitted. He was repeating for thoroughness. I appreciated the effort.

After finishing, Lasseter dropped onto the stool beside my stretcher and stared me in the eye.

He said, "I'm going to tell you something that doesn't leave this room."

I nodded, fidgeting with my thin, overly starched blanket.

"Two years ago an OR nurse died from complications due to a fall down the laundry chute."

He studied me for a moment.

"I know this because I treated her. She was unconscious. She died of internal bleeding within two hours of being admitted to the ED. We estimated that she lay at the bottom of the chute for about ten hours before being found. She probably would have lived if she'd been discovered earlier. It sparked an internal review. They looked at the policy for the laundry chute usage. Recommendations were made to change the design of the chutes. They're antiquated and in need of an update. You can see how far that effort went."

Dr. Lasseter looked tired.

"The one thing that differs in your case is the laundry bin was at the bottom of the chute – where it should be. In the earlier case, the laundry bin was missing. Of course, people in environmental services were questioned. Both the manager and the man responsible for changing out the laundry bins lost their jobs despite being loyal employees for I don't remember how long, and despite both of them swearing that the laundry bin must have been there unless someone had intentionally moved it. The police were called – we had to call the police – but there was only so much they could do. In the end, it was chalked up to a perfect storm. An accidental death. Not the first in hospital history, and probably not the last. Everyone was happy it never made the papers. Do you understand why I'm telling you this?"

I said, "Yes, I think so."

"Good," he said. "That's why I want you to think real careful about what you say next because I have to put it in my report. Earlier you stated that you believe someone pushed you down the laundry chute. How sure are you about that? Think about what that means. Would it be better to fade out and let bygones be bygones or do you want to fight this thing out to the bitter end? –because you better believe it will be bitter. I'll call the police. It might make the papers. There's going to be people who don't like you very much, and there's no telling how far they'll go to prove you wrong."

Lasseter ran a hand over his head. I noticed it was shaking. He was infected by Dortman's plague. I remembered what Dorothy said about a daemon, a parasitic spirit behind Dortman's sick ideas. Was this it? Could something control the thoughts of others beyond Dortman, warping them all to its own diseased will? How far had it spread? The ED always seemed like the last bastion, but even here there were signs and symptoms of infection. I felt like I was losing my mind. Correction, I *was* losing my mind. It's called a concussion.

I said, "You're saying this was a warning, right? That it wasn't dumb luck the laundry bin was there. They were sending me a message, and it's quite possible the entire thing was orchestrated for a night when you'd be working; so that you could warn me, and I'd get the message loud and clear to back off."

It was hard to keep the rage out of my voice. I felt like I was wrestling in darkness like I was still falling. I could have died, but I was no closer to knowing what Dortman wanted. One thing was certain: it wasn't just St. Rafa. He was planning something bigger. The atrocity show in OR Room 6 was a single part of a huge mechanism. That's the only reason he would risk keeping me alive.

Dr. Lasseter said, "Here's the thing, Ms. Neuman. There are times with a situation like this when it's better to just walk away. There's only so much one person can do."

I said, "I'm not backing down."

One side of his mouth rose in an exhausted grin. He glanced down at his missing finger and the grin fell away.

He said, "I'm going to retire next year. Move out to the ranch. I never should have left. If I had your kind of guts maybe I could have managed, but when you're young some things seem too big for you."

"This is definitely too big for me, but I don't plan on doing it alone."

Dr. Lasseter nodded and rose.

He said, "I'll have the charge nurse call the police. They'll want to take a statement from you and the woman who found you."

He moved quickly, threw open the exam room door, and stopped.

"I wish I'd had your guts when I was your age."

I barely heard him. I was staring over his shoulder at the empty space where Sam Filcher had been standing, eavesdropping until the door popped open.

Everything and everyone was infected.

65

Dorothy hurried into the room, grabbed my hand, and squeezed. As she searched my face, I avoided her eyes. I didn't want to cry.

I hadn't realized how much I wanted Mother until that moment. I knew better than to call her from the emergency department – not unless I was in a chronic vegetative state. Mother doesn't do hospitals.

Dorothy said, "Are you OK? How do you feel?"

I complained about the hair shave required for stitches. As I spoke, she passed me a note.

It read: "They're listening. Maybe recording. We have footage from the surveillance video showing Vanessa enter and exit the dressing room at the time you were attacked. Be careful how you play this. Dortman's bought off folks in the police. He definitely owns people in hospital administration. They won't play fair."

The note had a dehydrating effect. My tears evaporated.

I said, "How do you know?"

Dorothy said, "I'm a rad tech. The more you understand x-rays, the more you know how to expose what's hiding in the shadows. That's technique."

I said, "I don't understand."

She leaned in closer and said, "Here's how x-rays work. On one hand, you have quantity, milliamperage per second, mAs. It's kinetic energy. On the other hand, you have quality, kilovoltage peak, kVp. Potential energy. Without a proper balance of both quantity and quality, you don't have x-rays."

This was Radiography 101 stuff.

I said, "What does that have to do with seeing in the shadows?"

Dorothy smiled and patted my leg.

As she rose, she leaned in close to whisper, "Steer clear of Bunny."

Staring up at her in total befuddlement, I mouthed, "Bunny?"

She blew me a kiss and exited. I began to wonder if I had trusted my life to a senile old woman. What was all that about? And Bunny? How hard had I hit my head? The concussion jumbled the words around inside my throbbing skull.

One thing I was sure wasn't a delusion. We weren't just dealing with Dortman. There were other people trying to stop us, and they were willing to go to extreme lengths. What were they hiding? Why were they afraid of an x-ray tech?

I dropped my head back on the pillow and felt the immediate throb of pain from the suture site. Hot tears sprang to my eyes. I didn't care. Rolling on my side, I buried my head under the stiff, overly bleached blanket and wept.

66

Sergeant Coleman, the police detective who took my report, was a large white woman with cornrows and a Chicago accent. She wore a black suit a size too small.

After jotting down the details of the attack, she said, "Apart from the green clogs you didn't get a look at the perp, but I'm guessing you have an idea who it was."

I said, "Vanessa Flowers. She's an OR nurse."

"What's her motive?"

"She's had it in for me ever since this doctor she likes started dating my roommate."

"The jealous type."

"Exactly."

"Jealous enough to push someone down a laundry chute?"

I held up my hands.

"Anything else?"

I said, "Check the security cameras."

"We're on it, but it's going to take a warrant."

As Sergeant Coleman exited, Whitney Peppers the hospital VP of HR entered with two other women. One was Christina Auger. I couldn't remember her exact job title, but I knew she was a lawyer. The other woman I recognized immediately. I had seen her with Dortman.

She looked like she'd stepped straight out of Saks Fifth Avenue. Her outfit was the type of spaghetti western costume – alpaca wool poncho, suede pants, white cowboy boots – that had to be hideously expensive. Whitney Peppers introduced her as Bunny McCombs, the Vice President of Marketing.

I said, "Bunny."

She extended a hand for shaking. I indicated the IV line running to my arm.

Christina Auger closed the door. I felt exposed, dressed only in a hospital gown as three powerful women stared down at me.

Peppers was the first to speak.

"Ms. Neuman allow me to say on behalf of the administration of St. Rafael's Hospital you have our sincere sorrow for your accident and—"

"It wasn't an accident."

"Allow me to finish. Sorrow for your accident and sincere wishes for a speedy recovery."

"Not accepted."

Ms. Peppers said, "What?"

"It wasn't an accident. Someone intentionally pushed me down the laundry chute. Plus, it isn't the first time this sort of thing has happened. Nothing was done to fix the situation. So, I can't accept your sorrow or wishes or whatever."

Whitney Peppers is an older woman who looks perpetually harried and harangued. She exudes an air of incompetence: always late to meetings; frequently jokes about her inability to use computers; and she takes her sweet time doing whatever HR has to do to complete employment paperwork. She offered me her best, most harangued expression now.

Bunny McCombs leapt into the breach, laughing and actually shooing the disagreement away with a wave of her manicured hand. She plopped down on the wheeled stool by my side.

"We're all intelligent people," she said with an incredibly sincere-looking smile. "I'm sure we can agree this hospital provides vital services for our community. Vital services. But, if news reporters or social media gets hold of something suggesting staff are being pushed down laundry chutes, that could be a big black eye for St. Raphael."

I said, "Maybe that's what it takes to get things changed around here."

"If you're seriously claiming this is part of some conspiracy, they could shut the whole hospital down. Then what happens to all the people in our community who have come to rely on St. Raphael? Ms. Neuman, you can see why it's important that we keep this on the DL."

"What exactly do you mean?"

Ms. Auger, the lawyer, raised her hand and said, "Sometimes it can be difficult to make sense of things like this – especially in the heat of the moment. That's why we have policies to help guide our responses. There's a number of policies that I believe support Ms. McCombs point. Perhaps, the most important is 1-14. This is a general employee policy that applies to anyone employed or working at St. Raphael's Hospital. The policy states that no employee will discuss the business of the hospital with the news media or post about hospital events or activities in social media. There are of course exceptions detailed for marketing, public relations, and the legal team, but those don't apply to this situation."

I said, "Why not?"

Ms. Auger eyed me for a moment.

She said, "Primarily for the reasons Ms. McCombs just discussed. The point is we have a policy, and it is important that we stick close to policy on matters like this."

When did the battle between law and medicine begin? And what is it about lawyers that makes me want to punch them in the nasal bones?

I said, "Do we have a policy guiding what to do when employees are pushed down laundry chutes? Because it would seem that sort of potentially fatal eventuality should supersede other policies."

Wringing her hands, Whitney Peppers said, "I assure you, Ms. Neuman, the administration will work with the police to explore this matter in depth."

I waited, expecting more.

Bunny McCombs said, "What we ask in turn is that you will not disclose anything about these events to anyone except the investigators from the police department and the people present in this room."

I said, "Let me get this straight. You're going to explore this matter – I believe that's what you said, my head is still a little fuzzy – you're going to explore it, so that you can sweep it under the rug?"

Ms. Auger frowned, "That is not what we said. I would advise you to pick your words more carefully. We are not asking you to participate in anything untoward. Insinuating otherwise undermines the reputation of our company, which is precisely what we're trying to avoid. Will you please comply with this simple request to not disclose information about this event?"

I was five seconds away from a total meltdown. The only reason I didn't start screaming was I remembered what Dorothy said about Bunny. Plus, I knew I was compromised. I didn't trust my own perceptions. I felt loopy, and they were trying to use my state of mind to extract something from me. They wanted my word in the presence of a lawyer.

Beneath my blanket, I unclipped the lower ECG lead. The monitor chimed. I rolled my eyes back and let my head lull.

I said, "I don't feel so…"

Closing my eyes, I went limp. The three women panicked, calling for a nurse. I barely kept the smile off my face.

Trixie ushered the women out. She then radioed the doctor. She found the disconnected lead. I let my eyes flutter and then opened them. The alarms went silent.

I said, "Do not let them back in here. Tell them I'm sick and not to be disturbed. Anything. Just don't let them back in here."

Trixie said, "I'll see what I can do."

67

When the knock sounded on my exam room door, I winced involuntarily. I was certain it was the harpies back for the kill. Instead the dude of my dreams walked in - dressed in a slim fitting business suit, looking like Brendon Urie from Panic! at the Disco. I looked like a member of Slipknot.

It was Adam, the patient survey specialist. My first impulse was to hide under the sheets. The next was pure paranoia. Were they watching me all the time? Could they read my mind?

He said, "Hey."

"Hey."

Adam sat down on the stool beside me. I wanted to disappear into the gurney and roll myself down the hall away from him.

He said, "You look a lot better than I thought you would."

"Um, thanks?"

"That didn't come out right. I'm just relieved. I was really worried about you, but I couldn't just rush in here and see you."

A weird warmth spread through my body. He was worried about me?

I said, "Thank you. That's sweet."

"Then the alarms went off, and the nurse rushed in here. Are you OK? I mean you look good."

"I need a day or two of rest and a new hairstyle. That's all."

He said, "I'll text, OK?"

"Cool. I'd like that."

Adam did a funny thing. His face blanked, and he stared up at the vitals monitor for a beat too long. When he returned his gaze to me, he had changed. His demeanor was more professional. The words "compartment syndrome" came to mind, but I knew that wasn't quite right.

He said, "Now, I kind of need to do my job. There's other folks waiting."

I said, "Sure, I understand."

As he pecked his way through some menus on his tablet computer, I tried not to feel heartbroken. He said he would text. It wasn't exactly the stuff of romance, but I'm not exactly a romantic.

When Adam spoke again, the transformation was complete.

He said, "Dr. Lasseter is putting together your discharge papers now, but before you leave us today, we are interested in ways to improve the quality of care we provide. Would you be willing to participate in a survey regarding your treatment?"

This was awful. Love cannot abide a survey. All my hopes of being swept off my feet by a charming stranger were soon to be crushed beneath the Likert scale. He smiled in that terrible, seemingly genuine way people smile when they want to extract quantifiable data from you.

I said, "Nope, not interested."

His face fell. Glancing over my shoulder at the vitals monitor, I tried to determine what my heart was doing to make this dull ache in my chest.

Adam said, "Could I ask you to reconsider? The survey only takes five minutes and will not delay discharge."

I became engrossed in my armband. Making sure all the information was correct even though I had spent the last two hours reviewing it for correctness. Something about the spelling of my last name seemed odd, but I knew it was just the combined effects of the concussion and my weird last name.

If I looked into his hooded, wide-set blue eyes, I would have no choice but to say yes to his awful survey, which ironically would mean saying no to a relationship.

He wheeled a little closer to me on the stool, and I had this crazy vivid impression of him sinking down on one knee and taking my hand as he produced a ring from his suit pocket.

I said, "I do."

Adam said, "Do what?"

"Do not generally answer surveys. My mother is religiously opposed to statistics."

Oh my goodness, why was I talking about Mother?

He shifted in his seat and said, "My mom said the same thing when I took this job, but a job is a job."

That was precisely the sort of no-nonsense pragmatism that attracted me in the first place. He was right. Be practical, Claire.

Adam said, "You're an x-ray tech."

I said, "That's right."

"What are x-rays if they aren't statistical?"

I felt the capillaries in my face expanding as an epic, junior-high-grade blush threatened to make me the first patient in the history of medicine to go into cardiac arrest from shame. This was exactly the way I wanted a man to talk to me. This was the weird reason I found myself liking Dani. Regardless of all his flaws, he knew how to talk to a girl about x-rays. Now, here was a guy who was handsome, pragmatic, and he understood differential absorption. The heart monitor chimed. I spun around and silenced it.

I said, "I'll take the survey."

He said, "Thank you! They say there's not a quota, but there's a quota. Anyways, I appreciate it."

Tapping the app on his tablet, he scanned my armband, and read the lengthy, idiotic instructions. I signed my consent, and he started the questions. It was as awful as I imagined.

Survey completed, he thanked me again and exited.

When Trixie and Dr. Lasseter returned, the final diagnosis was stage 1 concussion and bruised ribs.

Dr. Lasseter said, "You're a very lucky young lady."

I didn't feel lucky or young. I felt old and hollow and crushed like an aluminum can in a recycling machine.

Dorothy drove me home. I fell into bed exhausted, but I couldn't sleep. That's the only way I can explain the haircut. I was sleep deprived, and there were electric shears in Dorothy's guest bathroom. I cut my hair to within a quarter of an inch of my scalp.

68

As I walked down the long white hall to the CT department, Sam Filcher stood outside the control room door, thumbs looped behind his fanny pack. His passive aggression couldn't withstand my active aggression. Dressed in scrubs, my hair buzzed, I'd been practicing mean looks in the mirror for the last two days.

He opened his mouth to say something. I cut him off.

"Saw you snooping around my room, Filcher. I'm watching you."

I shouldered passed him.

He said, "I'm telling Tim this isn't working out."

Badging through the department door, I said, "Do that."

Fortunately, CT was busy so I didn't have to sit around and watch Filcher brood. Becky and I teamed up to chisel away on the ED orders. We worked well together.

CT techs scan a lot of people who are so sick or traumatized they can't move. There's minimum positioning required for a CT exam. Once we have you on the table, the machine does the rest. The tricky part is moving the patients to the table.

That's were Becky and I played well together. We used a smooth mover (aka slider board). It's a long, thin sheet of stiff plastic. Once the stretcher is parked and locked next to the CT exam table, one tech takes the sheet the patient is laying on and rolls the patient – sheet and all – onto away from the table. The other tech slides the mover board under the patient from the table top.

We roll the patient onto their back, and they're halfway on the mover board. We then pull them onto the board and pull the board onto the exam table. Becky and I really meshed on this, moving patients in and out of the scanner quickly.

Spray a little floor wax on the mover board. It cuts down on static electricity and makes moving that much easier.

Part of the department protocol was to document a baseline blood pressure on any patient receiving IV contrast before we initiate the injection.

Becky said, "If a patient codes, we know what a normal blood pressure was."

Whoever checked the BP on the monitor would call out the numbers. The other tech would repeat the numbers back out loud and write them on the requisition along with the time.

This tag team approach allowed me the chance to scan more patients. Within an hour I had successfully completed my first abdomen and pelvis with IV and oral contrast. Maybe I was cut out for CT after all.

69

When Filcher stepped out for his lunch break, Becky asked if I was up for running a few exams solo while she worked on the other machine. We'd be within shouting distance.

I agreed and grabbed a brain CT from the stack of waiting exams. The patient was paralyzed. His body curled up in a rigid fetal position. No family members were present.

His nurse said he lived in a nursing home. The staff believed he had a stroke sometime after lunch because he was slow to wake up from his afternoon nap and had remained immobile and unresponsive. He had a history of stroke and a do not resuscitate (DNR) order.

I introduced myself to the patient and explained the exam as I wheeled the stretcher down the hall to CT. He was thin, bordering on emaciated, but it was difficult to place the smooth mover under him due to his rigid body position. He looked fearful as I slid him onto the exam table. He was unable to lie on his back. I worked to position his head in the head holder.

He became agitated, opening and closing his mouth soundlessly and twisting his head from side to side against the machine's head holder. I timed the scan between phases of agitation. The images were textbook.

Motioning to Becky, I said, "Take a look at that."

She whistled appreciatively and said, "Listen, you're getting the hang of this. I need to do kidney delays on mine. Why don't you take that one back and grab the next abdomen? By the time you're ready to scan I should be in the department."

I loaded the power injector with contrast for the abdomen exam before I transferred the gentleman to his stretcher using the smooth mover. We rolled out for the ED.

The next patient was a woman about Mother's age, Alice Gooden. I will never forget that name. Alice Gooden.

She looked like someone who could have been friends with Mother in high school or college. A free spirit, one of the many cheerleaders and groupies who played muses to the psychedelic second coming of Austin circa 1990.

She said, "Call me Alice."

I went over the questionnaire with her as I guided the stretcher down the hall to CT.

Alice transferred herself over to the exam table, and I flushed some saline through her IV and hooked her up to the power injector.

Becky was still out. Everything was good to go. I initiated the localizer images, and lined up for the exam. That's when I made my mistake. I pushed the contrast and started the pre-scan timer.

Alice sneezed, but I didn't think anything of that. It was only later that I learned contrast reactions often begin with a sneeze.

An adverse reaction to IV contrast is a strange thing. The term used in the research is "anaphylactoid," which means allergy-like. In other words, it's not a true allergic reaction. Before the scanner had started, Alice Gooden was gasping for breath.

The last thing she said was "I can't breathe."

I hit the stop button on the scanner and spun around to hit the code button on the wall by the oxygen valve.

After propping the scan room door open, I backed the exam table out of the CT gantry. Alice was clawing at her throat. I held her hand. Terror turned her gaze glassy. My blood pressure was up. I felt a steady booming beat in my ears. That's when I realized I had forgotten to write down a baseline BP prior to initiating the scan.

I glanced at her monitor just as the device lost power. That's when the code team arrived, running through the door with the crash cart in tow.

I switched Alice over to the department's vitals monitor as Dr. Lasseter gave orders for saline and epinephrine.

He said, "What's the BP?"

I said, "I'm working on that."

The department monitor was acting up. Becky brought in the monitor from CT Room 2. Was it that obvious I was screwing everything up? The patient began to convulse.

Dr. Lasseter gave orders for a second dose of epinephrine.

I heard him whisper, "What the hell is going on?"

Becky started the blood pressure cuff. I stepped back at a loss as to how I could help.

She said, "Get a piece of paper and start writing."

I hurriedly wrote down the time, the initial blood pressure, the doses of epinephrine, the next blood pressure. Nothing changed. The patient was rocked by another seizure.

Dr. Lasseter said, "This isn't a contrast reaction. We're moving out."

He rattled off commands to transfer the patient back to the stretcher. Becky and I assisted the team as they wheeled Alice Gooden back to the ED. I wanted to help, but Becky ushered me out of the chaotic room as the phlebotomist arrived.

The CT room was trashed. Filcher stood in the control room, vaping and staring at the wreckage.

He said, "What happened here?"

Becky said, "Contrast reaction. Don't act like it's never happened to you."

I cleaned up. Becky wheeled the monitor back to CT Room 2.

She said, "We need a new monitor. That one is acting up."

Filcher said, "Worked fine yesterday."

I said, "It's not working now."

He said, "What'd you do to it?"

Instead of reply, I picked up the plastic packaging material littering the exam room floor.

Filcher said, "How's the patient?"

He had a right to know, but I didn't want to tell him. I didn't want to have this conversation at all.

"I said, 'how's the patient?'"

Becky said, "She did everything she could."

Filcher said, "That's not what I asked, and you're not the person I'm asking."

My eyes filled with hot tears, but I forced myself not to cry. What was happening to me? Had I lost all professionalism?

Turning toward Filcher, I said, "The patient is not responding to epinephrine."

A contrast reaction causes the blood vessels to dilate. As a consequence, blood pressure bottoms out, mimicking anaphylactic shock. Epinephrine, which is basically adrenaline, causes the blood vessels to constrict, bringing the BP back up.

I can't be sure because my eyesight went smeary, but I thought Filcher smiled. He tried to cover it with a yawn. That's what stayed with me. That crooked maybe smile.

He said, "Fill out an event report."

70

After my shift, Ronnie called a meeting with me and Dorothy in the Cortina Brother's limo. We stayed parked outside the morgue entrance. It was a dismal place to sit in the back of a hearse, dark and stinking of garbage from the central dumpsters, but Ronnie had access to the hospital wi-fi and corporate intranet.

She said, "How are you doing?"

"I'm sore. It hurts to take a deep breath. I had a patient code on me."

"HR suspended Vanessa for investigation. I'm not sure if that's a good thing or a bad thing."

I said, "I'm glad she's out of the picture."
Ronnie said, "Sure, but it could be a dodge. There's been some strange activity in the security system. Detective what's-her-name? – Coleman sent them a warrant to review the security camera footage. That's a good thing. The weird bit is they changed the clock settings, which might not seem like a big deal but it makes the timestamp difficult to read. The point is they're trying to cover their tracks. I just don't know how."

Dorothy said, "The good news is we saved an unedited version of the camera feed. Anything they do to mess with the camera footage stands in our favor."

I said, "What about the financial stuff?"

Ronnie said, "Nepo is running the numbers."

I thought about the handsome young certified accountant. I should have been an accountant. Accountants don't deal with blood or vomit or anaphylactoid reactions.

Dorothy said, "What's the news from CT?"

I said, "The lead tech, Sam Filcher, hates me. He has to be on their team. I caught him eavesdropping."

"You said you had a patient code?"

"Some kind of contrast reaction that didn't respond to epinephrine."

Dorothy said, "What do you mean?"

I told her what Dr. Lasseter said and how they wheeled the patient back to the ED and were still trying to stabilize her at shift change.

She said, "That doesn't sound like a contrast reaction."

Ronnie said, "I've pulled up the ED board. What was the patient's name?"

The instant I said Alice Gooden's name Ronnie's face fell.

She said, "This isn't good."

Turning the laptop toward us, we saw the long black line on the ED board. Alice Gooden was dead.

I bolted out of the limousine. Dorothy called after me, but I ignored her, running through the back entrance, up the stairs, down the hall to the ED. The patient's door was closed. The chaplain was talking to a woman sitting stone-faced in a chair outside the room.

The family resemblance was strong. Alice's daughter. She was my age. My vision swam. My knees went limp. The woman started to cry. She wiped her eyes on the sleeve of her blouse.

I grabbed a box of tissues from a nearby supply closet and offered them to the chaplain.

He gave me a bewildered look. Then he offered the tissues to the woman. It seemed no one had ever made this simple gesture of understanding to him. Hospitals are busy places. Too busy for grief. Even for the chaplain, it was time to move on.

His face appeared tired and sad as he stopped me, he said, "Thank you. You are so kind."

I didn't feel kind. I felt like a failure. The door to the patient's room opened, and I saw the body lying on the stretcher. Hot tears leapt to my eyes. My mind went numb. I couldn't remember walking to Dorothy's house. When I came back to myself, I was sitting on the edge of the daybed, staring at my hands.

71

I woke-up early the next morning. Dr. Lasseter made me swear off running for a week until the stitches closed, but he didn't say anything about jogging. I pulled on my running shoes. As I padded up Cherry Road toward Mueller Park, the air felt good rushing over my head. I liked my new haircut. It was nice not messing with a pony tail or constantly brushing loose strands out of my eyes.

As I circled the lake, I thought about what Dorothy and Dr. Lasseter said about the patient not responding to epinephrine. What if it wasn't a contrast reaction? Were there other conditions – things not on the contrast history form – that could cause the sort of problems the patient experienced? What preexisting conditions caused interactions with epinephrine? As the questions multiplied, I typed them into a note on my phone. Back at Dorothy's house, I showered, pulled on a fresh pair of scrubs, and walked over to St. Rafa.

I used to be terrified of libraries. All those books lined up on the shelves left me cold inside. The way Mother tells it, books were the reason she and Dad hooked-up and the same reason they split-up. After the divorce, books looked like ticking timebombs to me, orderly systems of annihilation, capable of destroying lives.

The hospital library with its sterile shelves of medical journals and reference manuals felt safer than the stacks at the public library. Perhaps, it was the singular focus on health. Maybe it was simply that the St. Rafa library wasn't bigger than an x-ray exam room. Plus, it had a guest computer that didn't require any kind of login in order to access some high dollar medical databases.

The problem was the computer was currently in use – by Adam, the handsome patient survey specialist – and I could not for the life of me remember his name. He closed the browser as soon as I walked into the room.

Turning around and seeing me, he relaxed and said, "Claire, right? I like your new haircut."

"Thanks. I still feel a little weird."

"You banged your head pretty hard, and anyways maybe you're right. Things are a little weird around here."

I said, "Yeah? What do you mean?"

"For example, there was a patient last night who had a reaction to IV contrast, but nothing they did could bring her around."

"I know. I'm the one who injected the contrast. That's why I'm here. I want to look up pre-existing conditions that might have contributed to her reaction."

He shook his head and said, "What makes you think it was a pre-existing condition?"

"What else could it be?"

"A drug interaction. Maybe an over-dose."

I began to feel suspicious. Whose side was this guy on?

"Why are you interested in this. I thought you were—"

"Just a patient survey specialist? That's right, but I'm in my senior year of chemistry at UT, and I just applied to Baylor Medical. Anyways, I heard some of what they were saying last night, and it made me curious."

If he knew something, I didn't want him to say it. Not here.

I said, "Listen, would you want to grab a coffee? There's a place nearby."

The instant the words were out of my mouth, my heart rate spiked. The blood rushed to my face. I could picture Mother pronouncing all sorts of dire warnings over any relationship that could arise from a girl asking out a guy.

Adam followed me out of the library across the main lobby and out the front door of the hospital. He didn't talk, didn't ask any questions. I was grateful for that.

Once we were out on the sidewalk, I said, "What exactly were you researching in there?"

He said, "Promise you won't think I'm crazy?"

"I'm more worried you'll think I'm crazy."

He said, "Not at all. I'm glad you didn't want to talk about it in there. I think they're using the surveillance system to monitor employees. The whole place is bugged."

I studied him for a moment. How did he figure that out? How much did he know?
Shaking my head, I said, "That's not crazy. I've seen

how they're doing it. Is that what you were looking into?"

"No, I was researching drug interactions. Not sure if you know this, but they ordered a toxicology screening with the autopsy. That's not standard routine at St. Rafa. That plus the fact that the tech performing the scan was the same tech who set off a police investigation in the hospital made me wonder if there wasn't a connection."

I said, "You mean people are talking about the laundry chute thing? What about HIPAA?"

He shrugged and said, "People talk. It's not every day that an x-ray tech accuses a nurse of attempted murder. Some people think you're trying to frame the nurse? —what's her name?"

"Vanessa?"

"Right. That seems to be the going hypothesis. That there's some kind of bad blood between the two of you. You're both into the same doctor or something. So, you set it up to make it look like she pushed you down the laundry chute. That's what they're saying."

A wave of anger washed over me leaving me speechless. I clinched my fists, stalked across the road, shoved through the door of El Burrito Volador, and collapsed into the first empty table.

Adam lowered himself into a seat across from me and said, "I don't know if it makes a difference, but I don't think it's true."

I wanted to scream at the ceiling, but I clenched my teeth, sitting in silence. Adam seemed OK with that. I appreciated him having the good sense to keep quiet.

The waitress came around and took our drink orders. I excused myself and spent a long moment in the bathroom, staring at the tampon dispenser and thinking about mortality. Was this my life? My skin felt tingly. My head was a synthetic and weightless thing.

I was grateful my coffee had arrived when I returned to the table. I sipped the hot drink, clasping both hands around the warm mug.

Adam said, "What do you know about drug interactions?"

I said, "The main drugs we worry about are diabetes medicines, but they cause kidney problems not blood pressure problems."

He said, "So, you think it's a dead end?"

"Not exactly. It could have been an interaction with the epinephrine."

"Right, but Dr. Lasseter would have known if a drug the patient was taking was likely to interact with epinephrine. Which brings us to the last possibility. That it was an overdose."

"That would explain why Lasseter ordered the toxicology screening."

"Yep."

"But then why did the patient react to the CT contrast? It doesn't add up."

Adam studied me for a moment and said, "How do CT injections work?"

"We load a large syringe with contrast. Anywhere from 75ml to 125ml depending on the exam. Then we use an automated contrast injector to time the bolus."

"How quickly do you push?"

"Again, depends on the exam. Some studies you can get away with 1ml per second. Other exams you might push as fast as 5ml per second. Maybe faster."

He said, "Then CT is pretty much the fastest and largest IV push in the hospital. You give an average of 100ml of contrast at a rate of about 3ml per second. That's a 30 second injection time, right?"

I nodded, sipping coffee. He seemed very interested in the details on this. Why did he care? Was it just medical curiosity? – playing doctor?

Adam said, "How do you know that you have 100ml of contrast in the syringe? – not 100ml of propranolol for example?"

"We draw up the contrast immediately before the exam. Plus, we only have access to IV contrast and barium and maybe a few other things in the automated dispenser."

The automated dispensing machine is the electronic drug monitoring and storage system.

"It's all closely monitored."

He said, "What about propranolol? Is it in your department's dispenser?"

"The beta-blocker? Yes. We use it occasionally for CT cardiac angiograms. It slows the patient's heart rate so we don't have motion blur on the images, but we don't use propranolol for routine abdominal CT."

"How do you know there wasn't propranolol loaded in the automatic injector?"

"Because I loaded the injector myself."

"And you remained in the examination room from the time you loaded the injector until the injection was complete?"

The Mexican tile floor beneath me opened up, and I sunk three feet down. Halfway to my grave.

I said, "No. I loaded the injector, prepped the room, and went to get the patient from the ED."

"Is that wise?"

Damn, he was persistent. Was this how I came off to people? I didn't know whether to slap him or kiss him. This situation required Zoey-level apathy.

I shrugged. "It's routine. What are you getting at?"

"That's a bad routine," Adam said. "Think about it from the patient's point of view. They have to take it on your word that this giant robotic syringe is loaded with contrast, nothing else. Plus, it's possible someone could tamper with the syringe while you're in the ED."

He was beginning to make me feel bad.

I said, "I wasn't out of the room longer than three or four minutes, and the injector is a complicated machine. You'd need training to override the system and change the material in the injector. It has a lot of safety mechanisms."

He said, "But it's possible, right? In three minutes or so someone trained to use the power injector could override the safety mechanisms, dump a portion of the contrast, and draw up a different medication before you returned with the patient?"

"Time-wise, yes. But, Becky was in the CT control room some of that time, and it's a small department. She would have seen anyone come in the exam room. You don't seriously think someone loaded something other than contrast in the power injector do you?"

"I'm trying to understand what's possible. According to you, it's possible that someone could load a different drug in the syringe. Something that causes what seems to be a contrast reaction. Something like propranolol, which causes decreased heart rate and blood pressure, and the fake contrast reaction wouldn't respond to epinephrine, which is exactly what happened last night."

Pressure filled my chest. My ribs ached. I felt annoyed by this conversation, by him. I didn't like what he was insinuating or the way he half-smirked while he made his insinuations.

I downed the rest of my coffee and stood.

"I need to get back."

Adam looked up at me, "Was it something I said?"

"No. Yes. And yeah, I don't like what you're suggesting about me."

"I'm not suggesting anything except it's possible you're being framed."

I sat back down. My head dropped into my hands. He reached out and held my forearm. The touch was magnetic – a nail against a lodestone. Warmth spread from his hand across my skin like a topical administration of morphine. I don't know what the heck I'm saying. It's possible I went a little out of my mind because I had this moment of clarity where all my sensations focused, and I knew.

Looking up at him, I said, "You're saying the death of Alice Gooden might have been a murder."

Hearing my own words, I couldn't keep the tremor out of my voice. I sounded insane and terrified.

Adam said, "Be honest. How far does this thing go?"

I shook my head, "I don't know. If you want my advice, get out while you still can."

He said, "You're saying it's possible? You don't think I'm crazy that someone might have murdered a patient just to get rid of you? You must know something. Who wants you out of the picture that bad?"

"Dortman."

72

I remember reading the American Hospital Association Patient Care Partnership as a student in x-ray tech school. It details what to expect during a hospital stay, including: high quality care, clean and safe environment, involvement in care, discussion of medical condition and treatment choices, discussion of the treatment plan, discussion of personal information, discussion of health goals and values, discussion of who can make decisions, protection of privacy, preparation for exit of care, and help with the bill and insurance claims. When I was a student, all this read like a cure for insomnia.

Similar to the ARRT Code of Ethics, the words of the Patient Care Partnership underwent a miraculous transformation the instant I realized everything on the list is there because of multiple court cases claiming these obvious, commonsense things weren't done.

It's weird to imagine situations where healthcare workers wouldn't, for example, discuss treatment plans or provide a safe environment. This might be why healthcare workers are often the last to identify those situations. When faced with a violation of the Patient Care Partnership, the default setting for healthcare workers is this intense, vampire-shrinking-away-from-a-crucifix denial. Violate patient care? Caring for patients is like what I do. How dare you say I don't care.

The reality is more straightforward. According to the Patient Care Partnership, every time I've seen a piece of trash in the hallway of St. Rafa and walked by without picking it up I'm showing I don't care about the patient. I don't care about the patient when I simply end an exam with a "thank you" and send the patient on their way without explaining what to expect next. I show my complete apathy about the patient's health when I fail to seek to understand their personal goals for wellbeing and how their treatment choice relates to their religious or moral values.

What I'm getting at is that what Adam said about pre-loading the power injector stuck with me. He was right. While it definitely saved me time as a tech, pre-loading the injector was essentially a refusal to involve the patient in their care.

It's easy to fall into the trap of not caring. The traps often save time and make the job easier. There's instances where we might need to depend on the team to guarantee the success of the whole, like the surgeon who just spent ten minutes scrubbing for surgery doesn't need to pick up the gum wrapper by the sink, but the danger lies in our routines. The hazard is the unspoken protocols and unofficial policies. Those things we do because "we've always done it that way." Which isn't to say those things we've always done a certain way are of necessity wrong, but neither are they above questioning.

That night in CT, Filcher was annoyed by my determination to wait to load the power injector with the patient present in the exam room.

He said, "This is completely ludicrous."

I said, "You dig Ludacris? I had you pegged as more of a Lawrence Welk kind of guy."

73

Each power injector syringe comes in sterile packaging with a tear-off top made of polyethylene fiber paper. In a pinch, techs use the synthetic paper to jot down notes. Something about these exchanges with Filcher were what compelled me to start writing this story down. I outlined each event. Maybe it was because my life felt like it wasn't making sense – to myself or anyone else.

I began in the beginning or did my best to identify a beginning from the swampy sequence of events that had landed me in this predicament. That was a question in itself. Where in the past was the point at which life could be considered normal? That question, I realized, I had heard somewhere before.

We were hiking through an aspen forest. This was in New Mexico. It was Dad and me. Mom was doing a pottery class in Taos. At least that's what she claimed. I was fourteen.

I understood enough to know we'd come to some sort of family crossroad. On the drive up from Austin, I bought a notebook at a Walgreens in Lubbock and started writing stuff down, drawing little sketches, trying to convince myself I wasn't losing my mind.

The notebook had a black cover. It was spiral bound. Somewhere in those pages was where I first wrote about my feelings for Beth Nash. Most of what I put in the notebook was about my parents and this weird trip to New Mexico.

As I saw it, the problem was Dad didn't hike in the mountains. He sat in front of a computer. Mom didn't make pottery. She made mix albums from her large collection of vinyl records, transferring the vinyl song by song to her computer and burning discs. She'd give me the CDs, and I'd dutifully play them in my room while doing homework.

She'd ask me what I thought about this or that song from some long defunct Christian psychedelic band or Thai country music concept album. I remember she was always turning up the volume. She never thought I listened to it loud enough.

"You can barely hear it," she'd say. "Turn it up."

That was her measure of rock-ability. The turn-it-up test, which was the first sign that nothing about this little walk in the woods was normal. On the drive from Austin we didn't measure the rock-ability of Mom's ten newest mix albums. She didn't bring any albums.

Occasionally, Dad listened to the weather station. All twelve hours of that impossibly long drive, Mom never touched the radio. We drove in silence across the badlands of west Texas.

Walking through the quaking shadows of the aspen leaves, Dad leading the way, I had this awful feeling like something out of the Bible was about to happen. That he was leading me up the mountain to a bloody altar where he would sacrifice me to his gestalt therapist. I couldn't take it anymore.

I stopped in the middle of the trail and said, "Dad, where are we going?"

He took a couple slow steps and turned. He looked at me, and I could see that he knew I didn't mean 'where are we hiking to.' He hedged anyways.

Dad said, "Nowhere particular, Boo. I thought it'd be nice to get out of the city."

I said, "No, I mean, what on earth is going on? Why are you and Mom acting so weird?"

His shoulders slumped as he said, "No one is acting weird. Families go on hikes. It's something families do."

He never came clean. Never acknowledged there was a problem. I kept pressing him, and he kept hedging. Then we were joined by this boy maybe a year or two older than me. A nerd. Big curly head of black hair. I can't remember his name. He wore a Dr. Who tee shirt, looked like he spent way too much time in front of a computer. For some reason, this nerd was out in the middle of the mountains alone and, of course, Dad invited him to hike with us, effectively ending any further discussion.

Three days later, on the long drive back to Austin, Mother bought the greatest hits of Patsy Cline at a Love's gas station. We listened to it on repeat for ten hours. I can sing every Patsy Cline song word for word even now.

When we pulled up to the house, Mother popped the CD from the radio, carefully placed it in the jewel case, set the album on Dad's workbench, and smashed it with a hammer. She went to see the lawyer the next day.

I wasn't surprised. I knew before it happened. I wrote, "My parents are getting a divorce," in my spiralbound notebook the evening after our hike with Dr. Who. I burned that notebook in the patio firepit. I couldn't help but feel that what I'd written had caused the divorce, that writing was a poisonous and shameful practice. Something along the lines of black magic. Because what is a divorce except a curse, neatly written down, signed, and notarized?

74

Our monthly department meeting was at 600 hours the following morning. I stumbled into St. Rafa half asleep. We don't have a huge department – about seventy employees – and our meetings are pretty informal. There's an agenda. Timmy's admin, Gail, takes minutes, but that's about it for formal order. Once, we debated who makes the better ketchup – Heinz or Hunts – during a gripe session about the quality of the food in the hospital cafeteria. Heinz won.

I noticed a difference in the hospital auditorium before I made it to the coffee and doughnuts. The room was quiet. There wasn't the usual chatter about baby pictures and football. I stood sipping coffee as I surveyed the room. Bunny McCombs was sitting in the second row beside Timmy the Fearless. I didn't see her immediately because a man was leaning toward her, whispering something in her ear. She was smiling. He fell back into his chair with a loud laugh. Richard Dortman.

My knees buckled like I'd been kicked. I dropped into the nearest available chair. It was the first time I'd seen Dortman in over a week. I immediately felt out of my depth. What on earth was I thinking? How could I dream of challenging the CEO of the hospital? I ran a hand over my close-cropped hair. The stitches bristled at the back of my scalp. The thought that popped into my head was 'He's winning.'

Timmy the Fearless stood and took the podium.

He said, "Good morning. This is our last meeting of the year in this venue. I hope to see you all at the department Christmas party. We've booked a banquet hall at the Salt Lick."

The "Christmas party" Timmy was referring to was mandatory. It was technically the December department meeting. Our fearless manager had figured out a way to have the hospital pay for his all-you-can-eat BBQ dinner. Everyone else was required to buy their food. Never mind the Hindus, Muslims, and vegetarians. Oh, and it was a Christmas party – not a holiday party. Timmy was very MAGA on that point.

He said, "We have some guests with us today. Let's give it up for our new CEO, Dr. Richard Dortman."

Dortman took the podium to a strong round of applause.

I overheard an ultrasound tech whisper to her friend, "Gosh, he's dreamy."

My heart fell. She was right. In his five-thousand-dollar suit, Dortman was ready for the cover of GQ. To most everyone in the room, Richard Dortman was an ideal boss. A doctor who knew what it was like down in the trenches. Lots of money. Relaxed. Handsome.

Dani dropped into the seat next to mine, slipping an arm around my shoulders.

He said, "Good morning, beautiful. Did you miss me?" and kissed the top of my head.

I said, "Back off, or I'll punch you in the throat."

Dani raised his hands in surrender.

He said, "You're under a lot of strain. Let's go down to Red River tonight. You, me, M. It'll be like old times."

"I can't."

He leaned in, "Why not?"

"I'll want to get drunk."

"And, that's a bad thing?"

Dr. Dortman softened up the crowd with a joke about a dying rich man who tries to bring his wealth with him to heaven. He shows up at the pearly gates with a suitcase full of gold bricks.

Dortman said, "After inspecting the contents of the suitcase, St. Peter says to the man, 'You brought pavement?'"

Polite laughter. I wanted to die. I wanted Dortman to die. I felt sick – like this marginally funny, business class joke was somehow directed at me.

Dortman continued, "As I lead this great hospital, I often ask myself the same question. Am I carrying a suitcase full of pavement? What are the things that seem precious at the beginning of the journey but will prove worthless on arrival? Are there practices and protocols – gold standards – that have become substandard? As we work together toward improving our team, we need to ask ourselves what 'go-to' routines actually need to go away."

Heads were nodding.

Dortman looked directly at me and said, "With these questions in mind, I've asked all departments to reduce staffing by ten percent."

He paused. There was shuffling in the seats as people sat up straighter.

Dortman said, "I've made that ask along with a request to increase our patient numbers by twenty percent – in all departments."

I felt completely lost. St. Rafa is a hospital not a sandwich shop. We can't pay someone to put on a broken bone costume and dance around on the sidewalk to drum up business.

How are we supposed to increase patient numbers? – drive recklessly? – intentionally knock over old ladies at HEB? Give out carcinogenic cookies? How does a hospital increase sales?

I'm not a business person, and I'm sure there's plenty of ethical ways hospitals can increase patient numbers, but is sales revenue the best focus for a medical facility? I've always thought – and maybe I'm being ridiculously naïve – if you focus on providing high quality patient care the rest will fall into place.

I leaned over to Dani and said, "Red River it is."

75

M picked Cheer Up Charlies. She and her partner, Janet, were there when Dani and I arrived. Adam biked up a minute or two later. I invited him. We had been texting a lot, and I figured it was time to introduce him to the gang. M was more focused on my haircut.

She said, "Very Alien 3."

Janet said, "That's a compliment."

Janet was such a Janet. Like imagine Susan Sarandon dating a female Tim Curry. That's Janet and M.

It was Dani's first time in a gay bar, and he seemed genuinely surprised that the bartender was willing to take his money in exchange for alcoholic beverages. Maybe he thought they only sold rainbow oil and unicorn sweat?

Adam's presence only added to his confusion, and Dani wouldn't stop talking about the two for five-dollar PBR deal.

"Best beer deal in town," he said. "I mean wow. You think it'd be OK for me to drink in here solo? Like is some guy going to hit on me?"

M laughed. For such a skinny, gloomy looking girl, M's laughter was huge, open-mouthed, full-throated. She inhaled a strand of her long black hair and nearly choked.

Dani said, "What's so funny?"

M said, "Depends on whether they're downwind of your cologne."

Janet leaned over to me and whispered, "Who's Adam?"

I said, "A friend."

Dani said, "What's wrong with my cologne?"

M said, "It'd be fine if you didn't use half the bottle."

Janet turned to Adam and said, "How did you meet Claire?"

He told her about me refusing to take the survey.

M said, "Sounds like she was being a total bitch."

He shrugged, "Who wouldn't?"

"I'm joking."

He said, "We kept running into each other – the ED, the cafeteria, the library–"

"The library?" Janet said. "You poor pathetic soul."

M said, "Janet loves the library. Stop lying."

She swatted Janet on the rump.

Adam said, "We started texting. Then she invited me here."

I said, "Anyways, he knows about all the craziness going on a St. Rafa."

M said, "Now what?"

Dani said, "Two for five-dollar PBR is what."

M rolled her eyes. "I mean with everything at St. Rafa. Did they suspend Vanessa?"

"Yep."

"Anything new with the investigation?

"Nope."

Dani added, "I heard through the grape vine Vanessa is cleared to return to work."

Adam said, "How is that possible? Didn't you say you have security camera footage?"

"She told you about that?" Dani said. "You told him about that?"

I said, "He would have figured it out on his own."

Dani said, "Bro, you know what that means? She digs you hardcore."

I said, "Wait? What?"

"That's some secret sharing for sure. It took you like a year to tell me insider dirt like that, girl."

Adam said, "It wasn't like that."

Dani said, "Like what?"

M said, "She's blushing."

Janet said, "Leave her alone. Claire, just ignore these ignoramuses."

I said, "The point is if we're going to fix this situation, we're going to have to do it ourselves."

"The point is," Dani said. "Keep your head down and do your job. It's a paycheck."

He shotgunned his sixteen-ounce beer and started on a second.

M said, "He's right. Claire, you have to quit. Just no-show tomorrow. You've got money saved. Why stick around?"

"If I quit, they win, and who's to say they won't come for me anyways?"

Dani downed his second PBR. I raised my eyebrows.

"What?" he said, climbing to his feet. "Round two. I'm buying. What're y'all having?"

M and Janet ordered kale lime margaritas.

I said, "I'm fine."

Dani said, "Have another drink. It won't kill you."

He was tipping toward belligerent.

I said, "I don't want to get drunk."

"Yes, you do. Relax. Everything is going to be fine."

I had another drink. The DJ played J-pop. I flirted with Adam. We danced a little, but he seemed blind to my interest.

I snuck away when Dani went for his fifth round. Adam followed me to the parking lot.

He said, "Where's your bike?"

"Back at the house. I'll hail a ride."

If anything was going to happen, this was the moment. Away from the noise of the bar. The night was cool and neon lit.

Adam said, "OK. See ya around."

He turned his attention to his bike lock. I wandered off, hiding my hurt by burying my head in my cellphone. I looked up to cross 10th Street and put my phone away. I didn't need a ride. Walking felt good.

I made it to Dorothy's place in thirty minutes and dropped into a patio chair to rest. The walk cleared my head, but sitting alone, thoughts of Adam came crowding back. Had I made a complete fool of myself? Maybe he had a girlfriend? I couldn't believe he was so thick as to miss all my cues. Was I out of practice? What was I missing?

The garden was dark. The shadows deep. I couldn't shake the feeling that I was being watched. I walked to the backdoor. Something stirred in the shadows. I spun around, but the noise stopped. What was that darker shadow between the plum trees? Did it move? Were my eyes playing tricks?

I fumbled at the lock, letting myself into the house and latching the deadbolt behind me. Still, the feeling persisted even after I went to my bedroom and drew the curtains. It took a long time to quiet my heart. I must have drifted off to sleep.

At one point, I sat up in bed. I thought I heard footsteps on the brick walkway through the garden. I don't know whether it was real or a dream.

The next morning my mouth was dry. I hadn't slept well. I made coffee in the French press and wandered out the backdoor to the patio. On the table, in front of the chair where I sat the night before, rested an eyeball.

It stared at me. Flies swarmed. The organ was desiccated. A small dark stain surrounded it. The flies were so loud, too loud. And, it kept staring and staring.

It was too large to be human. A cow maybe. Still, it stared.

I lost my grip on the French press. The glass shattered on the bricks. I stepped back, fumbling for my phone, dialing Sergeant Coleman.

76

I did what I always do when I've got a problem I can't wrap my mind around. I worked. When we were slow, I cleaned. Every surface in the CT department sparkled like a cokehead's Porsche on a Saturday afternoon.

"Ms. Neuman," said someone behind me.

I turned and found Timmy the Fearless standing in the hall.

"Tim? Aren't you here kind of late?"

That's when I noticed the two security guards.

He said, "Ms. Neuman, will you please come with us?"

The security guards walked on either side of me as I followed Timmy the Fearless down the long white hall to the breakroom.

I said, "Would you mind telling me what this is about?"

Tim said, "Routine random locker check."

Nothing about this seemed random or routine. I glanced at the security guards. Neither looked familiar. One had a snake tattoo on his forearm. The other was gigantic, had to duck to pass through doors.

I said, "Do you always bring security with you for random locker checks?"

Timmy declined to answer. He held the breakroom door open ushering us all inside.

I felt embarrassed. I bike to work. My locker is far from clean. I tried to remember how much dirty laundry might be in there as I worked the combination lock.

Things were in pretty good order. As I pulled items from the locker for their inspection, my embarrassment turned to anger. In the five years I worked at St. Rafa I never heard of anyone undergoing a random locker search.

To Tim I said, "What's this about?"

When he didn't reply, I glanced up at him. He was staring intently into my locker. I pulled a cloth grocery bag from the back when I heard a sound of glass striking metal.

Reaching inside I found a glass medication bottle, propranolol 25ml, a beta blocker.

I said, "I didn't put this here."

Tim said, "Let me see."

He held it out for the security guards to inspect. I steadied myself against the locker. I felt faint.

I said, "I don't know where that came from."

Tim said, "Ms. Neuman, will you please come with us to HR?"

What choice did I have? As we walked, Tim was on the phone, texting someone. He took a photo of the medication bottle.

I followed him down the long, white hallway and out into the main atrium to the human resources office. Whitney Peppers sat behind her desk looking tremendously put upon.

She said, "Ms. Neuman, I'm surprised to see you here."

Tim set the medication bottle on her desk.

Ms. Peppers said, "I called Ms. Auger the minute I saw your text. She will be here momentarily."

I glanced up at the clock. Five minutes to 2000 hours. Peppers and Timmy were usually at home by now. Had they planned this?

The door opened. Dr. Lasseter entered. Stepping up to Ms. Peppers' desk, he grabbed the medicine bottle, inspected it, and set it back down.

Glancing at me, he turned toward Ms. Peppers and Timmy and said, "What's the meaning of this?"

Ms. Auger entered along with Dr. Dortman.

To Dr. Lasseter, Dortman said, "John, I didn't expect to see you here."

"I demand to know the meaning of this."

Dr. Dortman said, "The meaning is simple. A random locker search revealed this bottle of medication among Ms. Neuman's personal effects. Now, you know as much as any of us know, except perhaps Ms. Neuman."

Dr. Lasseter said, "Let's not jump to any conclusions."

Dr. Dortman replied, "My point exactly. Perhaps, Ms. Neuman you'd like to tell us how this medication bottle came to be in your locker?"

I shook my head and said, "I didn't put it there if that's what you're asking."

Ms. Auger said, "Please understand, we're all on the same team, Ms. Neuman."

The room went wobbly. I braced myself against the back of a chair.

Dr. Dortman said, "You admit the medication bottle was found in your locker?"

"Yes."

Dr. Lasseter passed a hand over his face.

"And you're familiar with the hospital's policy on locker contents?"

I said, "I think so."

Ms. Auger said, "It is every employee's responsibility to closely review the policy manual and sign paperwork annually to indicate that they understand and are in compliance with all policies."

Ms. Peppers added, "I have her signature on file from January of this year."

Dr. Dortman said, "Are you familiar with the hospital's policy on locker contents? —yes or no?"

I said, "Yes, I am."

Dr. Dortman said, "I believe that is all the questions we have for you right now, Ms. Neuman. Please remain available for further discussion when and if it is needed."

Goosebumps rose on my arm. Dortman's daemon was here in this room. It was pulling the synaptic strings inside several different brains at once. I wished I were an MRI machine. I wanted to make those protons sing just as the daemon's invisible claw pass through them. I wanted to see the diseased thing behind their thoughts.

I said, "I have a question for you."

Ms. Auger said, "Please, be advised Ms. Neuman that anything said in this meeting may lead to further inquiry."

"Good. I want to know - what am I being accused of?"

Ms. Auger said, "You're not being accused of anything at this time. This is a procedural protocol review that resulted from a random locker search."

I laughed. "Right. If you're not accusing me of anything then it begs the question who do you think put that propranolol in my locker? Because here's the thing. I know the patient who died last night did not respond to epinephrine. I know that's not a characteristic of an idiosyncratic reaction to contrast media. It's much more similar to an overdose of a betablocker like propranolol, and I know I did not put that vial in my locker. So, if you're not accusing me of anything, I have accusations of my own, and I believe

Detective Coleman will be interested to know about the proceedings of this meeting."

Ms. Auger said, "I'm confused. Our discussion here is in no way linked to the investigation of your accident—"

"It wasn't an accident, and neither is this."

Ms. Auger said, "If you value your job at St. Raphael's Hospital, you will refrain from any such course of action. Please understand, we're on your team."

I said, "Are you threatening me?"

"Absolutely not, but I will advise you to closely read over the hospital policy manual before you contact any outside parties about this matter. I assure you this is something we are prepared to handle in house without any external interference or negative publicity."

Ms. Peppers said, "As it stands, you're under review. It is not advisable to continue in your training in CT until satisfactory completion of the review. Please return to duty in the radiography department. I will have security make a new proximity badge. You can stop by there to exchange badges on your way back to the department."

77

In the hospital, we have a word for stuff that's been soiled by excretion or precious bodily fluids: contaminated. It's a fomite.

Ever wonder why practically no one in medicine pays cash? We've yet to see the data on the percentage of dollar bills passed through G-strings. That's why I felt like dropping my CT proximity card in a biohazard bag. This whole situation was fomite heaven.

The guy in security seemed to be having problems with his printer.

I said, "New printer?"

He said, "No, new prox card. I've never seen this style before. The printer keeps kicking it out. It feels thicker than the old ones."

Eventually he was able to make it work.

In the bunker, Dani said, "Glad to have you back."

I was glad to be back. I knew they were setting me up for a fall, but a total collapse would be more difficult to manage on my home turf.

Dani said, "Hate to be the bearer of bad news, but Dr. Dipshit has a laminectomy scheduled for 2200 hours, and he specifically requested you to run the C-arm."

It shouldn't have come as a surprise. He wanted me where he could see me. It occurred to me that maybe I wasn't back on my home turf. Maybe I was back on his.

Contamination is a big deal in the OR. There's some surgeries that require less time to perform than it takes to prepare the sterile field. Everything in the OR is either sterile or treated with suspicion.

Sterile packages have expiration dates and sterility indicators that change color confirming sterilization. They can't be open or punctured until it's time to begin preparation. All the surfaces are cleaned with "baby-killer" wipes.

Then there's the "Father, Son, and Holy Ghost." That's my way of remembering the steps for opening sterile packages. You open the package away from you, then the sides, then toward you. Just like crossing yourself at mass.

For beginners, start by memorizing the principles for asepsis – *touching reaching for the KY jelly don't pass alone for the erogenous zone.* That's my mnemonic: 1) Don't touch the sterile field or reach across it. 2) Discard moist stuff (KY jelly). 3) Don't pass between the physician and the sterile field. 4) Don't leave a sterile field unattended, and 5) Maintain a one inch "buffer zone" around field.

Once you've got those down pat, you're well on your way down the spiritual path we call "surgical conscience."

The Old Flame, my ex-boyfriend, Nat, was into mindfulness meditation and vegan clothing. He told me mindfulness is simply a matter of being fully present. That's how I think about surgical conscience. Only it's a holistic presence – mindfulness of the sterile field and all the possible contaminants. It involves a deep understanding of your moral, legal, and professional responsibility to the person splayed open and vulnerable on the table.

78

The second I pushed the C-arm into the operating room, I knew I was walking into a set-up. Vanessa was back and acting like I didn't exist. Walking around with her fake boobs stuck out like twin warheads. She and the scrub tech chatted away as I plugged in the C-arm and dialed in the laser sight.

I glanced at the EMR for the patient's information. It was a woman in her late twenties. Young for a laminectomy.

The scrub tech said something about the patient's husband demanding that there be no men in the operating room except Dr. Dortman. Hubbie was Dwight Ewing, CEO of an oil company.

Hubbie gets what hubbie wants, I guess. That's the thing about Austin. Try as it might to pretend like it's not in Texas, all the music fest harmony and hippy-turned-hipster peacenikery is fueled by big oil.

In the fall of 2010, Zoey and I saw Brad Pitt inside Lucy in Disguise with Diamonds, the huge costume shop on Congress Avenue. It stopped me in my tracks. That was the first time that I'd ever seen someone famous in real life.

It wasn't that he was stupid handsome. He was, but there was also something different about him. Something polished and meticulously detailed, almost glowing. It might sound crazy, but I remember thinking he was holy.

I guess that's what people mean by charisma. It was like someone was jacking with the gravity inside the costume shop, and I was being drawn toward this one person. I literally had to fight the urge not to run up to him and beg him for his autograph. Autographs are weird, right? Like religious acts of devotion or something.

It was the same when they wheeled the patient into the room. She was beautiful. Clearly a trophy wife. Tanned. Manicured. Her hair alone cost half my paycheck. I learned later that she'd starred in one of those Hallmark Christmas things that are basically Prozac in movie form.

She wore diamond earrings, a gold chain necklace with a diamond pendant, a diamond tennis bracelet, and a large diamond ring. The anesthesiologist tried to convince her to remove her diamond tennis bracelet from the arm with the IV.

The anesthesiologist said, "We can place it in this bag, and I promise I'll return it before you even wake-up."

The woman eyed the small plastic bag. A biohazard symbol covered most of the packaging. It was a specimen bag. Pretty much the only thing at hand for the situation.

The patient said, "You have to be joking."

Her words were slurred – probably Versed, a little Valium – but no less angry. She looked ready to spit in the anesthesiologist's face.

The anesthesiologist said, "I'm asking you as your doctor."

"You're not my doctor. Get that awful bag out of my face."

Dr. Dortman breezed into the room. He had not yet scrubbed in, and he was flaunting the rules of the OR by not wearing a surgical mask.

The patient said, "He's my doctor."

Dortman smiled and said, "Ah, my favorite patient. My beautiful, wonderfully wealthy, Jane Ewing. How do you feel Jane?"

She said, "Delightful as always, darling. Whatever is this stuff? I'd love to offer it to guests at our next little soiree at the ranch."

Dortman said, "Benzodiazepine. You know, 'Bennie and the Jets.' The wonderful thing about benzodiazepine is you don't remember a thing afterward. Jane, do you mind if I show all these nice people why we're doing this laminectomy?"

She said, "You can't be serious. I'm cold."

The anesthesiologist adjusted the patient's warm air blanket, but Dortman brushed her away. He raised the head of Mrs. Ewing's bed.

He said, "I didn't have a chance to fully appreciate them the other day, and I am something of an aficionado. I sincerely admire your determination to not harm them with some awful reduction surgery."

To the room he said, "Mrs. Ewing has elected to have back surgery to save her rack."

With a quick motion, he stripped the patient's gown off her shoulders exposing her breasts.

He said, "Ah, wonderful. All natural I hear."

The color drained from Mrs. Ewing's face, and her mouth fell open, hypnotized and horrified. She tried to lift her gown, but Dortman batted her hand away.

Groping her breasts, he said, "I can't wait to flip you onto the table and give you a good fusion."

I bolted across the room toward him. Vanessa jumped in my way. I dodged, crashing into the sterile field, contaminating everything on the table.

Dortman turned and sidestepped my headlong charge, tripping me as I careened passed him. I fell hard against the side of the anesthesia cart. The metal edge tore the sleeve of my scrubs and sliced my upper arm.

I'm sure I bruised another rib when I hit the tile floor.

Pain signals shot through my body like some awful neurodiagnostic test. I struggled to catch my breath and rise, but Dortman dropped his knee on my back, pinning me to the floor.

I screamed in pain, thrashing and kicking. He leaned harder against his knee. The stink of sterilization chemicals and dead cells filled my nose.

My eyes went molten with tears. Darkness strobed across my vision.

I remember thinking, 'Please don't let me black out.'

Pinned. Unable to run. Unable to move without pain dancing along each and every cell of my body. It was like my own fear had reached out of the shadowy corners of my brain and seized my thorax in enormous metal talons.

Dortman said, "Nurse, call security. Tell them this girl is unstable. She contaminated an entire sterile field. I want her escorted out of the building."

From where I lay, my face pressed against the floor. I didn't see Dorothy Hicks enter the room, but I recognized her voice immediately.

She said, "Steve."

The sound of that name shook Dortman. He leapt away from me. I didn't recognize the next person who spoke. It was a man.

"Dortman? What the hell is going on?"

Turning, I saw a great turkey leg of a fellow dressed in an expensive suit. I pulled myself onto my knees. Dorothy helped me to my feet.

The man continued, "What were you doing down there on the floor? Why is my wife uncovered?"

The man pushed passed Dortman to his wife's side, pulling the gown up around her shoulders. Vanessa had security on the phone. She was talking fast. Dorothy pulled the jack from the wall.

Dortman said, "We were preparing to transfer your wife to the table when the x-ray tech leapt at me, contaminating a sterile field—"

I said, "He was groping your wife. Feeling her up, right here in front of everyone. I tried to stop him."

The man said, "Jane, is that true. Was he touching you?"

The woman turned her stoned eyes up at him and said, "Dwight, darling. What are you doing here?"

Turning his fierce gaze back on Dortman, Dwight Ewing said, "Did you drug her?"

Dortman threw his arms in the air and said, "Of course we drugged her. This is surgery, Dwight. Listen, you know me, man. How many times have we seen each other down at the marina? Who are you going to trust? –me? – or a psychotic bitch? Nurse, why haven't you called security? I want Ms. Neuman ejected from the hospital immediately. She poses a risk to herself and others."

Dwight Ewing said, "I'm not some old-timey wildcatter, Dortman. I see what's going on. You stay away from my wife, my whole family. I'll sue. I'll report you to the state medical examiners for this."

He struggled to wheel the stretcher out of the room. The wheels were locked. Dwight kicked the stretcher and spun toward the anesthesiologist.

"You there, Dr. Whats-your-name, wheel my wife out of here and tell me what I got to do to get her sobered up."

The scrub tech scurried out of the room with the anesthesiologist, leaving me and Dorothy alone with Dr. Dortman and Vanessa.

They blocked the door.

Dorothy said, "Get out of the way, Steve."

He said, "You're welcome to leave anytime. Security will take care of Ms. Neuman. Assault of a physician will not stand. She is terminated effective immediately and will be turned over to the police."

Dorothy crossed her arms over her chest and said, "I wonder what Mr. Ewing will say about that."

"Dwight Ewing is a momma's boy. He doesn't care about anything except sucking on tits."

"He'll care about a subpoena. Then there's the anesthesiologist and scrub tech."

Dortman smiled and said, "They won't say anything if they know what's good for them. Hospital policy."

Dorothy's smile grew. "Then we might be talking obstruction of justice."

Dortman shook his head and said, "Good luck making that stick."

Dorothy said, "I don't need luck. I have the sound recording from the microphone you planted inside Claire's new proximity badge."

Dortman's face contorted with rage. Two security guards burst into the room. He lifted a trembling finger toward me, but whatever he had to say died in his throat.

One of the guards said, "You called, Dr. Dortman?"

Dortman spun on his heels and strode out of the room. Vanessa trailed after him, glaring at us both. The two security guards glanced at each other, shrugged, and shuffled off.

My knees were trembling. I could still see his face, glaring murderously. The vision was seared into my brain.

I said, "Dorothy, I—"

Interrupting me, she said, "Just a second, sweetie."

She yanked the proximity card off my scrub collar and pressed it against the corner of the anesthesia cart. The proximity card tore open. The little device inside cracked, spilling wires and circuitry. Dorothy clipped the badge back on to my scrub collar.

"Broken when you accidentally tripped and fell."

She held me by the shoulders and looked me over. Dortman was still inside my head. Maybe that's why something about the way Dorothy was looking at me reminded me of him.

Then again, the whole surgical department, practically the entire hospital, was tangled up with Dortman in my mind. I was left wondering if there was anything about St. Rafa worth saving.

Dorothy said, "Are you OK? Did he hurt you?"

"I'm fine," I said. "Probably rebruised a rib."

She saw the blood on my arm and said, "That will need stitches. Come on. Let's get you down to the ED."

I said, "I don't know whether to thank you or tell you to get the fuck out of my life."

79

Crazy to think that visiting the ED could become routine. That's how it felt to me. The same forms to fill out. Same questions. Even the mental confusion of struggling to reconstruct memories around a traumatic experience was familiar.

Dr. Lasseter was off. I saw Dr. Plum, a portly, angry-looking woman who is surprisingly nice but business like. I told her I tripped and fell against the anesthesia cart.

She made a smiling frown as she entered her notes. She didn't believe me, but she wasn't going to question me any further.

Dani wandered into my room as Trixie set up the sterile tray for more stitches.

He said, "Everybody's talking about how you stood up to Dortman."

The words felt like potassium on the heart. Ten minutes later, I could barely hear Dr. Plum has she explained something or other about the employee health nurse. I didn't feel anything as she cleaned the clotted blood from the laceration on my upper arm. The fancy word for that is pain agnosia.

Dr. Plum explained that I need to "practice self-care" and "be aware of the signs of depression." She closed the wound with 12 stitches. Trixie assisted. From entry to exit survey, I was done in under an hour.

Dorothy brought me a fresh pair of scrubs from the OR. My ribs felt like razor blades wrapped around my lungs, and the stitches left the skin of my arm stiff and fragile, but I was able to stand.

Dorothy said, "Chin up."

I took a moment to compose myself. She nodded toward the closed exam room door.

She said, "You know what's out there?"

I shook my head. At that moment, I wouldn't have been surprised if this mass-produced, faux oak exam room door hid a portal to hell.

Dorothy said, "Bones. Just old bones walking around inside rotting meat bags."

I shuddered and said, "You're not helping."

That was the first time I saw Dorothy smile. It was an awful, indelicate action of her face. Her jaw cocked back like the hammer of a revolver.

She said, "Just remember. You're an x-ray tech. You can see through them all."

Dorothy opened the door. Everything stopped in the nursing station. Doctors, nurses, techs, and staff all turned toward us. I stepped out into the hall.

I'm not sure where the clapping started, but we slow walked down the hall and out of the ED to a standing ovation. My eyes were clear. I saw it all – the admiration in some people's eyes. The anger and fear in others. All of them applauding whether they meant it or not. Sometimes the hardest person to see through is yourself.

80

Timmy the Fearless was back at the timeclock waiting for me before my shift the next day. He looked like he'd been partially digested by an anaconda. His cheeks were pale and hollow. His hair and clothes disheveled.

I said, "You OK, Tim?"

He said, "Who, me? Yeah, sure."

"You look awful. Have you been sleeping?"

Whatever was going on it required all his mental powers. He didn't have two neurons left to come up with a decent excuse. He said something or other about the baby not sleeping, but I knew his youngest was four or five. I didn't call his lie.

I said, "Did you need me?"

Timmy the Fearless almost winced at the question.

He said, "Yes, ah. We have a student. An x-ray tech student who needs some swing shift hours. I wonder if you wouldn't be her preceptor?"

"You mean because I'm such an exemplary employee who isn't currently in a knockdown, drag-out brawl with the hospital CEO?"

Timmy tried to laugh but only managed to look more nervous. He glanced down the hall, and I saw a girl standing at the corner. She was a skinny, awkward thing – barely eighteen all knees and elbows.

Timmy waved her over and said, "Ms. Day, this is Claire Neuman. She's one of our best techs. She will be your preceptor during the evening shift."

"Call me Claire."

"Mazzy."

She curtsied. Difficult to do in scrubs. I'm sure I looked at her odd.

Mazzy knit her brow and said, "I don't know why I curtsied. Sometimes I do things. Afterward, I'm not sure why I did them. Does that ever happen to you, Mrs. Claire?"

I said, "Claire is fine."

Her brows arched together in confusion.

She said, "Do you often talk about yourself in the third person, Mrs. Claire?"

"No."

I started walking, hoping she'd wouldn't follow. Unfortunately she did.

Mazzy said, "I used to. Talk about myself in the third-person. Until I was fourteen. Then I spoke in the first-person plural just to creep people out, but now they say I should only use the first-person singular.

How about you, Mrs. Claire? What do you think? Is the first-person singular best?"

I said, "Listen, Maz."

She wrinkled her nose and said, "I hate that name."

"Mrs. Maz, then, if you're going to follow me around, you probably need to know there's people at this hospital – powerful people – who don't like me, and those same powerful people won't like you just because you're around me. I'm a career killer."

Mazzy stared at me, blinked, and turned back to Timmy the Fearless who stood at the end of the hall.

She said, "This isn't working out, Mr. Tim."

I said, "Bingo."

Tim said, "I think we got off on the wrong foot. Let's not be too hasty. Follow Claire for a couple of days, and who knows? You might wind up best buddies. What do you say? Let's give it a try."

Mazzy said, "I'm not really the buddy type."

"Me neither."

I kept walking. Mazzy followed.

She said, "Anyways why would I want to be buddies with someone everyone hates?"

"Excellent question."

Tim shouted after us, "Don't let your emotions get the best of you."

Mazzy said, "People already don't like me."

"Stop whining."

"I'm not whining."

"And I don't have three bruised ribs and an arm full of stitches."

She said, "What? Let me see. Stitches are so cool."

"So, Maz. What's been the worst part of clinic so far?"

"I'm not good around needles."
"Venipuncture is where we'll begin."

81

Chemo nurses and CT techs are the best stickers in the hospital. Outside the hospital, EMTs rule IV placement. Who else besides an EMT can stick a 16-gauge catheter in the back of the hand while the ambulance hits the speed governor bouncing over potholes and swerving through traffic?

Explaining all this to Mazzy, I said, "The important thing to understand about veins is they have a mind of their own."

Fortunately, it's not a very complicated mind, but you still need to understand how veins think if you're hoping to stick a catheter in one. Chemo nurses, CT techs, and EMTs each have their own theory of the vein.

Chemo nurses know that veins love heat. The best of them learn to work with needles by sewing up little cloth bags filled with dry beans. They toss the beanbags in the microwave and drop their homemade heater bags on the patient's arm. The heat draws the veins up to the surface and causes them to expand.

CT techs understand veins like to wander. They go funny places. In CT you see the insides of enough people to know that every blood vessel is its own special little silly straw, and like silly straws, veins are happiest in the flow of their precious fluids. The hardest sticks are dehydrated patients.

The wisdom of the EMT lies at the point of insertion. They know that veins hate needles. The less the vein knows it's about to get stuck the better. All the bouncing and siren blaring actually works to distract the vein.

In the hospital, tell the patient to look away, have them squeeze a ball, stretch the skin, ask "how about them Cowboys?" just as you screw the needle to the sticking place.

All this I told Mazzy on the way to the oncology department. Then I left her in Roz's capable hands to sit at a desk and sew a little beanbag of her own.

I told her, "Don't leave until the beanbag is finished."

That would keep Mazzy busy for at least two hours while I figured out what to do with her the other six hours of my shift.

Mazzy finished sewing the beanbag in under an hour. She was ecstatic.

"You're so cool," she said. "At first you came on like a jerk, but I get it. The pressure."

I said, "Yeah."

"Working with the needle and thread and watching Roz do IVs I learned so much. That was the best lesson ever. Why can't hospital stuff be more creative?"

"Listen, Maz," I said. "The last thing a patient wants to hear is, 'Let's get creative.' You want creative – join a dance class."

Mazzy said, "X-ray is creative. It's like an art or something."

I couldn't disagree. She flipped her beanbag in the air. It was a little bigger than a hacky sac. The fabric was patterned like a Turkish carpet. It fit perfectly in her pocket.

I said, "I could use one of those."

"Already got you covered."

Mazzy tossed me a beanbag.

She said, "What's next?"

"Now you need to do some actual IVs."

We went to CT. My new proximity badge didn't work on their door. I knocked. Becky let us in. She was more than willing to take Mazzy for a couple hours. In fact, Becky was acting downright weird.

She looked like she hadn't slept in days, and she was smiling too much. She'd always been the helpful sort, but now she seemed almost too willing to accommodate my half-hidden request for a babysitter.

As I hoped, CT slowed Mazzy's role. Dani and I worked orders from the floor and the ED. After yesterday's drama in the OR, it was all quiet on that front. Mazzy returned around 2000 hours.

She said, "Who knew that blood vessels could be so odd? Speaking of odd, I don't think that Becky lady likes you."

I glanced at her, and she quickly switched to talking about scanning a brain and something about contrast.

I said, "What makes you think Becky doesn't like me?"

The comment stung. It was unexpected. I thought Becky was a friend.

Mazzy said, "She tried to be sneaky about it, but she kept asking me questions – so, how long have you known Claire? – did you hear about x? – did you hear about y? I mean, yeah, all the students know you're Killer Claire, but—"

"Killer Claire?"

Mazzy clamped a hand over her mouth.

She said, "You didn't know? I always figured you were in on the nickname like it was ironic or something."

"Where did you hear that? From Becky?"

"Gosh no. She was way dodgy about it. I started to think she was hiding something."

"Dodgy how?"

"That's what I'm saying. She was all like 'you know Claire's under investigation for the murder of a patient, right? Did you hear Claire attacked a doctor last night?'"

I half expected to find a knife handle sticking out of my back.

Mazzy said, "What do you think she was getting at? I mean it really seemed like she had something to hide, and she wasn't opposed to you taking the fall."

"Have you eaten?" I said. "I know a little place nearby."

"I don't eat while I'm at work."

"Well, I do, and you're with me."

82

I was becoming too much of a regular at El Burrito Volador. Mazzy was a biker, too. So, we pedaled across campus to the Drag.

I was grateful to be out of St Rafa and on my bike. Seeing Mazzy ride put her in a different light. She was a good cyclist. Her bike was a bright pink fixed gear she'd built herself. I had seen the bike locked up on the rack and wondered who's it was. As we pedaled past Littlefield Fountain, I realized we might actually become friends.

We found a Vietnamese place by the Scientology headquarters. I ordered tofu pho. Mazzy ordered a taro bubble tea.

As we waited for the food, I said, "Did Becky say anything about Dr. Dortman?"

"Only that he's the most amazing doctor in the world."

I blinked and said, "What?"

Mazzy shrugged, "That's all she said. She was like 'You know the world's most amazing doctor works here, and I heard Claire got into a fight with him last night in the OR? Is that true?' I knew she meant Dr. Hotpants –that's what the students call Dortman. I don't see it. Anyways, I was like 'How the heck would I know, lady. I'm a student. Don't try to pull me into your office gossip.' I didn't say that, but I thought it. That's when I realized she wasn't just gossiping. She was trying to screw with my head, and I don't appreciate that. I've got meds for that. That's pretty much why I left. You'd be proud of me though. I did two IVs. This bubble tea is too sweet. Try it."

The chill of anger settled into my bones. Was it possible? Could Becky have drawn propranolol in the power injector? Why? What was her motive?

Mazzy moved on to other topics, and I kept my questions to myself. Back at St. Rafa, Mazzy and I went on a portable run to the ICU. One of Dortman's patients needed a chest x-ray.

Vanessa stood in the hall outside the patient's room waiting on us. As I rolled the portable machine into the patient's room, she stepped between me and Mazzy.

"What are you? A student?"

Mazzy said, "Yes. And you are?"

"Don't act like Claire hasn't told you all about me."

"She doesn't gossip."

"Right. Can't you find a better teacher? Claire is worthless. You might as well give up and drop out of school if you have to learn from her. Totally incompetent."

Ignoring the diatribe, I drove my portable into the patient's ICU room. Mazzy helped me complete the exam.

As we wheeled the portable back to the department, Ronnie phoned me on the earpiece.

She said, "That was perfect. I have it all recorded. I've already emailed it to HR and the ethics hotline. That's exactly the sort of thing we've been trying to get on tape. After that little demonstration, they have no choice except to give Vanessa the ax."

I said, "What about Dortman's performance last night?"

She said, "It's not enough. Taking a nurse out of the picture. That's easy. A doctor is more difficult. The best we can hope from last night is that the husband will follow through with reporting to the medical board. It's going to take a lot more than bad behavior to bring down Dortman."

83

I had not been taking the best care of myself, and it was beginning to become a pattern. The concussion slowed me down. Swimming wasn't an option. It was too painful in my chest. Adam texted and asked if I wanted to go hiking. This might be love.

He pulled up in his Honda with a grande soy latte and a little present wrapped in pink paper with a white bow. A Digi-Flex finger exerciser.

He said, "I know how much you hate not being able to get out. I have one of these, and it helps work out the stress when I'm studying—"

"It's perfect. Thank you."

I leaned over and kissed him lightly on the cheek. He stiffened, hands clutching the steering wheel.

Adam looked at me, tried to smile. Failed.

I said, "What?"

We drove in silence.

He said, "There was a girl back home. Laura. She had a pretty messed up life, but we fell in love our senior year in high school and never looked back. We were talking about getting married, but..."

He squeezed the steering wheel.

I said, "If you don't want to tell me..."

Adam shook his head and said, "It's OK. I caught her with this total asshole..."

He trailed off. A tear rolled down his cheek.

"She said she'd never been true, said she hated me, that she was using me, but I knew it wasn't like that. She was disgusted with herself. It was written on her face. Anyways, I could never hate Laura, but after that..."

Adam parked at the trailhead, but we both stayed in the car. There was more.

He said, "You ever wonder if maybe we're asking too much of ourselves, I mean as animals, like biologically, with all this love stuff? The last two years being single have been amazing. Dating hasn't even crossed my mind. I've never felt lonely. Anytime I met someone I like I just remembered how it felt that night, and that's that. Then I saw you in the hospital, and something changed. I don't know what this is. I don't want anyone to hurt you. And, I really like being with you. So, can it just be that? That we're together. Together a lot, but not sleeping together. I want to do nice things for you. Look out for you, but I don't want anything more than that. Not now. Maybe never. I know that's not fair. I mean, if you want something more, I'm not that guy."

I said, "That's OK. I need my space, too. Maybe that's the best people like us can hope for."

We climbed out of the car. The sudden stab in my chest felt all too much like heartache. I knew it was the bruised ribs, but I forced myself not to cry, springing down the trail with a laugh.

I said, "I haven't been to Turkey Creek in forever."

We hiked beneath the scrub oak, hopping rocks and roots. At the first mile marker, I saw another hiker a hundred yards behind, but I didn't recognize Nat until he caught up with us. The Old Flame.

Seeing me, my ex-boyfriend stopped and said, "Claire? It's been too long. How are you?"
"Good," I said. "You?"

Nat glanced at Adam. I wasn't sure how to introduce one or the other and opted for no introductions.

He said, "Seriously, Claire, you look like shit. What happened?"

I said, "Had a little fall at work."

Nat said, "I knew it. You're such a bad liar."

I realized a second too late I was staring at him. His rugged good looks and self-assured, almost aggressive smile. I hated that I still had feelings for him. I hated that he knew I had feelings for him.

"Listen," he said. "I'll text you, or you text me. Either way. Let's get coffee. OK?"

I said, "Nope. Don't think so."

I'm not sure where the words came from. I had to force myself to look away from Nat.

He said, "You got to be kidding. Come on, Claire."

I turned to Adam and took his hand. "I don't feel like hiking anymore."

Maybe Nat watched us head back down the trail to the parking lot. I don't know. I forced myself not to look back.

It must have been almost five minutes before I realized how hard I was squeezing Adam's hand.

I said, "I'm sorry."

"Don't ever apologize," he said. "Not to me."

For a moment, I almost thought we were going to kiss. Just as suddenly the moment passed. We hiked back to the car in silence.

I was grateful that Adam didn't ask questions. I was grateful to have someone I could be quiet with. Someone I wasn't trying to impress. Maybe he was right. May be this was the best we could hope for.

84

I couldn't stop thinking about Becky. Of all the betrayals, her's stung the worst. Every time I thought about her, I felt like there really was something wrong with me. That I was the problem, not Dortman, not Vanessa. I thought Becky was my friend.

If I couldn't trust my judgement with her, could I trust myself with Mazzy? After all, Timmy the Fearless connected us. How do I know Mazzy didn't make up the whole interaction with Becky?

Mother called that afternoon to ask if I was up for dinner. She had a volunteer brunch thing to attend in the morning. She knew about the move to Dorothy's, but only the haziest sketch.

Mother figured roommate drama was inevitable. Equally inevitable would be the resolution. I had texted some with Zoey and Facebook stalked Alex, but they were still in you-need-to-apologize mode. I wasn't about to apologize to anyone.

My mother loved causes that have zero bearing on her life. Escapist causes I called them: freeing Tibet, Leonard Peltier, Pussy Riot. There was a steady rotation of bumper stickers on her biodiesel Mercedes.

Not that these weren't important social justice issues. They were, but Mother used them as distractions from all the many mundane injustices of everyday existence. Things she could actually work to correct – struggling public schools, illiterate adults, poor transportation, advocacy for people with disabilities – the sorts of things we all know need improvement in every community.

In Mother's case, those improvements come with personal sacrifice, and they lack the heroic flavor of saving the planet. Much easier to buy a $50 bumper sticker and go on with your life.

I love my mother, but nothing had changed in her insulated world since we last sat across the table from each other. Or, if anything changed, the marijuana candy and psychedelic country music buffered the transition, producing one continuous groovy cartoon of phenomenon.

Meanwhile, I felt like a completely different person, like someone pushed down the stairs, suffering a traumatic brain injury. The person I was at the top of the stairs was different from the person gazing up at the ceiling from the bottom.

Mother said, "I don't know if that hairstyle suits you."

"I don't give a shit."

She smiled and said, "I take it back. It's perfect."

Buttering a roll – we were at a French café on the east side – she said, "What's troubling you, darling?" I said, "You don't want to know."

"You're right, but it would be impolite of me not to ask. Here's the thing, Claire. I love you. I don't care who you're trying to rescue from what. I've given up praying you'll come to Jesus, marry a doctor, and settle down. I just love you. You're weird and wonderfully frustrating and there's days – months at a time – when I can't understand how you're my daughter. Still, I can't think of a more perfect daughter for me. Sure, you think I'm a phony – no hear me out –"

(It was weird being called weird by Mother, but I hadn't tried to interrupt. I was hanging on her every word.)

She said, "— I'm the only person who will ever love you just because you're you. I've got the scars to prove it or at least the stretch marks. My vagina was never the same—"

"Mother!"

"There's that goofy grin I love."

"I don't—"

Her hand came down on mine, clutching my metacarpals so hard it hurt. I started to protest, but Mother locked her eyes on mine.

She said, "Stay alive or I'll kill you."

She released my hand and waved the waiter over for another glass of wine.

85

That evening Dorothy was waiting for me at the kitchen table. She'd found Alice Gooden's obituary in the paper. The funeral was delayed due to the autopsy. I decided to go to the visitation.

I'm sure the Gooden family had no desire to hear my condolences, but I needed this for myself. I biked to a resale shop on Lamar and found a black dress. I wore the dress out of the shop and biked to the funeral home.

People who work in hospitals have a unique aversion to funerals. Beyond the soul-sucking guilt, the sense of incompetence, you know it's all improv. The script flew out the window. Maybe you played the part of the consummate fixer. Now there's nothing left to fix. The mask falls away. All that remains is the intertwined paths of rage and acceptance.

That's the thing. When you work in a hospital you start to believe that it's your job to fix people. That fixing people is who you are. Working in a hospital, you could live your whole life believing that bullshit.

The reality is people aren't problems to fix. If anyone needs fixing, the job lands squarely in God's lap – if there is a God and if he/she/it has a lap – so thinking you're a people fixer only makes you part of the problem.

I'm not an atheist. I don't know what I believe. Specifically, I don't believe my belief matters. My thing isn't do I believe in God? It's does God believe in us? I don't believe in heaven or an afterlife. I believe we need death. We need an end to all our fixing and doing. Without death we would be as insensible as rocks.

Death makes us who we are. I don't mean humans. I mean every living thing. Maybe even rocks.

Wandering around Alice Gooden's visitation, I had this uncanny feeling. We spend so much time trying to forget – keeping busy – acting like death doesn't exist. We're in denial.

Without death, who are we? I can't define life except that beyond it is death, and I'm grateful there is an end to the will to survive.

I'm not talking about acceptance. Fuck that. I need the fight. Win or lose I don't care. No acceptance. Just fight. But, I'm also grateful for the bell that ends the fight.

Alice's fight ended too soon. Someone fixed it that way, and there's nothing I can do to change the results there in the casket. I certainly can't fix the person who made that choice, but I can hunt them down.

I will know them as a person, not a problem. That's what they want me to do. Deep down at the center of their being, they are screaming "Stop me before it's too late."

I have to believe that. Have to believe it just as much as I have to believe I can and will stop them.

It's too late for Alice Gooden. My duty to her is over, but my duty to her murderer has only begun. It is not too late for them.

86

Ronald called me down to her lair as I left the funeral home. I wasn't due to work for another three hours, but I biked to St. Rafa. Dorothy and Nepo were there when I arrived.

They had surveillance footage from the board room. The sound quality was awful, but it wasn't necessary.

Basically, HR fired Vanessa earlier that day, and Dortman was having a temper tantrum in front of the entire hospital board. He stalked back and forth down the long table. Behind him was a slide showing hospital revenue. The lines were pointing up. Everything looked good. It wasn't good enough. Dortman demanded more.

Maybe it was as simple as that. Greed. He was trying to make the hospital make more money than it was ever meant to make, but there was a desperate quality to his wild pacing.

Vanessa was gone. Maybe, he was feeling the loss. She'd been something of a stabilizing force, a corrective.

The word that came to mind as I watched him lambast the hospital board members was unhinged. That was confirmed when, one by one, the board members rose to their feet and exited the room. They'd had enough.

Ronnie stopped the video.

She said, "They're out. All except one or two have already sent their resignation emails. Dortman doesn't have a board. Without a board he can't change policy. He can't mess with the budget. He's weak. This is our time to strike."

Dorothy turned to me and said, "Your call."

I said, "Nepo, what have you found?"

Nepo said, "Nothing. He's squeaky clean on the financial side. The only thing I couldn't review was the finances for Dortman's office."

"Why not?"

"He must be using a separate system."

I said, "Ronnie, any chance we can get access to the records for his office?"

She shook her head, "Nepo already asked, and I already tried. The only way we can access Dortman's office files is directly. I mean sitting at one of his office computers and using someone's login."

I said, "Then that's what we're going to do."

Ronnie said, "Can't. It's illegal as hell."

"Girl, please. Like you care about legality."

"OK well, it's impossible. How are we going to get the login and password?"

"Pinhole camera. We put it over Dortman's desk."

"What gold-plated shit do you think we're going to find in his office files to risk charges for breaking and entering, identity theft, and who knows what else they might throw at us if we're caught?"

I said, "Dortman is intentionally botching surgeries. He's elevated it to an art form. He knows which surgeries to screw up and exactly how to screw them up."

Ronnie said, "This is your theory?"

"How else do you explain it?"

Ronnie said, "My theory starts with psychotic and ends with asshole."

"Sure. But this psychotic asshole has a method. Otherwise he would have been caught by now. Instead he's been successfully performing surgeries at St. Rafa for over a decade. He's wormed his way up to the top.

He must be using some kind of metric – insurance type, patient income, assets – I don't know. But if he's keeping separate records on a separate system, the answer is somewhere in his files. We need access. Then we can bust this wide open."

Nepo said, "If you want to really do this, you need to talk to my cousin, Angelique."

"The Legal Angel?"

Angelique's billboards were a prominent feature in the parts of town where bail bond and checks cashed services flourished.

Nepo said, "What? She'll cut you a deal. Nothing else she knows who we should talk to on the legal side."

I said, "Screw that. I'm not talking law suit. I'm talking criminal charges. What I want is evidence. Something we can give to the cops."

Dorothy said, "How do you know we can trust Detective Coleman?"

"I don't trust Detective Coleman, but Dortman can't buy the entire police department."

I returned to watching the video footage. Dortman was on the phone, pacing the boardroom.

"Who did he call?"

Ronnie said, "Marketing. Then someone in the hospital from the sounds of it."

"What do you mean?"

"He asked about a medication. There was some kind of hold up administering the dose."

"Play it back for me."

After listening closely to his side of the phone conversation, I said, "This is code. He's talking about the propranolol they planted in my locker. He's making arrangements to take me permanently out of the picture. He doesn't have the toxicology report. That takes too long. He's going the scandal route."

Ronnie said, "That's crazy. He just had his whole board walk out, and you think he's going to feed a scandal to the news?"

Dorothy said, "Claire's right. That's exactly what he's going to do. He's crazy. He doesn't think like us. He's constantly drawn to whatever will cause the most pain, which gives me an idea. We call the local news stations and tell them that the board of St Raphael's just walked out on Dr. Dortman amid rumors that he is intentionally injuring patients. Then we call Dr. Dortman's patients. Ronnie has a spreadsheet of the suspicious cases. We tell them that Dr. Dortman intentionally injured patients – that the story is going to be on the news tonight. Soon the injured patients and their families will be calling the news stations, and the news stations will be calling St Rafa's administration."

Ronnie said, "And we use the ensuing circus as a smoke screen for sneaking into his office and planting the pinhole camera."

I said, "The only problem is if we turn the pressure up too much he might start destroying evidence before we can get back into the office with the username and password."

"That's a risk we'll have to take."

I said, "I like it, but if it's going to work, we better hurry."

87

That afternoon at the hospital was the strangest of all my strange afternoons in radiography. Everybody –

nurses, doctors, techs – either loved me or drew away from me like I had Ebola. Work in a hospital long enough and even the most jaded person will develop a sixth sense for trouble. Whether they knew all the details or not, my co-workers could intuit there was a hurricane brewing, and I was standing at the eye of the storm. Some folks became my best friends and others decided they'd sooner ship me to the morgue.

Sam Filcher slunk his way into the bunker when no one else was around.

He said, "Claire, I know we didn't hit it off. Funny thing is I thought maybe you were working with Dortman. That he was using you to keep tabs on me."

I wanted to laugh, but I kept my face stony and impassive.

Filcher said, "I understand if you don't trust me, but something happened. I think you should know about it. Three nights back I did the department medication audit. Everything was accounted for, but something didn't add up. When I compared the audit with the department exams performed, we had used one extra vial of propranolol. I thought that was odd. So, I reviewed all the records on propranolol usage. We mostly pull it during the day for cardiac studies, but there was one that had been pulled at night. There weren't any cardiac studies that night. I figured it must have been a mistake, and the bottle would go back in the system a few hours later maybe. It was never returned. Then I realized that was the night of the contrast reaction. Listen, Claire, if that patient wasn't responding to epinephrine, there's a possibility they were overdosing on propranolol."

"Can you show me the records?"

"I have the print offs, and they're time stamped, but here's where it gets spooky. Someone scrubbed the system. The missing count isn't there anymore. It's like it just disappeared."

"It didn't disappear. It showed up in my locker."

Steve Filcher slumped against the wall.

He said, "It's worse than I thought."

"Who pulled the propranolol, Filcher?"

"Becky."

88

When I was eight years old, Mother sent me to cotillion. I didn't last long. All the talk of restraint and decorum sounded like a hostage situation. This marked me even at an early age for hospital work. If a person is dying and you're trying to save them, you can forget being polite.

Instead of politeness and decorum, we use physical restraints to prevent people from injuring themselves or others. That means tying people to their bed with straps. Restraint is physician ordered. Without physician orders, you're talking lawsuit for false imprisonment.

Regardless, I had never seen a physician in restraints until they wheeled the anesthesiologist into the ED, both wrists and ankles tied to the stretcher.

I asked Trixie, "What's that about?"

She said, "That's about a need to know basis."

"She was the anesthesiologist who saw Dortman grope Jane Ewing."

Whitney Peppers, VP of HR, and Ms. Auger stalked down the ED hall and into the anesthesiologist's exam room.

Trixie leaned toward me and said, "The rumor is she was found with stolen pain pills—"

"It's a set up."

"—Let me finish. Strung out on ketamine. That's like a horse tranquilizer, but you didn't hear it from me."

"Who found her?"

"Becky? The CT tech. Apparently she was in an unused patient room…"

Trixie continued talking as my vision contracted to a single point. My ears filled with a warm, buzzing tone. All I could think was "We have to hurry," but I couldn't have said where or for what purpose.

I slumped back in the chair like I was stoned, unable to move, watching Trixie talk, hearing only that warm buzzing tone and the echo of "Run, hurry, now."

That's how Dorothy found me – near catatonic.

She said, "Claire, what are you doing?"

I shook myself and stared up at her.

Dorothy said, "Now's your chance."

She grabbed me by the elbow and hauled me to my feet, pulling me toward the ED exit.

I said, "Chance for what?"

"Dortman will have his eyes on the ED for at least the next hour, maybe two. If you're going to do what we talked about, this is it. Take Dani with you."

Ronnie came on over the earpiece: "Heads up. Dortman's headed your way down the back hall to the ED."

Dorothy said, "Go! Take the sub-corridor entrance in the supply room. Ronnie will help you locate Dani. I'll slow Dortman down."

As I ran, I turned and saw Dorothy step into the hall's intersection. A smile spread across her face.

89

I was able to locate Dani quickly enough with Ronnie's guidance. We left the radiology department in the capable hands of the two travelling techs and punched out thirty-minutes early. If we were doing anything remotely outside the provisions of the law, we would not be on the timeclock. It was 2300 hours.

We took the stairs to the third floor and used my master key to enter Dortman's office through the backdoor. The lights were on, which creeped me out more than if they'd been turned off. Ronnie assured us that no one was in the offices. She'd kept close watch on the cameras ever since we'd hatched our plan.

She guided us to Dortman's personal office, and then Ronnie said, "Y'all I have to go check on something. I'll be back online in five minutes."

"This isn't a good time, Ronald. We need you watching the cameras."

"Trust me. I have to do this."

"What is so all important?—"

"You guys do what you have to do. Dortman won't be back that way for a while. I'll stay in contact on the earpiece."

Dani and I went to work. We slipped on nitrile gloves and tried to access the computer, but the screen lock was activated. I spread a sheet over Dortman's desk. Dani jumped up on the desk and placed the camera over the ceiling tiles, making a tiny hole in the tile for the lens. The entire operation took less than four minutes.

I said, "Ronnie, can you tell us what you're seeing on the camera."

Her voice sounded heavy. She was out of breath. She said, "Two minutes."

"Ronnie, this isn't the plan. You're supposed to be there."

"Sit tight."

A door opened and shut in the hall outside the office. Footsteps approached. Dani slipped down from the desk, and we folded up the drop cloth, accidentally upsetting a coffee cup full of pens. The footsteps stopped. My eyes darted around the room, looking for any kind of cover.

Dani and I saw the closet door at the same time. It was unlocked. We stole inside, closing the door as the office door swung open. Someone walked in and stopped in front of the desk. My heart filled with dread. The upset coffee cup gave us away.

I heard the clank of something metal. Then a phone blared a Bootsy Collins ringtone.

A woman answered: "What? Nothing. Cleaning my last office. I'm off in an hour. Where you at?"

I exhaled in relief. It was environmental services.

Ronnie came on over the earpiece. "You there?" Her voice sounded ragged. I texted back with the details.

Ending: "Where the hell did you go?"

In the earpiece, Ronnie said, "Dorothy is hurt."

She burst into tears.

I texted: "What happened?"

"I don't know. They were standing at a blind spot in the hall. I heard it. I heard her screaming and screaming. I just started running."

I texted: "Calm down. We need you level headed."

"I think he snapped her neck. Bashed her skull in. I don't know what all. There was blood on the floor. Claire, she might be dead."

"Did you tell the ED?"

"They were already there. Nurses and doctors all over the place. He wasn't. I don't know what I would have done if I saw him. I never wanted a gun so bad."

I texted: "It's not going to do her any good if you lose your crap right now. We need you to calm down."

The office door closed. We heard the footsteps fade into the distance. On the line, Ronnie drew a ragged breath.

I bit my lip, staring at the ceiling, thinking about how stupid I was. How did I ever wind-up here, hiding in a closet? If Dani and I were discovered, we'd lose our licenses. What right did I have to drag him into this? I could see the doubts and dread playing out on his face.

I remembered my dad on that long drive back to Austin. The mask of horror on his face in the rearview mirror. Why that image came to me in this moment of panic I couldn't say. I often think about dad, wonder where he is, what he's doing. Was this all because I had daddy issues?

Ronnie said, "OK, the camera is in position. Everything looks good. The cleaning lady is moving toward the front desk. You guys can roll out."

I motioned Dani to open the closet door. He went to work setting the desk to right. I glanced around the closet. In the light, I noticed the shelves were full of files.

267

Still wearing my nitrile gloves, I went through the folders. They were patient charts. Before this moment, I had never seen an actual patient file. Everything was electronic now.

Among the records I found, Jess Walden, M's patient. The woman from Janet's work with the botched spinal fusion. I pulled her file and opened the folder.

There, in neat manuscript, were Dr. Dortman's notes.

I read, "Fully insured. Roughly $500k in assets. Process level 2."

I snapped a photo with my smartphone, shelved the file, pulled another, and read, "Fully insured. $2 million in assets. Process level 2."

I snapped a pic and grabbed another. Why did he care about assets? What was level 2?

Dani said, "What are you doing?"

I said, "This is it. He's not keeping electronic files. It's all here. Grab charts and start snapping pics. Make sure to keep them in order."

On the earpiece, Ronnie said, "We have a problem. Dortman is headed your way. Someone or something must have tipped him off."

Dani and I replaced the files and closed the closet.

Ronnie said, "He's headed for the office back door. The cleaning woman is still in the reception arena."

I said, "What do we do?"

She said, "Hide. Somewhere. Just get out of his office."

We exited Dortman's office and moved toward the back door away from the reception area. We took a hall that branched away from the back entrance.

Shortly after we turned the corner, I heard the office's back door fly open and footsteps hurrying down the hall. I ducked into an exam room and pulled Dani in after me.

Dani said, "That was close."

Ronnie said, "Where are you? I'll guide you out."

I struggled to slow my breath and steady my shaking hands.

Ronnie said, "He's in his office now."

"What's he doing?"

"Nothing. Just staring at his desk."

"Now what?"

"Still staring," she said. "It's like he knows something isn't right."

"How? Does he have access to the pinhole camera."

"Impossible. No, there has to be another explanation. Photographic memory, maybe. Claire, he's got a gun."

I was shocked. Of course, a gun was an obvious move for Dortman, but I couldn't quite explain how much the idea of it jolted me. How many times had I walked past the signs on the hospital's front door declaring a prohibition against firearms inside St. Rafa and said a little prayer of gratitude? It seemed at times I worked in an enchanted place where no one need ever fear a mass shooting.

Now, I saw the sign for what it was. Painted plastic, an illusion of safety, but an illusion based on policy. If there was a sign, there was a policy. Dortman was breaking policy.

I said, "Ronnie, listen. Record him with the gun. Get it on file. It's not much, but it's something."

She said, "Done."

To Dani, I said, "There has to be access to the sub-corridor in the employee breakroom. We can avoid the main hallway. The problem is if it isn't there we're trapped."

Dani said, "That's our only option."

We quietly crept down the hallway toward the breakroom.

Ronnie said, "He's looking at the closet now. It was like for a moment there he went to the door and heard the cleaning woman in reception, but then he spun around and started staring at the closet door."

I tuned her out, focusing on moving as quietly and quickly as possible down the hall.

Ronnie said, "He opened the closet door. Claire, he knows you were there."

We made the breakroom. The door was behind a table. We carefully lifted and moved the table.

"He's out of his office and moving fast."

I said, "Call a code blue to this location."

"But no one's coding. That's—"

"If he can break policy, so can we."

Ronnie went silent.

I heard her voice on the PA: "Code blue. Third floor. Neurology offices."

She repeated the code three times.

Dortman screamed in rage. He ran down the hallway toward us. I heard doors opening and slamming shut. I used the master key to unlock the sub-corridor door, and we slipped through, quietly pulling it closed behind us.

We ran down the dark, red-lit sub-corridor, turning a corner.

I stopped and looked around the corner, waiting. The breakroom door flew open. Dortman stood, framed in light, listening. I was certain he could hear my heart. It was hammering inside my skull. I was pinned in place. Unable to move.

Dortman turned, slamming the door after him, and the breath I had been holding flew out in a ragged gasp.

90

I never imagined I might feel safer among the dead than the living, but in a matter of minutes, Ronnie had turned the morgue into a fortress, barricading both the main entrance and the sub-corridor with steel bars.

She said, "No one short of the SWAT team is getting in here."

I said, "Where's Dorothy?"

Ronnie said, "In the ED."

"What about Adam?"

"What about him?"

"We need all the help we can get."

"Do you trust him?"

When I hesitated, Ronnie turned and looked at me, glaring from underneath her pink mohawk.

I said, "Yes, see if you can track him down."

Ronnie pulled up the security monitor on her computer. Dorothy lay unconscious on a stretcher bed. Trixie busied herself transferring the IV bag and vitals monitor to the stretcher.

I said, "Where is she taking her?"

Ronnie said, "CT."

Becky stepped into the room.

I said, "No. We have to stop her."

Dani said, "What? Why?"

Ronnie said, "She needs the CT."

I explained about the missing propranolol, and my suspicions about Becky. Just then we heard a fist pounding on the morgue doors.

They said, "Security. Open up."

Ronnie said, "It's a trap. Dortman's trying to flush us out."

I said, "We can't stay cooped up in here forever."

Ronnie said, "Maybe you can't, but I can."

She gestured to the shelves full of nutrition bars and bottled water.

I said, "I'm not going to let them kill Dorothy and make it look like an accident."

Ronnie said, "What do you suggest we do?"

I said, "I'm heading to CT. You two can either come with me or stay here."

Dani said, "You're sure about this?"

I nodded. Ronnie raised the barricade bar and opened the door.

Dani said, "In the name of Allah, the most merciful and the most beneficent, protect this psycho bitch."

I said, "Amen."

And ducked through the door.

Dani said, "Wait."

He ran after me. Ronnie closed the door, dropping the bar in place. Dani grabbed my shoulders, spinning me around.

I said, "What are you doing?"

He slipped his arms around my back. I looked up into his eyes. His face was strange in the red lights of the sub-corridor.

Dani said, "Claire, I love—"

I clamped a hand over his mouth.

"Right now we have a job to do."

He said, "Right."

His face went blank, set with determination. He squeezed me fiercely and let go. As the pressure of his embrace released a sudden fountain of rage welled up in me. I was so angry, as I stormed down the sub-corridor, I didn't notice the plastic material until I was through the aperture. Sections of the sub-corridor held tarp enclosures, dust covers for sensitive machinery.

Dani said, "Wait. Hold up."

I turned around, staring at him.

He said, "Get out of there."

Or, I think that's what he said. The words jumbled up in my head. I noticed a sound, a sweet smelling, shushing sound. Dani reached for my arm as I tumbled backward, crashing through the plastic tarp on the opposite side. My head hit the cement floor, and I was out.

91

The soundbite played over and over, drawing me toward consciousness. Electric guitar, drums, piano, the announcer's voice. Pause. Electric guitar, drums, piano, the announcer's voice.

I had a ringing headache. The sort that carves the brain in half with lightning bolts. I blinked my eyes. Tried to rub my face only to find my hands were restrained, tied to the gurney where I sat upright.

The room was shadowy, lit only by a computer monitor. Out of the corner of my eye, I could see the screen. The video was paused. It was an exterior view of St. Rafael's Hospital.

Someone sat at the controls, adjusting the placement of an audio track. The video played: zoom in on St. Rafael's hospital, electric guitar, drums, piano. There stood Dr. Steven Dortman, waving at the camera, beckoning the viewer through the automatic doors.

Cue the announcer's voice as the video swept through a montage of medical innovations: CT scanning, robotic surgery, stock footage of people staring into microscopes. I couldn't follow everything that was being said. Where was I? How long had I been here?

At the hazy center of my aching head was a vague recollection of a red hallway and plastic curtains. I could feel a goose-egg on the back of my scalp. Dried blood clung to the gurney's fitted sheet. What hit me? It felt like someone had smacked my skull with the entire hospital.

The video rewound and played again. I strained against the restraints. Nothing. Hence the name restraints.

"You're awake?"

I couldn't see the speaker. They spoke through a voice modulator. The tone was unnaturally low - like Tay-Zonday-on-Dimetapp low.

"Untie me."

I fought the restraints. It was no use. I screamed.

A woman's hand appeared, dangling a remote control in front of me. She pushed a big orange button. Electricity wrapped through my body like barbwire. I yelped in pain and panic.

My body fell limp on the stretcher bed. It was an obedience collar for dogs. I could feel the two electrodes protruding into my neck.

I said, "Who are you? What do you want?"

The computer monitor continued playing the ad.

I said, "Let me go."

"Don't be a bore."

"Says the dork with the voice modulator."

I was only gradually becoming aware of my body. I wasn't in a good place.

I said, "I need to use the bathroom."

"Be my guest."

I have never so much in my life wanted to spit in the face of someone I couldn't see. Even through the modulation software, the voice oozed smugness. I don't know the first thing about spitting.

My face reddened, and I fought the straps. The woman's hand dangled the remote in front of me. I gave up the fight, dropping back onto the gurney. She shocked me anyway. I grimaced but held back the scream. I didn't want to play her sick game. I lay there.

"You're no fun."

Where was I? Turning my head, I could see downtown Austin through the floor-to-ceiling windows. The neon glowed against the light-polluted night sky. None of it seemed real. I felt stoned.

I said, "If you're planning on keeping me, I'm going to need a tampon."

"Gross."

I was lying about the tampon. I figured my only option was to come up with some kind of excuse to get these restraints off and make a run for it.

I said, "I'm going to need that tampon soon."

Nothing. I lashed out against the restraints. Fighting for my life. The woman hit the shock button over and over until I was burned numb against the electricity. I kept fighting, pulling, trying anything to wrench myself free.

The door opened behind me. I fought harder. Dr. Dortman stepped into view, settling into an executive chair at the side of my stretcher. His face was a foot away. I swung my head at him trying to break his nose with my forehead.

He grabbed my throat pinning me to the stretcher. At his touch, my body went slack. All the fight ran out of me.

I said, "I can't breathe."

He pressed harder. Stars swung across my vision. I choked. He smiled, easing his grip. He wheeled the gurney away from the monitor into a dark room. The blinds were drawn. Out of the corner of my eye, I saw a king-size bed. What was this place?

Dortman studied me for a moment, he said, "Have you ever seen *Lonesome Dove*?"

"Go to hell."

"Great movie – more a miniseries really. A classic. Robert Duvall, Tommy Lee Jones, Danny Glover. You have to see it. No spoilers. I promise. The idea is you got Texas. There's all these ranchers competing for the land because they have more cattle then they know what to do with. Cattle back then was money. Stock and trade."

I said, "I know your game, Dortman."

"Do you? Anyway, a couple of these cowboys get the bright idea to put their stock somewhere else. The Montana territory. But we're talking tons of cattle. It's like people today with a lot of money. They have to keep it somewhere. To avoid the taxes and regulations and such. In the movies it's always a Caribbean bank account. You follow?"

I stared at him hatefully.

He said, "The problem is the same. A lot of money, too much regulation. Only the solution changes. Back in the day it was moving cows to Montana. Then it was transferring cash to off shore accounts. Then Florida real estate. Now, it's South Dakota."

I said, "I couldn't care less about the money. I'm going to stop you from hurting people-"

He set his hand back on my throat, squeezing the air out of me.

"That's better. You don't need to say a thing. You're not going to remember this conversation anyway. Where was I? Sioux Falls. Ever been there? Me neither. Call it the inevitable result of globalization. *Lonesome Dove* all over again."

His grip relaxed.

I said, "Is the plan to kill me with boredom? If so, I need to visit the bathroom first."

He shook his head. "The plan was to frame you with the murder of that CT patient – whats-her-name?"

"Alice Gooden."

"Whatever. Dorothy Hicks and that stupid anesthesiologist were your accomplices. We had it all worked out – a life insurance scam. Anyways, that was the plan, but plans change."

"Why? Seems like a pretty good plan for someone with your limited intelligence."

He gave me a last good choke and released his grip. A weird smile came over his face.

Dr. Dortman said, "She didn't tell you, did she? I mean you have zero idea what this is about."

"Who? Becky?"

"No. That bitch. My mother. Dorothy Hicks."

92

The questions and doubts overwhelmed me like a drug. My head dropped back against the gurney. Why didn't Dorothy tell me Dortman was her son? What had I gotten myself into? How much of this was some dumb family grudge?

Dortman said, "You should see this."

He turned on a flat panel TV on the wall opposite the bed. Security feeds from around the hospital populated the display. First, he showed me the footage from the morgue. A security detail was working on the steel door with a battering ram.

I said, "They're going to be there for a while."

He frowned and changed the view to the hospital's exterior. Armed security approached the Cortina Brother's hearse, guns drawn. I kept my face as placid as possible. Inside I was screaming, 'Get out. Run.'

The guards drew down on the driver. I couldn't hear the shouting or the shots fired, but I saw the muzzle flash from their guns.

The hearse roared to life, barreling out of the parking space, toppling one of the security guards off its hood and onto the cement. They fired at the retreating car, but the hearse didn't stop.

Dortman was engrossed with the action on the monitor. I used the distraction to work on my restraints. If you're in your right mind, and you have enough time, you can free yourself from hospital restraints. They're more like a straitjacket than handcuffs. The trick is not to fight it. The more you fight the tighter the restraints get. Stay relaxed.

I began to work on the knot securing my right arm to the stretcher. Dortman was sending off a flurry of texts, touch typing them. He seemed to have never learned how to use his device's microphone.

He was clearly agitated, working the delete key more than any other. I told myself, 'Easy does it, Claire. You have plenty of time but only one shot at this.'

There wasn't a plan beyond free myself from the restraints. Oh, and if possible, pick-up Dortman and throw him bodily through the floor-to-ceiling window.

I managed to free my right arm when he spun and looked at me. He was still distracted, thinking. I could see the little gears in his head working frantically to maintain that aura of control, but the situation was quickly getting the best of him. I didn't want to be anywhere nearby when he finally realized how screwed he was. That's when he would do something desperate.

Dortman smiled. From the pocket of his lab coat, he drew a tampon.

He said, "I heard you might need one of these."

My stomach lurched and my vision swam as he stepped up to the foot of my stretcher bed.

I said, "Rot in hell."

"Ms. Neuman," he said. "I am a doctor. I'm only here to help."

"You're a fraud and a very sick person."

With a sudden movement he reached up my hospital gown and pulled my panties down my legs. His hands were rough and professional. Butchers hands.

I tried to kick, but my legs were tied. My only hope was to wait for the right moment and grab him with my free hand. If I timed it right, he would pull back, and the stretcher bed would topple over on top of him. The metal safety rails would strike his legs, hopefully breaking a bone and pinning him to the floor. From there I might have a fair fight.

Dortman said, "Spread your legs."

I said, "No."

He ripped the wrapper off the tampon. No gloves. No hand hygiene. He was filthy and disheveled.

The realization of how deranged Dortman looked standing at the foot of my stretcher bed came as a shock. It was like the scales finally fell away from my eyes. It was then that I saw passed the mask of medical authority and caught a glimpse of the monster underneath.

He said, "Spread 'em."

I couldn't control the shaking in my legs. I told myself, 'This is the price of victory. It will be worth it when you hear his tibia snap beneath the stretcher.'

Dortman said, 'Lift your knees.'

He roughly threw the gown over my head. I tossed my head from side-to-side, fighting to keep my face uncovered. He was staring at my crotch. He smirked at me.

"I've seen too many twats. They all start to look like hemorrhoids. Doesn't matter how pretty a bitch is. There's a giant stoma between her legs. You though, let's face it, you ugly, but it's like an ugly bitch makes the gash look good."

He leaned closer. That's when I moved. I grabbed a handful of his shirt and latched on tight.

Dortman shouted in alarm.

I screamed, "This bitch has claws."

Startled, he lurched backward. I yanked hard, and the stretcher rocked wildly to the side, crashing down on top of him. I felt the railing strike his leg.

Dortman screamed in pain and struggled to free himself from my grasp.

I held firm. My left hang hung in the air, tethered to the opposite side of the stretcher. My legs were useless.

The first punch came as a shock. His fist caught me squarely in the side of the head. My ears rang. The room swung around. I ducked the next blow, and brought my elbow down forcefully onto his crotch.

Dortman howled in pain and thrashed wildly.

He yelled, "Get her off me."

That's when I saw Vanessa. Just before the bolt of electricity shot through my body. My arm went limp. My fist unclasped. I felt the stretcher shift, and Dortman squirmed out from under the railing.

He stood, limped in a circle, and kicked me in the stomach, knocking the air out of my lungs. He kept kicking, lashing out at my chest, neck, and head. I tried to fend him off.

Dortman scream, "You can't stop us."

I barely heard him, but I was beginning to believe him. If he kicked me again, I don't remember. I blacked out.

93

I woke-up to Dani's voice. He was saying my name over and over. He sounded tinny and far away. I blinked against the darkness. I couldn't move my body. Something covered my eyes. Gradually my senses came online. I was laying prone and shivering with cold.

Dani said, "Claire, wake-up. Wake-up, Claire."

I tried to say, "I'm awake," but I struggled to speak.

He said, "If you're awake, wiggle your toes or something."

I wiggled my toes.

"Good, OK. Praise Allah."

I could hear the emotion in his voice, but I couldn't see him. What was going on?

He said, "You're in the OR. Ronnie and I are still pinned down in the morgue. I don't know where Adam wound up. The Cortina brothers are long gone. Looks like things didn't go according to plan."

My clothes were gone. I was dressed only in a hospital gown. The room was freezing. I tried to rise, but I was strapped to the operating table.

Dani said, "That isn't going to work."

I said, "What's happening? Where's Dortman?"

"He's in surgical supply."

The dawning realization spread over me. I wanted to scream, but I forced it down. Tears fell from my face onto the tile floor.

"Is there anyone else in the OR?"

Dani said, "No. The main entrance is closed and locked. He's headed back your way. We don't have much time."

"What about the news, the police? Were we able to contact Alice Gooden's husband?"

"Yes, but it's too early to say if that did anything. I have to go now. Stay strong. I'll find a way. I'm coming for you."

I heard the pounding of the battering ram on the intercom as Dani spoke.

He said, "Try to keep him talking. The man can't talk and chew gum. I've seen it a million times in surgery."

His voice cut out. The OR door banged open.

Dortman said, "Wakey wakey."

I said, "What? Where am I?"

Dortman said, "Time for your operation."

"What operation?"

"Oh, something or other with your spine."

"I refuse. I don't need an operation."

"The unfortunate thing is we're currently short staffed in anesthesia. So, I'll be performing surgery without sedation."

I said, "You can't. You wouldn't dare."

"Oh, I can, and I do dare."

He dropped a tray of metal instruments on a table nearby. The sudden noise made me jump against the straps. I fought.

"Let me go."

"You're not going anywhere, and if you struggle, you'll only make this worse."

He yanked the straps tighter, forcing the air out of my lungs.

I said, "Why are you doing this?"

"Why? Because I can. Because you can't stop me. Because I love power. That's if I'm completely honest."

"What's this all about? I mean that's what I don't get. Why are you doing what you're doing? It just doesn't add up."

Dortman said, "Nope. Won't work. I see what you're trying to do. You're trying to distract me."

My cellphone rang. It was somewhere on the other side of the room.

Dortman glanced at the screen and said, "It's your boyfriend."

My first thought was: 'Dani? Why is he calling?'

Dortman said, "I'm going to answer this and you're going to tell him everything is just fine."

He leaned in closer: "And if you don't I'm going to make it to where you'll never have sex again. Do you understand?"

I nodded.

Dortman answered the call and put it on speaker phone. It was Adam. I think the feeling I felt was deep disappointment, but it's hard to process through your love life when you're strapped to an operating table.

Adam said, "Claire?"

"Adam. Are you OK?"

"Yeah, you?"

"Yep, just laying low."

"Right. I take it Dortman is there."

"No. What are you talking about?"

Adam said, "Listen up, Dortman. You need to paddle your douchecanoe over to the marketing department like immediately. We sent the video, and the hospital is getting tons of calls from the news media. Bunny needs help answering the phone."

Dortman said, "What? What video?"

"Ask Bunny. She'll give you the deets."

Without another word, Dortman hung up the phone.

That's when I realized that I've got this. I don't need to run anymore. Dortman is the one on the run. I can stand my ground. I've got a team behind me. There are protocols in place. There's social media, the news, the police. Everything that happens in this room is being recorded.

He leaned in close and said, "What video?"

I said, "Sounds like you can watch it on the evening news."

He screamed in rage and stormed out of the room. I heard him talking to someone in the hall. Everything went quiet.

94

I hoped and prayed that Dani would come back on the intercom system and give me the all clear. As far as I could tell, the phone call with Adam was just another ruse, and Dortman was outside the room watching through the window.

I began to work on the straps, shifting my body from side-to-side. It was painfully slow work that required every bit of my strength, but the straps began to loosen. I had no idea what I'd do if I got free of the table. There was no use thinking about it. I had to concentrate on the straps. If I wasn't careful, I'd shift too much and pull the operating table down on top of myself or get hung up on the restraints.

Footsteps approached down the OR hallway. I froze, listening. The sound was softer than Dortman's heavy trod. This person was lighter, smaller.

I couldn't see, and I wasn't free enough from the straps to escape. The door swung open, and the person stopped. I heard a sharp intake of breath. Whoever they were, they were nervous.

I said, "Hello? Who's there? Let me go, please. I didn't agree to this surgery. This is illegal."

A woman spoke. She said, "Shut up."

I said, "Becky? Is that you? Dortman tied me down. He said he's going to make it to where I can never walk again. You have to let me go."

Becky said, "I'm here to do your IV."

I said, "Don't do it, Becky. It'll be a big mistake. I don't know what Dortman told you, but the news and the police will be here any minute."

"You're the one who needs to worry about that."

"Becky, it's over. We have Dortman on tape accusing you of killing Alice Goodman. He's going to sell you out like he did me. Whatever lies you're believing, they're all about to come crashing down."

"Wrong."

"Fine. Don't believe me, but listen, don't do whatever he sent you in here to do. Just turn around and walk out that door. Come back in fifteen minutes. If he says anything, say you were delayed. If I'm wrong, you'll know in fifteen minutes, but if I'm right, you'll spend the rest of your life thinking about it behind bars."

She stood in silence. I heard the door fly open and her footsteps pounding down the hall. I began to work on the straps.

The locks were tightening even as the straps loosened. It took everything I had to gain those last few fractions of an inch. I began to squirm my way free.

Falling gracelessly across the floor, I knocked over the entire table of instruments. I was getting really good at contaminating sterile fields.

I grabbed a surgical scalpel from the pile. It wasn't much, but the blade was sharp. I retrieved my clothes, shoes, phone, and Bluetooth earpiece, exiting the back door through surgical supply. I went down a couple doors to a darkened operating room. There I ripped off the hospital gown, hiding it in a nearby drawer, and changed into my scrubs and shoes.

95

I called Ronnie on the Bluetooth. She answered on the second ring.

"Where are you?"

I explained about Adam's call and my escape.

She said, "I'm with Dani and the Cortina brothers. We'll have access to the security cameras in two or three minutes. I can guide you out of there."

I asked, "Have you heard from Adam?"

"No. He must be hiding in the hospital. Security has that place locked down tight. We were lucky to escape."

"Try calling him. I'll send you his number. Maybe you can help us connect. We'll have a better chance of getting out of here together than alone."

"Are you sure that's a good idea?"

"Yes, I'm not leaving anyone behind. Do you have footage from the pinhole camera in OR room 6?"

I heard typing on the other end of the line.

Ronnie said, "Yes."

"Can you make a video of the last ten or fifteen minutes and send it to the hospital monitors?"

"The ones used for advertisements and stuff?"

"Exactly."

"I honestly don't know. It's worth a try."

"Send it to the news, post it to social media, anything."

"OK. I'm into the security system. Dortman's headed your way, and he's got four security guards with him."

Perfect, I thought, five against one, and they've got guns, tasers, who knows what all.

I asked, "How close is he?"

"At the OR main entrance."

"Tell me there's a sub-corridor entrance around here."

"Nope."

"Of course not."

"How do I get out?"

Ronnie said, "Two choices: the main entrance or the breakroom."

"Which is right by the main entrance."

"Exactly, Dortman's through the door and headed down the south hall."

The surgical department is three long hallways: the south hall, the supply hall, and the north hall. Between the halls are the operating rooms.

I heard Dortman and the guards hurry down the south hall passed the room where I hid. They would be at Room 6 in a matter of seconds. I ducked through the door to the supply hallway and through a room headed toward the north hall.

Ronnie said, "Hold up. There's a fifth guard at the main entrance."

I whispered, "So—"

"You're trapped. They're in Room 6. Dortman has the guards fanning out to search. Hide. Somewhere. Anywhere."

I said, "No. I'm done hiding. I'll take my chances with the fifth guard."

I sprinted down the north hall.

Dortman came over the PA, his voice calm and reasonable.

He said, "Claire, it doesn't have to be like this. We need someone like you on our team."

A guard emerged from a room ahead of me. I barreled straight into him. He fumbled at his belt for a stun baton. I buried the scalpel in his hand.

Dortman continued: "Surrender, and I'll make it worth your while."

The guard stumbled backward, clutching his hand, his mouth opening and closing in silent shock.

Dortman said, "Keep fighting, and I'll kill your parents, your friends. You'll live out the rest of your putrid life in a nursing home."

I ripped the stun baton from the guard's belt and struck him in the head. He went down hard and stayed down. I ducked into the breakroom, but not quite fast enough. Another guard saw me and gave a shout.

Racing through the breakroom and locker room, I exploded out the door hitting a trip wire strung across the lower portion of the threshold. I went down hard.

Popping up on my knees, I buried the stun baton's electrodes in the thigh of the security guard. He convulsed once, twice, then dropped to the floor. That's when I felt the needle hit my bicep.

I spun around and saw Vanessa. Her smile was a flash of bleached white on her otherwise orangish-brown face. She stepped backward, watching me hungrily. Her eyes flicked down to my shoulder and back up to my face. I looked down at the syringe sticking out of my arm, the plunger fully depressed. I yanked it out of the muscle, throwing it aside. I raised the stun baton, struggling to my feet.

"What did you give me?"

She said, "Wouldn't you like to know."

"Haloperidol," Dr. Dortman said, stepping through the OR door, followed by three guards.

I spun around. The hallway tilted on its axis. Just slightly. I held the stun baton out, electricity crackled between the electrodes. I pushed them back toward the OR doors.

He said, "Frequently used in psychotic patients to end agitated and aggressive behaviors before they hurt themselves or others."

I said, "I don't want to hurt anyone."

"Tell that to the man with the scalpel buried in his hand."

"I didn't have a choice."

He shrugged, "Sure. Whatever. Doesn't matter. I'm giving you a choice now. Join us."

Dortman extended a hand toward me.

He said, "We need someone like you, a real fighter. You're smart and tough, and I like it."

I lunged at him with the stun baton, but my reflexes were slow. I managed to take down one guard. The second kicked the stun baton out of my hand, and the third punched me in the stomach, knocking the wind out of me.

Gasping, I dropped to my knees. The hallway stretched and elongated sickeningly. A cold sweat passed over my face.

I struggled to rise, falling sideways against the wall. Dortman picked up the stun baton and depressed the button, watching the electrodes spark.

Struggling to catch my breath, I said, "I will never join you."

Dortman shrugged and said, "Who cares? I was just trying to say something nice before I did this."

He swung the stun baton down. I leapt back, and he stumbled. I brought my foot down hard on his knee.

Dortman yelped in pain, dropping the stun baton and falling into the two guards. I grabbed the stun baton and ran. The hall lurched sideways.

I heard him scream, "Get her," as I rounded the corner.

96

Ronnie guided me to a sub-corridor entrance, and I used my master key to slip inside just as the guards rounded the corner. Pulling the door closed after me, I stumbled down the dimly lit corridor. The guards pounded on the locked door. They were hired thugs. Dortman hadn't given them keys to the building.

On the Bluetooth earpiece, I said, "I'm safe in here for a little while, but Vanessa dosed me with a tranquilizer. I've got maybe five to ten minutes before everything goes Wonkaland."

Ronnie said, "I'm way ahead of you. Keep moving. I'm texting with Adam. He'll find you and smuggle you out the back door on a gurney. Take the next left, and use the ladder to go down three floors."

"I don't trust myself on the ladder."

My words were slurred, everything turned smeary.

Ronnie said, "OK, stay there. Adam's headed up the ladder. He'll find a gurney on that floor."

I braced myself against the wall, listening. Soon I heard someone ascending the ladder. When I saw Adam's face in the red sub-corridor light, a wave of relief swept over me.

He caught me just before I collapsed, holding me close. Somehow the Bluetooth earpiece popped out. I heard it crunch underfoot.

Adam said, "It's OK. I'm here. This way."

He tucked the stun baton under his belt, swung my arm over his, and helped me down the narrow corridor out into the blinding light of the hallway. As we lurched together down the hall, a girl maybe eleven years old rounded the corner in a wheelchair followed by a woman talking on a phone – probably her mother.

The little girl stopped, stared at me.

I think she said, "Is she OK?"

Everything was fading in and out.

Adam said, "She's hurt, but we're going to help her get better."

The girl said, "I was hurt, but now I feel better. I like this hospital. Watch me."

She popped a wheelie and managed to hold it for a second or two before her mother said, "Gabby, what did I tell you about that? It's not safe. Leave those people alone."

Adam led me to the stretcher bay. He helped me onto a gurney, locking both the side rails up. He covered me with a sheet. My legs and arms felt like over-filled water balloons, heavy and floppy.

He said, "I'm glad I found you."

I nodded. The walls and ceiling lurched and wobbled. The lights dimmed.

He said, "You've made more trouble than I ever imagined."

Even through the drug, I heard the shift in his tone of voice. I struggled to focus on his face.

Adam said, "I never thought I would say this, but I was genuinely hoping you'd escape so I could bring you back. This save will go a long way for me."

I said, "What do you mean?"

"You'll have to speak up I can barely hear you."

"Let's go. Let's get out of here."

Adam shook his head and said, "Oh no, we're not going anywhere until everyone is here."

"What are you talking about? Ronnie is going to meet us outside."

"You stupid bitch."

I sprung at him. He grabbed my shoulders, easily pinning me to the stretcher.

Shaking me, he said, "I know what you think. That you're fighting for the good guys, but you're not. You're really not. There's no good guys or bad guys anymore. Not at St. Rafa. Not anywhere in the whole healthcare system. The insurance people control the cash flow, and the politicians are too stupid to see it."

I squirmed. Adam pressed me harder into the mattress.

He said, "By the time I'm done with medical school, I'll be so deep in debt it hardly makes it worthwhile. Sometimes I think Dortman is the only one who gets it."

"Dortman is a psychopath. He has to be stopped. He's hurting people."

"You mean the back surgeries he botches?"

"You know about those?"

"Of course, that's what won me over to his cause. The patients are self-selecting. They're the assholes who demand back surgery because they're too busy sitting around eating junk food and watching TV. They want a bad back, Claire. They want an excuse to draw disability and lay around strung out on hydrocodone. It's a win-win. The drug companies benefit. The hospitals benefit. The doctors benefit, and the patients get what they want. The only group left out in the cold is the politicians, and frankly, fuck the politicians – all of them – they never should have messed with us."

I said, "You're crazy."

The words were barely audible. My strength was fading. Adam shoved me down further into the mattress.

He said, "What was that? I'm crazy? How about the system is crazy? I could buy a house with the student loans I'll take out for med school, and that's permanent debt – non-transferable – thanks again to politicians. How am I going to pay it off if those same politicians have structured the system so that insurance companies control how much they pay for services? Not to mention I'll have to pay liability insurance just to practice medicine because everyone who walks through the door is a lawsuit waiting to happen. At the rate things are going, I'll have my student loans paid off around the time I die an early death from the stress."

Dortman stepped from behind the curtain. I tried to fight, but I couldn't lift my arms. I was paralyzed by the drug.

He said, "Adam's right. People seem to forget. If there's a god in this world, he's a doctor."

Adam pulled the stun baton from under his belt, handing it to Dortman. The doctor activated the electrodes.

He said, "Fuck with god, you're dead."

Dortman hit me again and again with the stun baton. Shimmering, pain-filled darkness fell from the ceiling, driving me down through three floors of concrete and steel, straight into the side of the earth.

97

I figured I was dead. Everything was dark. The air was warm and close. I smelled a scent of new car. My ears were filled with rushing sounds. I remembered Adam and Dortman and reflexively clenched my fists.

My hands were numb. My wrists tied together with zip ties. My body felt wooden. I was in a car trunk, drugged into submission, and I was about to die.

Worse still I gave exactly zero craps about my death. The fight had run out of me. Probably a side effect of the sedatives. When Dortman popped the trunk revealing the shiny white interior of a meticulously clean three car garage, I didn't even feel disoriented just apathetic.

He said, "Here we are."

Adam wheeled up a gurney. That's when it landed. I remembered the stories circulating St. Rafa about the operating room at Dortman's house. Panic seized my chest and shook me. Just as quickly the anxiety ebbed away. I couldn't hold a thought.

They transferred me to the gurney. I tried to struggle, but my arms were useless. They wheeled me down the hall to the operating room, rolling me onto the table and strapping me down. I was prone, face down on the table. Rough hands tore off my clothes.

Dortman said, "She's not much to look at in the face, but she has a nice ass."

Adam said, "I've seen better."

"Want to do the honors?"

I heard a clink of metal, a scalpel.

Adam said, "You mean it?"

Dortman said, "Sure, why not?"

All I could see was the tile floor below. I heard Dortman pass Adam something.

He said, "Usually, we use x-ray for localization, but this time it hardly matters. Go ahead and make an incision along the full length of the spine."

I felt the scalpel slice through the flesh of my back, felt my skin peeled open with retractors. I screamed and screamed, but the sound was quiet. Muted by the tranquilizer.

Through the fog of pain and drugs, I heard a phone ring. Dortman answered the call on speakerphone. It was a woman. Her voice sounded familiar, but I couldn't place it.

She said, "I hate to interrupt, but you both need to see this."

Turning my head as much as I could, I saw the screen of a laptop. I caught the sounds of Dortman's voice on video. It was the feed from the operating room. Ronnie must have posted it to social media.

Dortman said, "Fix it."

Adam and Dortman turned toward me. They both wore surgical gowns, masks, hats, and gloves.

Dortman said, "How long had you been recording in OR Room 6?"

I said, "Long enough."

Dr. Dortman stepped closer, but Adam held back. Even through the surgical clothes I could see the fear in his eyes.

Dortman said, "Who posted the video online?"

I stayed silent.

He screamed, "Who?"

I heard the retractors click, and the skin and muscle peeled back from my spine. I ground my teeth against the agony coursing through my body.

Adam said, "It was one of her stupid friends. Dani or Ronnie. It doesn't matter, Dortman. Time is up. We have to kill her and dump the body."

"I'm not done with my experiment."

Adam said, "Yes, you are."

The gun was small. I didn't see where Adam pulled it from. I saw the single dark eye of the barrel, stark and black against the baby blue of his nitrile gloves. It was pointed at me. It had a pronounced sobering effect. I was completely awake.

I fought against the straps.

Dortman said, "Adam, listen to me. Put down the gun. If we need to get rid of her, trust me, there's cleaner ways to do it. I have a helicopter out back. We can dump the body in the Gulf of Mexico."

I could feel the straps loosening, slick with blood. Every twist and turn felt like I was tearing myself open.

Adam said, "You said 'if' like 'if we need to get rid of her.' There's no 'if' Dortman."

297

The doctor had moved out of my line of sight. I was still staring at Adam and the gun in his hand as I fought against the straps, but I heard the awful menace in the Dortman's voice.

He said, "No 'if'? Why do you say that? Could it be because you're not on the video? Because you aren't tied to any of this? Because if she takes me down, you're still in the clear? It seems like you've forgotten something."

Adam said, "What's that?"

Dortman said, "I'm the doctor."

It happened so fast, I almost missed it. Dortman slapped a surgical towel over Adam's face. The gun discharged. Adam fell inert on the tile floor.

At first, I thought Adam had been shot. I saw Dortman fall backward drunkenly, dropping the small towel on Adam's face as he ripped off his surgical gloves. Chloroform.

Dortman spun and staggered toward me. I drew a sharp breath. His surgical mask was blackened by gunpowder. He shook his head. Blood trickled down his cheek. The bullet had barely missed his face.

He said, "I underestimated you."

The straps loosened. I slid off the surgical table onto the tile floor. I heard something snap in my left wrist. Bloody tissue retractors scattered across the floor behind me. I was too wired on adrenaline to notice anything more than this gut level voice insisting 'you're gonna feel that in the morning.'

I sprung to my feet, naked and covered in blood. Dortman stumbled back two steps. I was Godzilla — a radioactive lizard bitch goddess. He was still reeling from the effects of the chloroform when I hit him in the head with the metal surgical tray.

He fell backward, stumbling over Adam's body. He grabbed the gun, aiming at me. I scrambled behind the surgical table, as he fired two shots.

That's when Dani ran in. I'm not sure what he was thinking. Or, if he was thinking. Seeing the gun, his eyes grew wide, and he backpedaled toward the door.

He said, "Claire!"

I screamed, "Dani, get out of here."

Looking around, I spotted a heavy steel mallet laying on the floor a few feet away. It was the sort of surgical device Thor might use if Thor was a doctor. Dortman's eyes darted from the doorway to me.

He was still too disoriented from the chloroform to stand. A trickle of blood ran down his forehead toward his left eye. He wiped at it angrily. I snatched up the mallet.

Dortman said, "She's right, Dani. You're too late."

Dani said, "Wrong again asshole. The cops are on their way. Claire, I'm not leaving without you."

Dortman laughed low and mean.

He said, "It's the blind leading the blind. Two x-ray techs who can't see a damn thing. I own the police. I own the hospital. I own you."

Yelling, Dani ran at the doctor. The gunshot exploded in my ears, shaking my entire body. Dani fell forward, sliding across the tile floor. Strange as it sounds, that's when I realized I loved him. It wasn't something I planned – like the thing with Adam. There wasn't any thought or obsession about it. It was a desire, not exactly sexual, more elemental, something ripped out of me, extracted by some strange reverse gravity that shoved my entire body toward the ceiling. When I saw Dani fall, I was on my feet and running.

I've always been a clumsy girl. Not quite as bad as M, but there's a reason we're such good friends. What I'm saying is I completely surprised myself when I buried the mallet head in Dortman's skull. I'm not exactly sure where the strength came from. I hadn't meant to kill him, but then yeah.

His eyes rolled back into his head. The mallet handle stuck up in the air. He went down on his knees and fell face first on the tile floor. His body jerked and twitched. Just as quickly he went deathly still.

I ran to Dani and knelt beside him. Tears flooded my eyes. The shock was beginning to wear off, and the incision along my spine pulled at my back like an enormous barbed fish hook.

"Dani, are you OK?"

His face twitched and eyelids fluttered open.

He said, "Did I get him?"

"Not exactly. Where are you hurt?"

"My left thigh."

I looked down. Blood had begun to soak through his scrub pants. I pulled them down. The bullet hole was in the outer meat of his thigh. A ragged exit wound in the back. Removing his shoes, I pulled off his pants and used the fabric as a bandage, applying pressure to the wound. Dani didn't scream.

I said, "You're tougher than you act."

He laughed, "Not really, I just can't get over it. Damn girl, why didn't you tell me you had a Brazilian wax? You know I love that shit."

I almost slapped him, but given the state that we were in, if he thought I looked good maybe it was meant to be.

There was a scrape of metal behind me. I spun around to see Dortman rising to his feet. The handle of the mallet protruded from his skull like an antenna. His surgical mask and face were bathed in gore. His hand didn't shake as he raised the gun. He said something, but the words came out in an awful, rasping whisper.

He stopped. A single eyebrow raised. He tried to speak again. The words were inaudible. His free hand went to his ear, tracing the contours of the mallet. He found the handle.

With a single, swift motion, Dortman pulled the mallet from the concavity in his skull and dropped into a heap on the floor. Blood poured from his head, pooling on the tiles.

I stepped over to the body, kicking the gun away. I hadn't wanted to kill him. Now that he was dead, I felt empty, weightless. Like Dani and I and all the many things around us were floating off into outer space. I swam out into the darkness among the stars, staring down at the tiny planet below.

Out among the cosmic radiation, light filled my whole body from the outside in. I didn't feel sorry for killing Dortman, but I was sorry to see him go. He had – in the end – taught me something.

He showed me the way to this empty and untethered self, naked and unashamed. Those were the words that went through my head as I helped Dani to his feet. We hobbled together out of the operating room toward the sound of the approaching sirens, naked and unashamed. A new creation.

98

I've never been out of the United States, which I guess explains why I felt so nervous boarding the plane in Houston. It seemed silly considering everything I had been through, but then again I'm in my feelings more now. If I'm scared, I'm scared. No use denying it.

I'm saying I was grateful for the Ambien Dr. Lasseter prescribed. Worked like a charm. I went to sleep somewhere in the air over east Texas and woke up in Frankfurt.

Dani rented a BMW, living out some adolescent dream of redlining his way across Deutschland on the Autobahn, blasting gangster rap. We stayed that first night in a hostel near the modern art museum.

M spent the next morning bumming around the museums and galleries. I reassembled my bike, and we all met for lunch at a little café by the river before I set off down the bike paths along the Main toward Wurzburg.

I stopped outside a nightclub in Offenbach called – of all things – Robert Johnson. I took a selfie by the sign for Mother. As I cycled away, Dorothy called. I picked up on my Bluetooth earpiece as I continued down the road.

She said, "You're never coming back, are you?"

I said, "I was just thinking that. I mean Germans really get it. This place is biking heaven, but I would have a hell of a time with the language."

Dorothy said, "A pretty young thing like you would have no problem finding tutors."

"How are you doing?"

"The good news is I started physical therapy today. The bad news is I started physical therapy today. You?"

I said, "I'm still not 100%, but I'm not trying to break any world records."

"Take my advice and stop at every biergarten between Frankfurt and Wurzburg and you'll be fine."

"Do you know how many biergartens there are between here and Wurzburg?"

"What are hostels for?"

"At that rate I would get there by my 40th birthday."

"You're the one who said you wanted to stay in Germany."

"I would miss you too much."

"Girl, please."

"I'm sorry I wasn't there to see your first day of rehab."

"Bullshit. You and I both know you're grateful you missed it. I only wish I could have missed it, too. Do me a favor and relax for once in your life, Claire. Have fun. Drink a lot of beer, take a lot of pictures, find some hot German guy with a big bratwurst in his lederhosen—"

"You're breaking up, Dorothy. I'm going to have to let you go."

She said, "The point is – this is your special celebration. You earned this. Make the most of it, you get me?"

"Yes, ma'am."

"Listen Claire, I only talked to your dad for a minute or two there in the hospital, but I remember him saying how proud he was of you. I want you to know that. He didn't seem like the type to say it."

"He's not."

"So, I'm passing it along for him, and I'm going to remind you of it a lot. You've made us all very proud. I'm going to hang up now because I'm going all mushy. Drink a beer or five for me today."

In Karlstad, I met up with Dani and M at a local tavern. After a couple beers, M attempted in broken German to survey the locals for the whereabouts of a haunted castle – any haunted castle. Dani massaged my shoulders, moving the tension out of my neck and spine.

My phone rang from a number at St. Raphael's. I immediately thought of Dortman. Told myself I was being ridiculous; it was only Cat, our newest tech, or one of the others I'd hired recently, wondering where the barium was or how to complete an exam in fluoro Room 2.

Beneath the polka music and crowd noise, I heard Dorothy saying, "That's right. You can see through them. Let them learn how to see through things, too."

I tucked the phone away in a saddle bag.

Dani said, "The hospital?"

I nodded. He settled into the seat next to me, an arm slung over my shoulder. This familiarity felt new and exciting. There were more questions than answers, but I'd learned to appreciate the questions. They were questions worth asking. A shiver passed up my spine.

Dani said, "Don't."

"What?"

I tried to play it off, but he knew me too well, knew I was back in that operating room under the straps, feeling the blade lacerate the flesh down my spine.

He said, "Drink."

We both drained our glasses.

He led me outside the noisy tavern. Down the narrow cobblestone streets of the fairytale village to the bank of the ancient Main River.

The sun was setting over the hills. I kissed him. True I was a little drunk, but I still felt that irresistible pull. Felt myself melting into his body, all the tension running out of me, and again there was that weightlessness.

Was it true love? I don't know. It was too soon to say. All I knew was I was grateful we were together. No one could ever take that away. Once you've given yourself in love to someone, that way of being, that in love feeling, is always yours to return to. That's when I knew I was going to sleep with him.

M bounced up and pushed us apart.

She said, "Knock it off. Hey! You guys won't believe it. There's a haunted castle like just on the other side of the bridge."

Dani said, "Do they have any vacancies in their dungeon? Because I'd love to leave you there."

99

The road along the Main into Wurzburg could have been a highway along the Colorado River anywhere in the hill country. Minus a few castles, the heart of Texas has a German feel. I hadn't really appreciated it until I came here.

What I'm trying to say is my days biking along the Main were making me feel less like an American citizen and more like a citizen of the world. I had picked up quite a bit of German along the way, listing to language lessons on my Bluetooth earpiece as I cycled

So, I was daydreaming, and the next thing I knew my rear wheel lifted up into the air, and I rose up over my front handlebars, and in the slow-motion seconds that followed, as I pitched headlong into the sky, I noted, somewhat philosophically, that I'd managed to hit the one pothole on this Teutonically well-maintained stretch of road. It was a deep pot-hole. Just wide enough to permit a bike wheel. The perfect pothole to catapult a daydreaming cyclist over their handlebars. The moment gradually passed there among the angels and sensible scenery. I landed in a heap on the roadside.

You know how – when you close a car door – there's that sound like "fwump," the vehicle body shakes slightly, and the atmosphere adjusts? I felt that same set of sensations inside my left shoulder as I toppled through a cloud of dust and my bike cartwheeled through the air overhead. I felt like someone had slammed shut a car door inside my body.

I climbed to my feet, bicycle shoes clacking on the pavement. My shoulder felt funny, but I was more worried about my bike. Attempting to lift the handle bars to inspect the front wheel, I couldn't make my left arm cooperate.

That funny, car-door-closing feeling in my shoulder compounded, multiplied, descended from my shoulder to my heart in this breathtaking lightning bolt of pain. My body knew before my brain. I'd messed up.

I nearly sat down and had a good cry. The one thing that stopped me was I didn't know how I'd get back on my feet. Only in the past week had I begun to feel somewhat normal, and the prospect of more doctors and hospitals was almost too much to bear. I hadn't even lost all my stitches yet.

I pushed my bike down the road fighting back the tears. I was too shook-up to call Dani.

A nice German truck driver pulled over. He was a cyclist. He had a bike rack behind his cab where he stowed my bike. He took me to a hospital that looked like an old royal palace from a Disney movie where I was quickly seen by a doctor.

The x-ray tech spoke some English. Her name, she told me, was Billie, and she was very curious about my trip to Wurzburg.

A light of recognition flooded Billie's face.

She said, "You are bad ass."

She said it like Bad Ass was my Christian name.

I said, "Well, not exactly. Just biking through really. Nothing special."

She said, "No, I know you. You are in paper. You stay. Move nothing."

I stayed, moved nothing. Billie returned with a newspaper clipping.

She held it out for me. I thought, "Oh no."

I couldn't read the article. Didn't need to. My picture was at the top of the piece.

Billie said, "You are bad ass. Kick ass x-ray tech. That you."

I blushed. Even attempted a shrug, and painfully realized that wasn't happening.

I nodded, "Yep. I'm bad ass."

Billie was a large boned woman with a face given to severe expressions, but she actually jumped up and did a little dance.

She said, "I never believe in God. Now I do. He have you fall from bike. We write to you. Ask you to come to Wurzburg."

None of it made any sense.

I said, "What are you talking about?"

Billie said, "I not tell you. You talk to doctor. I take you there."

Sometime around then, Dani and M arrived. They sat with me while the doctor – a thin, gnomish man with long eyebrows – replaced my dislocated humerus.

Then there was all the normal business of monetary exchange and paperwork. They gave me a CD with the images for the orthopedic surgeon, but in all likelihood, I would be fine with three or four days of limited use. As we walked toward the door, Billie came running.

She said, "I tell you. You no leave."

Honestly, I had a little pain medication on board, and my memory of our previous conversation was hazy.

I introduced her to Dani and M.

Billie couldn't have cared less.

She said, "You come with me."

I followed her out the door and across a courtyard toward the street.

Dani said, "What's going on?"

Billie said, "I no tell you. How you say? It is *überraschung*?"

Dani said, "We are not going anywhere until you tell us what this is about."

Billie said, "She bad ass. We give *überraschung*."

M said, "Surprise?"

Billie nodded, "That is it. Surprise."

Dani, M, and I exchanged glances.

I said, "Can you at least tell us where we're going?"

Billie said, "No. I no tell."

That settled it. We walked two or three blocks in silence. I began to recognize some of my surroundings. I had seen these streets on online maps and virtual tours, and I recognized our destination immediately. It had been on my phone for the last week of cycling. The Roentgen Memorial. I wanted to bike to Roentgen's lab.

The coincidence left me feeling oddly underwhelmed. X-ray techs are a pretty tight knit group. I know almost every x-ray tech in Austin. Like even a big city feels like a small town to techs, and Austin is almost ten times the size of Wurzburg. So it was no surprise that an x-ray tech in Roentgen's hometown knew people at his memorial museum.

Still, I hadn't realized how close the hospital was to the memorial. We walked maybe four blocks, which was good because I was already feeling spacy. But, feeling spacy in Germany isn't a scary feeling because every German town is almost painfully nice and neat. Even the garbage dumpsters seem artfully arranged.

The Rontgen Memorial isn't big, but it's a surprisingly modern set-up. Walking through the glass doors into the small lobby, I was surprised to see so many people there. Many of them dressed in hospital scrubs. They cheered loudly.

Dorothy Hicks emerged from the crowd. She held an award plaque. Taking care with my injured arm, she gave me a side hug and introduced me to Tomas Sebold, the German council member of the World Council of Radiological Technologists.

When the cheering quieted, Tomas said, "Ms. Claire Neuman, as a fellow of the World Council of Radiological Technologists and a board member of the Roentgen Memorial, it is my distinct honor to present you with this plaque recognizing your work making the world safer for patients and medical practitioners."

Dorothy said, "We would also like to award you a lifetime membership in the World Council of Radiological Technologists."

The crowd began to chant: "Speech, speech."

Holding the plaque in my good hand, I nearly passed out. A chair was brought, and I settled into it. Slowly my strength returned.

I said, "I'm not big on words, but I'll say one thing. I came to x-ray mostly for personal reasons, just a small-town girl from Texas, but being a technologist has opened me up to a completely different way of seeing things. I understand now that I am – we all are – citizens of the world. Members of one race, the human race. With a single home, this planet. So, let's make this place a caring place, full of healing with everything we do."

I wish I could remember more of that night. It was a flurry of laughter and toasts and meeting people from all over the world. What I have is more a sense that I had come home. That this was my family.

Late that night at a tavern around the corner from the memorial, we got drunk and made wild promises. And I do remember later still, after two or three bottles of Chimay, Dorothy Hicks told me the story of her failed marriage and wayward son, confirming my opinion that I would never, ever have children.

Part of seeing through things works because of the things you can't see through. If you saw through everything, you wouldn't see anything. For example, bones. X-rays can't see through bones; so, you see the bones.

The skeleton of Dortman's system was still there, sprawled down the halls of St. Rafa. It lacked muscles. It could not move on its own, but bones are the last thing to go.

I shivered, staring across the table at Dorothy. The contagion spread by Dortman seemed for a moment to have wrapped around the entire planet to find us. I thought about Adam and Becky awaiting trial for their parts in Dortman's plan. I thought about Vanessa. She had vanished, and along with her went any insight into Dortman's strategy, his method.

Maybe I'm trying to explain how I landed in Dani's bed that night (and the next three nights). Maybe it doesn't require an explanation.

100

One of the hardest x-ray exams to nail is a lateral knee. Taking a picture where the femoral condyles are perfectly superimposed regardless of the patient's anatomy takes years of study and practice, but there's not a lot of things that give me much more satisfaction than seeing a perfect lateral knee image, and I can't take a lateral knee or any of the x-ray views I enjoy seeing without a patient.

That's why, when it's all done, I thank the patient. I don't say "have a nice day" because people who are sick or in pain don't have nice days and they will (correctly) dislike me for suggesting they should. I don't say "Goodbye" because that seems too final. I definitely don't say "See you later" because in a hospital that's equivalent to saying "Hope you're injured again sometime soon."

I say, "Thank you," and I say it with meaning. I show my gratitude with my eyes, my voice, my very bones because I'm an x-ray tech, and what has passed between us defies explanation. You allowed me to see you in a way I may never see my closest friends and family members, and this way of seeing has a life of its own. This way of seeing deserves respect. I say "thank you" because I saw someone else in a truly personal, living way, through the skin and bones and vital organs down to the entangled photons of that other hidden being beneath the surface of everything. To that being, I say, "Thank you."

Acknowledgements

This humble book would not exist apart from the inspiration and creative work of the triune God. To God be all glory. To the Father, you give all things: goodness, beauty, truth, and the Word. Life is a gift from you. To Jesus Christ, the Son, you teach the most important writing lesson of all. "Every scribe who has been trained for the kingdom of heaven is like a master of a house, who brings out of his treasure what is new and what is old." Creative work directed toward this world is futile. Writing must be directed to heaven. The task of the writer is to entertain our guests – both earthly and heavenly – with a few of the old stories and some of the new. Finally, to that third, most self-effacing person of the trinity. You are my muse. This whole enterprise is my feeble attempt at knowing God better. It is, in the weird way of intercession, a prayer. Thank you for your love, for the creative joy that flows endlessly out of you, for the riches of your presence here and now and forever. Amen.

Questions for Students

1. Claire offers a number of thoughts about patient care. Did you find yourself agreeing or disagreeing with her line of reasoning? What support have you found for or against Claire's approach to patient care?

2. In Chapter 10, Claire discusses being able to see through things. What traits does she list as contributing to this ability? Do you think x-ray vision, as described by Claire, is something people can achieve? Why or why not?

3. The book presents a number of medicolegal concepts and situations. What legal aspect of patient care stood out to you as the most important? What presents the most challenges?

4. Chapter 29 briefly discusses "nosocomial" infection. Define this term in your own words and list methods of prevention.

5. Chapter 45 introduces an fMRI polygraph test. What are specific safety considerations for patients undergoing MRI test?

6. Dorothy argues that medicine is very different from health. What differences do you notice between medicine and health? What are areas of overlap?

7. Selman and Dorothy argue whether it is OK to take an x-ray of Claire's hand. Which one of them do you think is correct and why?

Based on the ARRT Content Specifications

53 Free Questions

Vol. 1 - Radiography Patient Care

EDITED BY BENJAMIN ROBERTS

Find us on YouTube at Rock the Registry!

Printed in Great Britain
by Amazon